Books by Joy Collins

Second Chance 2007

Coming Together (with Joyce Norman) 2009

Second Chance

A Novel

Joy Collins

Desert Spirit Press

Arizona

Author's Note

This book is a work of fiction. Names, characters, places, and incidents are used fictitiously, and any resemblance to actual persons, living or dead, and actual events is entirely coincidental.

Desert Spirit Press, LLC
www.DesertSpiritPress.com
DesertSpiritPress@cox.net

ISBN:
978-0-9844319-1-5 [pbk]
978-0-9844319-2-2 [ebk]

Printed in the United States of America
Third Edition

To John—
For loving me,
and for always believing in me.

Acknowledgements

Every writer has that list of special people to thank and remember and I'm no exception.

Thank you -

To my parents – Millie and Pat – for giving me my first library card. That card was my passport to a completely new world and you encouraged my exploration.

To my Aunt Mary and Uncle Al – for listening and never laughing at my first feeble attempts at becoming an author. Your support meant a lot to me.

To the many readers of the gazillion revisions of this book – Deejah, Judy, Claudia, Shelley, Kathy, and Pat. Your help and suggestions were so appreciated.

To those whose encouragement kept me going when I wanted to scream and run from my keyboard – Linda, Viv, and Sherri.

To the many women I met online – second wives,

stepmothers – who shared their lives and struggles with me. You were there in spirit with me on every page.

To my fur-kids – you helped me more than you will ever know just by being.

And last, but never least, many thanks and much love to my husband and best friend John. You gave me courage when I had none, and hope when I thought I was a fool for even attempting this. This book would never have happened without your support and encouragement.

Prologue

"Mom? You home?"

Sara threw her book bag on the floor in the hallway, next to her mother's sewing machine. Neat piles of folded material lay on the floor next to the old machine waiting to be completed. Her bag knocked the small heap over but she didn't notice.

Her mother's car had been in the driveway. It was almost dinner-time and that meant Mom should have been in the kitchen getting supper ready. Her mother's shift at the hospital should have been finished hours ago. Where was she?

Sara stuck her head in the living room doorway. The room was quiet except for the ticking of Grandma's old cuckoo clock.

"Mom? You here?" Sara looked in the kitchen. She had wanted a snack as soon as she walked in. Maybe an apple before dinner. Walking home from the library had made her hungry but these days doing almost anything made her hungry. Mom said that was just because she was fourteen and growing.

Sara's stomach tightened. Instead of hunger pangs, she was feeling painful butterflies, like she did when Sister announced a surprise quiz at school and she knew she hadn't studied.

This wasn't right. Ever since Dad had left, Sara needed order in her life. Sure, Mom had gone back to her nursing job and that made things harder, but there was a schedule. Sara and her younger sister Angela went to school. Mom went to work. Angela came home; the old lady from across the street stayed until Mom came home. Mom made dinner and helped Angela with her homework. Sara came home. They ate. Watched TV. Talked. Went to bed.

On some weekends, they went to see Dad. Lately, Dad's new wife Eleanor had been there, too. Mom hated that and made no bones about telling Dad how she felt about it. But Dad hadn't backed down. Eleanor was his wife now, he had said. He loved her and she was staying.

"Mom? Where are you? Angela?"

"We're in here," her mother finally called from the bedroom Sara shared with her sister. She heard soft sobs now and panic gripped her. She ran into the bedroom and stopped short in the doorway. Angela and Mom were seated on Angela's bed. Angela was curled up in her mother's lap, her head on her mother's shoulder, her short brown curls bobbing as she cried. Helen Cavaleri was still dressed in her nurse's uniform. Something wasn't right and the fear in Sara's tummy grew.

Helen rubbed her daughter's back and made soothing sounds. Small for her age, Angela looked even younger now than her ten years. Sara expected to see Angela sucking her thumb, something she did when she was stressed. But Angela wasn't sucking her thumb. Instead, she clung to her mother's neck with both arms.

Helen saw Sara immediately and motioned for her to come and sit beside them.

"Mom, what's going on? Is Angela hurt?"

"No, sweetie. Angela's not hurt." Helen stopped, took in a breath. "Honey, I don't know how to tell you this. I have some very sad news about your father." She put her head down and Sara felt her fear increase. There was something in her mother's eyes that she couldn't name.

"Daddy? What's happened to Daddy? Aren't we going to see him this weekend?" Since the divorce, Sara didn't see her father as much as she wanted. Sometimes, the fights about Eleanor and schedules meant that plans were often changed. It had been weeks since she had seen her father and she had been looking forward to it. Part of her, too, was anxious to be away from home and her mother's complaints. She hated her mother's tirades. Sara tried to understand but sometimes she just wished she could live with Daddy and Eleanor. They always seemed so happy. There were days she was even tempted to tell her mother she wanted to move in with them but she knew the trouble that would cause. Better to just keep quiet.

Helen put her arm around Sara's shoulder and pulled her closer. "Sara -"

"Daddy's dead," Angela blurted out. "Eleanor killed him."

"No, Angie, Eleanor didn't kill him, sweetie." Helen kissed her little girl and then turned to Sara. "Honey, your father was very sick and the doctors couldn't help him. He died."

"What? What do you mean he died?" Sara watched those medical shows on TV. She knew patients could be saved. Her mother was wrong. "You must have misunderstood. Where is he? I want to go see him." She pushed her mother away and stood up. The bedroom window was open and she could hear the neighborhood kids playing outside in their yard. Their screams and laughter hurt. She hated them. Their fathers were coming home for dinner tonight. It was bad enough when she had to explain to them that her Daddy

11

didn't live with them anymore. Now this? Mom was wrong. She had to be.

Helen reached for Sara's hand. "Sara, listen to me. I know how hard this is for you. For all of us." Sara swung her hand away so her mother couldn't touch her. "Please, honey. Don't be like this. It's going to be okay. I'll always be here for you. We're a family. We have to pull together now. We still have each other."

"I'm calling Eleanor. I have to talk to her." Sara ran back into the kitchen. She knew if she could just talk to Eleanor the misunderstanding would be cleared up. Mom had to be wrong. She grabbed her mother's address book out of the kitchen drawer and began leafing through it. Tears formed and she had trouble seeing the words. Eleanor and Daddy had recently changed their phone number and Sara didn't know the new one yet. Mom must have it somewhere. Where was it?

Helen dumped Angela on the bed and ran after Sara. She grabbed the little phone book out of her hand and threw it back in the drawer, slamming the drawer so loudly Sara jerked from the noise.

"The number's not in there. Besides, you can't call her. I promised her we would leave her alone." Helen grabbed Sara by the shoulders. "She has a lot to deal with right now and she said she's taking care of everything. She doesn't want us there. You know how she is. I promised her, Sara. Please, promise me you'll leave her alone."

Sara looked into her mother's eyes. Her mother looked genuinely frightened. What had Eleanor said to her?

Angela was beside her mother now, whimpering again. Sara looked at Angela's smudged face and her mother's words finally sank in.

"It's really true? Daddy's..." She couldn't make the word come out.

Helen nodded. "I'm so sorry, baby." She reached for her daughter again.

Sara wrenched herself free of her mother's grasp and ran to her room. She slammed the door as hard as she could.

Throwing herself on her bed, she cried.

For Daddy.

For herself.

For what would never be.

Chapter One

I should have known it was not going to be a good day. Saturday was usually my favorite day of the week. Whether it was running errands, playing with the dogs, or just cuddling on the sofa with my husband – Saturdays always filled me with a sense of home and peace that I enjoyed and cherished. Now with summer approaching, I was looking forward to barbecues and afternoons in the pool, as well. As I neared the mailbox at the end of our driveway, I breathed in a whiff of orange blossoms from the neighbor's front yard and sighed. If we really can create our own heaven when we die, orange blossoms were definitely going to be a part of mine.

The Arizona sun was already warming the morning air and it felt good on the back of my neck. I decided it would be nice to eat supper on the deck that night. Since moving here from Philadelphia, I never tired of the warm weather. Sure, Phoenix was becoming congested and was downright oppressive in the summer, but as long as we stayed in Fountain Hills, our little oasis in the desert, I could pretend the city was far away. The stifling summers were a small price to pay for the more than pleasant rest of the year. I definitely didn't miss the snow. I daydreamed about our romantic dinner. I'd make my chicken recipe that Paul loved. We'd have some wine, cuddle under the stars, and just see where it took us.

Thoughts of romance quickly vanished, however, when I pulled out the day's mail offerings and saw the letter on top.

A letter from Mona.

Sweet Mona.

Sweet, vindictive, conniving Mona.

Yes, the signs for upcoming trouble had definitely been there that day. I had risen early while Paul was still in the shower. I threw on a pair of sweats and put a pot of coffee on. I wanted to get an early start on a report for work that was due in a few days. I pushed the start button on the coffeepot and let the dogs out into the back yard. They ran and chased each other while I went back into my office, booted up my computer, and spent a few minutes going through my email.

When I heard Paul get out of the shower, I thought I would surprise him with a cup of hot coffee and spend time with him before he rushed off to do some errands. As I approached the kitchen, I wondered why I didn't smell the coffee, though.

As soon as I saw the coffeemaker, I realized why. I had forgotten to put coffee grounds in the basket. I now had a pot of very hot water.

Paul just smiled. "I'll grab a cup of coffee on the way to the junkyard." He was going to look for parts for an antique car he was working on.

"I don't know how I could have done that."

"Sara, it's okay. Things happen."

No, they don't. Things happen for a reason. I truly believe that the Universe sends us messages. Some are subtle. Some are as obvious as the Italian nose on my face.

15

But the signs are there.

I watched Paul while he pulled on his jeans. He was standing in front of our walk-in closet in the bedroom. At fifty-two, he was still handsome. Since he had started his own construction firm, he didn't do as much manual labor as he used to but he worked out and kept his body trim. He was much taller than I was (just about the entire rest of the world was, it seemed) and I liked the way I fit under his chin when we hugged. His chocolate colored hair was getting thinner and, in retaliation, he had recently grown a beard. I thought it made him look distinguished, especially when it started to come in a little gray. But it wasn't his hair or his height that I was admiring. I watched him shrug his tight butt into the jeans and fantasized about ripping them off and dragging him back to bed. It had been a while since we had made love and my hormones were in overdrive.

Paul stopped zipping up his fly. "What?"

My daydream ended in mid-rip. "Hm? Oh, nothing. Go. Enjoy your junkyard adventure." I kissed him on the mouth, lingered just a second longer than usual.

Paul hugged me closer. "You sure you want me to go? I could put this off if you have something else in mind."

"It'll keep."

Paul kissed me again. "Remember where we were when I get back."

I could hear the dogs barking in the yard as his car drove off. Afraid the dogs would annoy the neighbors, I let them back in the house and went back to work. Paul loved shopping for car parts as much as I loved shopping for shoes so I knew I would have a few hours to myself. An hour later, my computer locked up. I rebooted and re-loaded my document only to find that I had lost two pages of the report, which was almost all of the work I had done that day so far. Cursing myself for not saving my work more frequently, I started back at the beginning. Minutes later, I heard the mail truck rumble up the street and decided I needed a break.

Despite all the electronic communication I received, I still looked forward to the daily snail mail.

As I walked down the hallway, I tripped over a dog squeaky toy and twisted my ankle.

"Toby! Did you do this?" Toby was our rescue dog from the local animal shelter. His breed could best be described as "hairy". As I dangled the offending toy in front of him, he put his head down, more in response to my voice than any idea that he had done something wrong. The look of doggie contrition melted my heart but my ankle still hurt. I hung onto the wall and rubbed my sore foot.

Today just wasn't going right. First the coffee, then the computer, and now my ankle. I limped slowly to the mailbox at the end of our driveway, working the kinks out of my foot. I absently kicked some gravel from the driveway back onto the lawn. Arizona lawns were certainly an anomaly. Nowhere else had I seen "lawns" made entirely of gravel and stones. When we first bought this house I had thought all the earth colors were boring but now I had come to love them. And the critters! My city roots hadn't prepared me for our almost daily visitations from jackrabbits, coyotes, javelinas, and quail. Especially the quail. Their silly noises as they scratched under the feeder in the front yard never failed to make me smile. Paul had hung the feeder on the tree outside my office window just for me. No matter how often I heard them, they always sounded ridiculous and brought a smile to my face. Today was no exception.

But my smile froze and my stomach knotted as I grabbed the batch of envelopes from our box and immediately recognized the handwriting on the top one.

The envelope said it all. It was addressed to Paul in Mona's usual perfect handwriting and the return address only said MLW.

No name.

No address.

Just the initials.

M L W.

Mona Louise Weber.

I saw it as an implied intimacy that he would know it was from her. That she still used his last name after all these years (and her re-marriage and subsequent divorce) was not lost on me, either.

Oh, crap. What did she want now?

Paul and I had been married for fifteen years and we still fought over Mona, his ex-wife. Emphasis on the *ex* in my book. Emphasis on the *wife* in hers. I felt he let her get away with so much because of Claudia, the child they shared.

It was amazing how a simple #10 envelope could throw my emotions into a tailspin. Mona had trained me well, though. I had learned from bitter experience that most communication from her was going to be trouble.

Like when she sued us for more child support right after I landed a new job a couple of months before our wedding and then had the papers for child support modification hand delivered to our apartment the day of my bridal shower.

Or the time when she just "happened" to be cleaning out some old boxes and came across some baby pictures of Claudia that she thought Paul "would just love to have." So she sent them to him.

For Father's Day.

Right after I had a miscarriage.

Or the letter from Mona's attorney demanding payment for braces that Paul never said he wouldn't pay for.

Right after we signed the mortgage on our new home in Arizona.

Or the umpteen demands for more child support, or private school, or dance lessons.

No, no letter from Mona was ever good news. She had a knack for turning my home into a battleground, often for no other reason than what seemed like her sheer joy in causing trouble. I swore she was addicted to the drama. Even when Paul agreed to whatever she wanted, she felt the need to involve her attorney and threats of court. It had gotten to the point that I dreaded every piece of mail from her, knowing full well what it was going to mean.

"It's going to be all right. Trust me," Paul had said more times than I could count. "I won't let Mona interfere. You'll see." But Paul was incapable of seeing her for the controller that she was. It amazed me how blind he was regarding her. And he never admitted the role that he played in any of it. When I complained, the problem then became my fault.

Mona manipulated. Paul caved. We fought.

It was a vicious dance that had been going on for years.

At forty-seven, I had expected my life to be more settled. No little girl played "Second-Wife" when she was young. I wasn't prepared for the role. My life seemed to be clearly divided. To the outside world, I was a successful and happy businessperson, a nurse consultant, a wife, a confident woman. But inside, I felt frustrated. Sometimes angry, often unhappy. I loved my husband. In my heart, I knew he loved me. It was just that one little area....

I had even gone into therapy over it, in the third year of our marriage. I wanted to make things better. The therapist was a woman, a second wife herself.

"Sara, you need to stand up for yourself. Help Paul to see that you and he are a team and you're on his side. He needs to put your relationship with him first."

She even brought Paul into the sessions, but it didn't help.

"I do put my marriage first," he had insisted. "If I give in to Mona, it's because, in the long run, it makes things easier for me and Sara. I know it looks like I'm placating her, but it's only so she doesn't take us back to court and we can see Claudia more. It really is the best way to reduce the stress, not add to it."

He never saw that his plan never worked. The more he gave in to Mona, the more she took. After six months of trying to convince him otherwise, I gave up and quit therapy.

I knew that once Paul got an idea in his head, it was hard to change his mind.

My desire for a passionate dinner evaporated. The kink in my ankle returned as I walked slowly back to the house. The day was going to hell quickly and it wasn't even lunchtime yet. I placed the mail on the breakfast bar in the kitchen, making sure Mona's letter was on top. I wanted Paul to be sure to see it first. I poured myself another cup of coffee (I had made another pot by this time, grounds included!) and came back to stare at the letter again, as if staring at it would give me some clue as to its content.

I opened the other letters, threw away the junk, and left the bills for Paul to look at. I told myself I should go back to work. But Mona's letter drew me like a magnet. I had to admit that I was more than a little fixated when it came to her. Paul wished I was less obsessed but I couldn't help it.

"Let it go, Sara," I had heard on more than one occasion.

My answer was always the same. "I feel better if I know what she's up to. If I make contingency plans, she can't hurt us as much." Paul would just shake his head and retreat, usually to the garage.

I ran through all the possible reasons why Mona would be writing to Paul at this particular time. She used email occasionally, but only just to send short chatty news about Claudia. Important information (meaning demands for money) was always sent via regular mail and was always cc'd to her attorney as well. I assumed she wanted the paper trail and didn't trust email copies. So, I knew this letter had to contain something that was going to prove to be upsetting. Braces were long over with. Claudia wasn't planning a visit any time soon that I was aware of, so it couldn't be that. I stared at the envelope and willed it to burst open. No luck.

Jesse, our Golden Retriever, ran up to me and started whimpering so I let him out the back kitchen door to relieve himself and chase the birds. As soon as I did, Toby wanted out, too. I watched as they scampered and ran in the yard, like the two best buddies they were. I tried going back to work but my mind kept wandering back to Mona's letter.

I gave up on getting the report finished. Instead, I tried to focus on the day ahead and made a mental list of the things I wanted to do.

1. Shop for groceries
2. Take the dogs to the dog park
3. Color my hair (the gray was starting to win over the brown again!)
4. Clean out the pantry

I loved my lists. I loved making them. I loved crossing things off them. Sometimes I added things I had already done just so I could cross them off. Paul considered it more than a little weird. I even had a computerized list that I used when it was time to pack for trips. He laughed at me on more than one occasion while I checked things off as they went into the suitcase but he never arrived somewhere missing a tie or a belt or those navy socks that he just had to have, thanks to me.

I found a certain comfort in my lists. Once something was crossed off, I knew I didn't have to deal with it again. And when my world was out of control, I compensated by making more lists.

I did that when I had divorced Kevin.

1. Call attorney
2. Find place to live
3. Hire moving truck
4. Move my savings to a safe new account
5. Forward mail
6. Pack my things
7. Pack up the cat
8. Place note to Kevin on fridge
9. Leave

No, it wasn't very nice to just leave a note.
I wanted to write:

Dear Kevin,
Life with you sucks.
See ya.
Bye,
Me.

But I didn't.
Instead, I took the blame. I said I hoped we could work things out.
We didn't.

Life with Kevin had not always been bad. He and I had met a few years after I graduated from nursing school. I was working on a medical floor in a hospital in New York City. Kevin was one of the new group of residents starting that July. I wasn't looking for a new love. I had just broken up with a fellow nurse that I had been dating for over a year. But Kevin and I struck up a friendship and within a few days of our first meeting he asked me out to dinner. Within weeks, it was obvious to everyone that we were a couple. He took me to the best restaurants. We vacationed in exotic places. After a year of whirlwind courting, he asked me to marry him. We married in a small church in the city. I planned everything right down to the color of our napkins (I was a list maker back then, too). My mother was there, beaming at all the relatives. My sister was Maid of Honor but I was The Bride. I thought I couldn't be happier. I only wished my father had been there to see me, to walk me down the aisle.

After a week's honeymoon in Mexico, Kevin and I settled into our apartment in a high rise in Manhattan on the fashionable East Side. I threw myself into the role of the happy housewife. Kevin opened a city practice in internal medicine. Soon, however, what had started out as networking meetings turned into heavy drinking. A year and many drunken nights later, I had to face the fact that Kevin was battling alcohol and the alcohol was winning. His angry outbursts were frequent. His practice deteriorated.

Kevin blamed it on the stress of the heavy competition in the city. Thinking a change of location would help, we moved to a town outside Philadelphia to be near his elderly parents.

It worked, at first. I wanted desperately to make my marriage succeed. We tried for babies. To our sorrow, I lost two of them. Kevin was there for me but after the second miscarriage, he started drinking again. He had car accidents. He got into arguments at the hospital. His practice was failing again.

When his rages became physically violent, I knew it was time to leave. I secretly found a place to rent and one day, while Kevin was at work, I packed up my belongings, put Mr. Smudge in his cat carrier, and left a note on the refrigerator.

My happiest list was the one I made when I married Paul.

1. Ask Lea to be Maid of Honor
2. Buy dress
3. Hire caterer
4. Find a judge to marry us
5. Invite/tell immediate world

Crossing things off that list had been a lot more fun.

I also made a list when I started my own legal nurse consulting business. That was a scary time and having that list made it a lot easier. It was my lifeline whenever I thought I had to be crazy to consider my own business.

1. Incorporate

23

2. Design stationery
3. Make marketing packet
4. Talk to my boss about working from home
5. Market to other attorneys in town
6. Clear office space in spare bedroom
7. Succeed

Paul didn't know it, but I had a secret list for when his child support ended. It only had one item on it, though, and it was only for me.

1. Celebrate

Maybe it was mean, but I felt I owed myself that one indulgence. No more child support meant no longer dealing with Mona. I had been marking down the time in my mind. Two more months. Then, Claudia would be eighteen years old and out of high school. Claudia was planning on going to a community college in New Hampshire where she and her mother now lived. As far as we knew, no provisions had been made for Paul to contribute to that as costs would be minimal. Mona wasn't very good about keeping Paul informed. But regardless of what Claudia did after graduation, it would not be something we *had* to contribute to. Paul and I could decide what we wanted as a couple. No more edicts from Mona.

I shut down the computer for the day and went out on the back deck. Once again, I was allowing Mona to gain control over me. I could almost hear my therapist warning me. "Sara, stop giving her rent-free space in your head." But with no one there to scold me, I let my thoughts run free. I sighed in frustration. I didn't expect Paul back for a few more hours. That letter was going to sit on the kitchen counter and bug me until then.

Chapter Two

I needed a distraction and working wasn't going to do it. I needed shopping...and a friend. I called Judy. She was always up for spending money.

A phone call, a change of clothes, and an hour later, I was sitting in a coffee shop in Scottsdale waiting for Judy to arrive.

Judy was the paralegal in my favorite lawyer's office and the reason I was at Thompson and Concetti in the first place. One day, after another failed attorney interview in Phoenix, I was in an elevator on my way down to the parking garage feeling miserable. Why the irritable attorney had agreed to meet with me when it was obvious he didn't want or need a nurse consultant was beyond me. I tried to console myself with the notion that at least the interview had been good practice. But practice for what, I couldn't decide. The idea of being a legal consultant seemed like the stupidest idea I had ever had. I should just go back to working in the hospital. I was a good nurse. So what if it meant working nights again? Paul and I would adjust.

As the elevator door was closing, a hand shot in and popped the door back open.

"Sorry," said a woman carrying too many files. She was young and thin and looked very professional in her navy pantsuit. Except for her hair. Long, blonde and curly, it refused to stay confined by the combs on either side of her head. She blew a strand of hair out of her eyes as she punched the button for the lobby with her elbow. She smiled at me. "Thanks. I'm late for a meeting."

I smiled back. "You sure have your hands full." I never knew what to say in elevators. Do people want you to acknowledge them? Is that too forward?

"Yeah," she said as she adjusted the stack. "Medical case. It's amazing how much paperwork they generate."

My ears perked up at the word "medical". "Are you an attorney in this building?"

"No, I'm a paralegal, and I don't work in this building. Our office is in North Scottsdale. I just came here to pick something up. Hi, my name's Judy, by the way." She extended a couple of fingers while she attempted to hang onto the pile of records as they started to slide.

"Here, let me help you with that," I said. I grabbed a couple of the folders from her. "I'm Sara. And I know what you mean about medical files. I'm a nurse."

"Really? Ever work for an attorney?"

"I'd like to. I just interviewed with one in this building but it was a disaster."

"We could sure use you in our office. We just lost our nurse. Here, hold these a minute."

She plopped the rest of her burden on top of the files I was already holding and rummaged in her purse.

"Where are those? Oh, here they are." She offered me her business card but I had no hands left to take it with. "Oh, sorry."

We exchanged files for card.

"Call me tomorrow at that number," she said. "I think we

26

can help each other out."

And the rest, as they say, is history.

Judy took personal pride in the fact that she had brought me to the firm. She made me her special project and took me under her wing my first week. I was twelve years older than her but despite our age difference, we became close friends. Judy was a little scattered. I was anything but. I was fascinated with her carefree approach to life and she seemed to want my dating advice. Judy had had a brief marriage to her college sweetheart that lasted only a year. Since her divorce several years ago, she had become a social butterfly. I loved hearing her dating war stories and she, for some strange reason, enjoyed hearing about my trials as a second wife and sometime stepmother. It worked for us. We formed a lasting friendship.

I was halfway through my carrot cake, rationalizing my guilt over the icing when Judy breezed into the coffee shop finally and sat down. She was out of breath, as usual.

"Sorry, I know I'm late. But I got a call just as I was leaving the house." She raised her eyebrows. "I had to take it. It was Sam." Sam was her latest fling. Judy was head over heels.

"And how is Mr. Tight Ass...I mean buns?" Judy had complained that she liked Sam but he was a little cheap.

"He's fine and not as tight as he used to be...in the wallet, I mean. His buns are still quite nice, thank you."

She eyed what I was eating. "That any good?"

"It's OK. I've had worse."

"Hmm. Maybe I'll just have coffee. Be right back."

A few minutes and a latte later, Judy was sitting back down. "Ok, spill it. What's wrong? Don't tell me you just had to have coffee fifteen miles from your house on a Saturday afternoon."

"*She* wrote a letter to Paul. It came this morning."

Judy immediately knew who I meant. We had discussed my feelings about Mona at length. "And...?"

27

"And what? She sent him a letter. I don't know what it says. I didn't read it. Paul is out car part shopping. He hasn't seen it yet."

"Sara, Sara, Sara." Judy clicked her tongue. "Have you learned nothing from me? Let me get this straight. The ex wrote to your husband. You have the letter and you haven't read it."

"Yeah."

"And you say your husband is the one who avoids things?"

I took a sip of coffee to stall. Judy had hit home and it hurt. "I guess."

"So, you're upset but you don't know what you're upset about?"

I suddenly felt foolish. "It doesn't sound so earth-shattering when you put it like that."

"I'm not saying she isn't trouble. You certainly know her better than I do. But it may not be as bad as you think."

I was slowly allowing myself to believe my friend even though experience had taught me otherwise. Hearing Judy's reaction made me think that I was blowing this way out of proportion. We brainstormed a few things that Mona might be asking for and then we spent the next couple of hours shopping. On the drive back home, I replayed my conversation with Judy. She was right. I was making more of this than I needed to. I should just read the darn letter. I knew Paul wouldn't mind. He shared everything with me when it came to Mona anyway. But a part of me really didn't even want to know.

Mona upset me...a lot. On the one hand, the less I knew about her and her life the better. Denial was a wonderful thing. In between contacts from her, I did very well. I could almost delude myself into thinking that she wasn't out there somewhere. But knowing what she was up to was vital as far as I was concerned.

Mona had tried to do a lot of damage to me/us in the first

few years of my marriage to Paul. And I have to admit, I did not handle most of it well. And that's not like me. Raised in Queens, I prided myself on what my friend Lea used to call my "New York brass". I usually gave as good as I got. But for some reason, when it came to Mona, I fell apart.

Most times, I cried. Sometimes, I yelled (I blamed that on being Sicilian, and sadly, my mother's daughter). There had been days, especially if we were going through anything that caused us to have to work through lawyers, that the mere mention of Mona's name would cause me to shake and get nauseous. Mona brought a primitive fear out in me that I just couldn't explain.

While part of me could understand her frustration, anger - and yes, unhappiness - at losing her husband, I could not understand why she hated me so much. I had done nothing to destroy their marriage. Paul had already left Mona before he and I became a couple. Mona, however, always contended that I was the reason she and Paul were not back together again.

Paul was in the kitchen going through the mail when I got home. The letter from Mona was on the counter, unopened, set aside to be dealt with after the bills and junk mail. I tossed my keys on the kitchen counter and tried to sound casual. I kissed Paul on the cheek and nodded toward Mona's letter. "Putting off the inevitable?"

"It's just going to put me in a bad mood," he grumbled.

"Oh, just buck up and open it. Maybe she's dying and she wants to apologize for everything she's ever done to us."

Paul looked at me and smiled. "Don't get my hopes up." He grabbed the letter opener and slit Mona's envelope open. I found myself holding my breath while he read the letter.

"Well? What does she want?" Please let it be simple.

And cheap.

And nothing that involves court.

Paul hesitated. Not a good sign. He slid the pages back into the envelope and placed it back on the counter. "We can

29

talk about this afterwards. Why don't we do that after dinner?" I could feel my stomach tighten. He knew I wasn't going to wait that long. Guess he had to try.

"No, let's talk about it now. I can deal with it better if I don't have to worry about it."

"What Mona wants shouldn't worry you." I sensed the irritation starting to come into Paul's voice and knew we were starting down a well-worn path. Soon, he would be raising his voice and accusing me of making his life difficult. Why couldn't she just go away?

"Paul, just tell me what she wants. This affects me, too. Apparently, it's something that is upsetting you." I was trying to be nice, hoping he wouldn't get defensive. My resentment was returning. Why couldn't Paul put my feelings first for once?

"Her letter isn't upsetting me. What is upsetting me is knowing that you're going to get angry and then I have that to contend with." Paul grabbed the envelope and pushed it across the countertop at me. "Here, read it for yourself since you're obviously not going to let this go." He got up and walked out of the room. I guess he wanted to be out of range when I blew.

Hands shaking, I picked up Mona's letter. She had once again invaded my home. I pulled the sheets out and scanned the first few paragraphs. It was just silly chatter about Claudia. Claudia had won this award. Claudia was dating this guy. Blah, blah, blah. Nothing important - until I got to the middle of page two.

There it was. Claudia and college and what was Paul going to contribute? My face felt hot and I clenched my teeth.

What did she mean what was Paul going to contribute? What part of nothing didn't she understand? There was no provision for college support in Paul's divorce decree. As far as I had always understood, once Claudia graduated from high school we were through with mandated support.

Apparently, Mona thought differently. As usual, Mona and Claudia had left things to the last minute. Now, all of a sudden, Claudia had apparently decided she wanted to go out of state to a four year college. Her high school was helping them make applications but it didn't look like any scholarships were going to be forthcoming since most deadlines had passed. In her letter, Mona was claiming that Paul had verbally agreed at the time of their divorce to help her and Claudia out with college expenses. She was threatening that the state of New Hampshire would award college support to her if she went back to court. Mona also said she had already consulted an attorney about this. She was hoping it wouldn't come to that and was appealing to Paul's desire to "help their child" and cough up some money. But the threat was obviously there. If you don't give me what I want, we will be in court - again. And Claudia wasn't even accepted anywhere yet. Leave it to Mona to start some fireworks over next to nothing.

No wonder Paul didn't want to be in the same room with me when I read that letter.

I controlled the urge to crumple the letter and throw it across the room. Instead, I fantasized slapping Mona across the face. I took a deep breath and tried to control the panic that was starting to swell. I swallowed but my mouth was dry. This was going to be huge. I assumed from his reaction that Paul wanted to make some kind of compromise with Mona and was anticipating an argument from me. He was right. I felt strongly about giving her any more money. I had been counting the months until child support would be over and our finances would no longer be an open book for Mona to peruse at her leisure.

Over the years, she had periodically asked for increases in child support based on one reason or another, many of them fabricated. No matter. Each time, we would have to hire an attorney to go with Paul to a hearing at the local courthouse where our financial records would be scrutinized

31

so that the judge could make a decision. Each time, I felt so violated.

Mona knew every job I had had, and how much I made. Where my savings went. What small inheritance my aunt had left us. How much life insurance we had. What make and model car I drove. How much we owed on our home. All of it.

Granted, her finances were on the table, too, but I felt that was only right. She was the one crying poverty and asking for the handout. I had no problem with Paul's finances being looked at, either. Just not mine. After all, he and Mona did have a child together and they owed Claudia a good life. But enough was enough. I had thought the end was in sight. Now this. When was the gravy train supposed to end?

Jesse came over and licked the back of my leg. Little Toby followed right behind him as usual. Some days I didn't know what I would do without those two. They always sensed when I needed them. I absently reached down and scratched both of them behind their ears. Then I bent down and hugged Jesse and the tears started to fall. Toby licked them off my cheek and that made me laugh. I hugged each of them again and stood up. Time to face the music. I could hear Paul puttering in the garage and I went out there.

Paul had the hood of the antique Mercedes sedan up and was busy inspecting something very grimy. Whenever he had something on his mind, he worked on his car. It was his therapy. Mine was shopping. Paul's way was cheaper but not as much fun.

"Paul, can we talk about this?" I asked.

"Talk. I'm listening." I could hear the anger in his voice. His head never came out from under the hood. He wasn't going to make this easy.

"What do you want to do about Mona's request? I thought we weren't obligated to pay for college for Claudia. Maybe we should have talked about this sooner but I was under the impression we were through with child support when Claudia graduated high school. Besides, I thought Claudia was going to go to a less expensive community college."

Paul's voice was a little muffled, his head still bent over whatever he was tinkering with. "I guess she's changed her mind. And *we* (Paul put an emphasis on this word that I did not miss or like) are not obligated to pay for anything. Claudia is my daughter and I might want to help her out with college. I didn't know I needed your permission."

I waited a second before answering. This was going to end up in an ugly argument if I wasn't careful. When Paul got defensive like this, I was the one he attacked.

"Okay, I can understand where you're coming from. I had just thought we would talk about this, that's all. This is a big step and I would like to be included in this."

No answer from under the hood.

"Paul, can we just talk? Did you hear me?"

He stood up and looked at me, all the while wiping the dirt from his hands on a rag. He sighed. Maybe he was softening his position. Encouragement started to replace fear.

"Look, Sara, I don't want to fight about this. I know you resent Claudia."

I opened my mouth to protest but he put his hand up to stop me.

"It's okay. I'm not criticizing. I know this hasn't been easy. I know dealing with Mona has been hard – on both of us. But Claudia is my daughter. I would feel like a real louse if I didn't do something to help her out with college. I'm not saying I'm going to write Mona a blank check. I'm going to talk to her and see what she has in mind and then you and I can talk about it. But I'm not going to tell her a flat no, either. I don't want to wind up in court over this and you know we will if I refuse to help out at all. Why can't you see it from my point of view?"

Why can't you see mine? I felt like screaming but didn't.

33

Instead, I just asked, "When are you going to call her?"

"I'll call her in a little bit. It's three hours later back east and I don't want to call too late. You want to be there?" He knew I did. Whenever he was on the phone with Mona, I felt compelled to be in the room with him even though hearing her voice upset me. For one thing, Paul was bad at remembering details and he hated to answer my questions about the conversation afterwards. He said he felt like I was grilling him. My response was that if he remembered things better, I wouldn't have to grill him. But I think he forgot most of his conversations with Mona because he didn't like to remember unpleasant things. We had agreed that he would always speak to her on speakerphone so that I could listen. I never spoke to Mona. She wouldn't respond to me if I did anyway but she knew I was in the room listening and it tended to keep the conversation civil if she knew it was being monitored, so to speak. In the old days, she would get very argumentative and use the phone calls as an excuse to berate Paul, especially if it was about making arrangements for visitations. Sometimes, she did this right in front of Claudia but this had all stopped when Paul told her I was acting as a witness. Our attorney had suggested this. Mona complained at first but eventually complied when she realized it was the only way Paul would talk with her.

"Yes, I want to be there. I want to know what we will be up against." Paul made a face when I said that but didn't say anything. "I'm going to work in my office a little. Let me know when you're ready to make that call."

Paul's head went back under the hood. "Fine."

Chapter Three

I went back into the kitchen and just stared at the pages of Mona's letter still strewn on the countertop where I had left them. I couldn't believe all that had happened in the last hour.

I needed to do something. Despite what I had told Paul, I knew working on my report was a bad idea. It was too hard to concentrate. I kept hearing possible conversations between Paul and Mona in my head, none of them good. Instead, I peeled potatoes and chopped vegetables for dinner. Cutting florets off the broccoli stalks was cathartic. I kept imagining it was Mona's head.

I hated feeling so insecure. But that's what thinking about Mona reduced me to. I could recite a long list of the things she had done. In the early days of my marriage to Paul, I used to replay many of them over and over in my mind, a masochistic game I inflicted on myself when I was feeling especially wimpy, which back then was a lot.

Most of them centered around the few things she had said to me (when she would let herself acknowledge my existence at all) and the snappy comebacks I had...three hours later. I was not good at standing up for myself with Mona. Dealing with her made my knees go weak, my throat close up, and my armpits sweat. And I was sure she knew it. Paul excused her behavior by saying it was hard for her to see us together and so happy and that things would get better with time. Poor delusional Paul. He hated conflict. Always did. He just couldn't stand having to deal with Mona when she went off on one of her rants. I really think he thought it would get better. He also truly believed that as long as he appeased her, he would have easy access to Claudia. I remember telling him once that I was going to enroll him in the "Bucket of the Month Club".

"What's that?" he had asked.

"Every month a new bucket of sand is delivered and you stick your head in it. Works great."

Paul didn't always enjoy my sense of humor as much as I did.

Half an hour later, Paul came back into the kitchen and began washing the car engine grime off his hands.

"I'm calling Mona now if you want to hang around," he said. He knew I did. Maybe he was hoping I'd changed my mind but this was an important call. I had no intention of skipping it.

"OK, I'm ready. Let's get it over with."

Paul frowned at me but didn't say anything. He dialed Mona's number and put the phone on speaker. I felt my stomach lurch when I heard the phone pick up. It had been several months since Paul had spoken to her. I never got used to it.

"Hello? Weber residence," she said. Oh, that annoyed me but I said nothing. Now wasn't the time to be petty.

"Hi, Mona, it's Paul. I got your letter today. I thought we'd talk about this a little."

"Am I on speakerphone? I think I need to know that before we continue."

"Yes, Mona, you know you are. Now, can we talk about this request of yours regarding college? I thought Claudia was planning on going to the local community college."

"Well, yes, Claudia was thinking about that but she and I have been talking about it some more and we decided it would be better for her to go away to a four-year program. So, I wanted you to know that and to find out what you plan on contributing. You can't expect us to foot the entire bill and you not contribute anything toward her education." Mona was on a roll. You could tell she had either been coached or she had practiced this speech. "I have already contacted my attorney and he has informed me that I have a very good case if I take you back to court for more support."

"Whoa, let's back up here a little. I think it's premature to talk about going to court already. You haven't told me any details regarding this. You haven't even given me a chance to say yes or no and already you're threatening to go to court. I don't think that's fair." I could see Paul's face start to redden. I made a motion for him to relax. He smiled weakly at me and nodded. "This has taken me completely off guard."

"Well, Paul, I was just anticipating what you were going to say based on past experiences. Any time Claudia has needed extra things, I always had to beg to get something out of you." Paul's jaw tightened and I could see his muscles tense. He took a deep breath.

"Look, Mona, I didn't call to fight about this. I just want to know what you and Claudia have in mind. Where is Claudia planning on attending? I need details and then Sara and I will talk it over and get back to you about our decision."

There were a couple of seconds of silence followed by a snort or something. "What does Sara [*insert snotty tone here*] have to do with *my* daughter's education?" All of a sudden, Claudia had gone from "our" daughter to "my" daughter as soon as my name was mentioned.

"Sara and I make all our financial decisions together and that's all you need to know. Now are you going to give me any details or is this conversation over?"

"Well, Claudia hasn't definitely decided where she wants to attend college." Mona liked to maintain an air of control by being in charge of information. This was a ploy she had used over the years to her advantage. She rarely gave Paul information about events in Claudia's life and when she did she often left important details out. I sensed she was doing this now. "She has several places in mind. I know Boston College and the University of Pennsylvania are two that she's mentioned. I know for sure she wants to go out of state."

Yeah, probably to get away from you.

"She will be applying for grants and loans and scholarships but she may not get anything much for the first year. I think both of her parents should help her out as well. I don't want her graduating with a big hefty bill to pay off."

Paul sighed again. Mona didn't really seem to have this fully thought out and he wasn't getting anywhere. "Look, I'm not saying yes or no at this point. I think you and Claudia need to come up with some numbers before I can make up my mind, and we can't do that until we have some idea of what the final cost is going to be. Maybe I need to talk with Claudia about this, too. I don't even know what she plans on studying. What her major is going to be. That should influence where she goes, I would think."

I could hear the sneer in Mona's voice. "Well, maybe if you talked to your child more often, you'd know these things."

I watched the color rise in Paul's cheeks and knew Mona had stepped over the line. "Okay, I think this conversation is over. I don't need a lecture. Have Claudia call me if she wants to talk about this. You and I can discuss it again after that. Good-bye, Mona."

"We'll definitely be talking about this again." Then,

without even saying good-bye, she hung up. I looked at Paul. I didn't know if I should say anything or not.

Paul let out a sigh and then smiled at me. "I think that went well, don't you?"

I had to laugh. At least, it broke the tension. "Wonderfully, but you forgot to ask her to come for Sunday dinner."

Paul shook his head. "She's one of a kind, isn't she? I keep expecting her to grow up or change and she never does." He looked down at the phone and then at me. "What did you think?"

"I don't know, Paul. She really didn't give us much to go on. What are you feeling? What do you think you want to do?" I was glad to see that Paul and I were at least talking again.

"Well, I think some of it depends on Claudia. Let's see if she at least calls and talks to me about this. I'll give her a couple of days. I'll call her if she doesn't call me. Then, I guess we'll see. I'd like to help her out. I know you don't feel I should or that I'm obligated to. I know that. I'm not doing this because Mona asked me to. I want to do it for me, for Claudia. Maybe to make up for the lack in our relationship right now. Maybe I'm thinking if she knows I'm helping her, it will give me a second chance with her. I hope you understand." He shook his head. "Here I am asking you to understand and I'm not sure I understand myself."

I sighed. What could I say? This was my husband, the man I loved above all else and he was obviously hurting. I didn't want to be the cause of any more hurt. "Okay, let's wait for Claudia to call. We'll see where she wants to go to college and then go from there. It might be fun to talk with her about this." I put my hand over Paul's. He was still sitting at the breakfast nook, next to the phone. "We're together on this, Paul. It'll be okay."

Paul looked at me and smiled. He looked so grateful, my heart melted.

He squeezed my hand. "Thanks," he said.

I felt lighter. I hated the fact that Mona still had this control over my life. I knew that I gave the power to her to some extent. But I really felt unable to change that.

Paul went back out to the garage and I continued making dinner.

While I peeled potatoes, I kept replaying Mona's conversation with Paul. How could she think that after all she had done to destroy Paul's relationship with Claudia that he was just going to roll over and hand her a check? Mona's sense of entitlement knew no bounds.

According to Paul, Mona was used to running the show during their marriage. Paul had met Mona when he was Best Man at his brother Gregg's wedding. Mona was the Maid of Honor, best friend to Carol, Gregg's new wife. Paul and Mona started dating immediately afterwards. Even though Paul was still in college (he was a late starter, having recently left the service), Mona wanted a big wedding with all the trimmings and a house and children. All right away. Paul was able to put her off a little because of school. He got her to agree to no kids for a few years until they were better off financially. What often struck me when Paul talked about his early years with Mona was that he never mentioned falling in love. My marriage to Kevin wasn't happy toward the end, by any means, but at least I had some good times to look back on. Paul didn't seem to have that. Some days when we were in the thick of Mona battles I used to ask him what made him marry her. Why? He could never really say.

"It was just the thing I felt I needed to do at the time" was the best answer I got from him. Maybe he thought it was time to marry and Mona happened to be the person at the right place at the right time. Maybe it was a guy thing. I don't know.

As it was, Paul's plan didn't last long. When Mona got tired of waiting, she went off the pill behind Paul's back and within months, Claudia was in the making. Paul was angry and he later told me that that was the beginning of the end for him and Mona.

No, that's not right. That was Act Two of The Beginning of the End. Act One started pretty soon after the honeymoon. Mona complained – often - that Paul did not pay enough attention to her. They didn't go out enough. They didn't have enough money. He wouldn't visit with her friends. Blah. Blah. Blah.

I know, it sounds like I'm really blaming Mona alone for their troubles but she and Paul did have an agreement. Paul has a methodical nature. I've learned that over the years. When he made a plan, he stuck to it. Paul's plan was for he and Mona to marry, which they did the summer before his junior year in college. The next part of the plan was for Paul to stay in school and work part-time until he finished his undergraduate degree in Architecture. After that, he would apply for his licensure and start his own business. Mona already had a license in Real Estate and she was supposed to work to help support them until Paul finished. Then they would start a family. Paul had told me he knew it wasn't the greatest plan but it was the one he was most comfortable with.

Much to his surprise, Mona had agreed to it.

Then, I guess fears about her biological clock running out of time set in. Soon, fights about children, or the lack of them, among other things, became frequent and long, according to Paul. Mona's weapon was the silent treatment for days on end afterward, including in the bedroom. In an effort to make peace, Paul dropped out of school and took a job selling pharmaceuticals. The deal was that he would make some serious money and then they could start a family. After a few months, Mona became impatient and the fights about children started again. Paul told me that he had had a short-lived affair right around then. He felt that the marriage was so shaky at that point, he was actually afraid to have children with Mona. He even considered leaving her. But he

41

felt terrible about the affair and ended it after just a few weeks. He didn't think Mona ever found out but it was shortly after that that she went off the pill.

I had just put the chicken in the oven when the phone rang. Thinking it might be Claudia calling Paul, I picked it up on the first ring.

"Hi, there!"

But it wasn't Claudia.

Chapter Four

It was my sister Angela, calling from New York. She barely acknowledged my greeting before she started in.

"Do you know what she did today? I found food all over her room, stashed in the weirdest places. And dirty underwear in her drawer. She's driving me crazy."

Angela was, of course, referring to our mother. Mom had been living with Angela ever since it became painfully obvious that she could no longer be trusted living alone.

"Sara, I swear it's time to put her in a home." Angela and I had had this conversation many times before. We were in agreement that Mom was getting worse but neither of us wanted to place her yet. It was such a final step. I was grateful, too, that Angela had taken her in, something I was unwilling to do. My feelings toward my mother were tainted by bitter memories of my childhood and my mother's tirades after Daddy had left her – and us. Going away to nursing school was the best thing that had ever happened to me. I had lived on my own ever since and not once had I ever looked back.

"Well, Angela, if that's what you think we should do, then let's look into that."

"Well, that's not something I want to do all by myself. That's too much responsibility and, frankly, I don't have the time or the energy to do it right now. I have a business to run, you know, and I don't have a husband to do things for me like you do."

I took a deep breath. Sometimes, Angela sounded eerily like Mom. "I know, Angela, you have a very tough life. What would you like me to do?"

"There's no reason for sarcasm. I'm just saying that you need to pull your share of the load, that's all."

"Look, Angela, I'm sorry that I live across the country and that makes life inconvenient for you but I told you last year when this first came up that all you had to do was call me and I would come out. If you want to look into nursing homes or some kind of assisted living situation for Mom, tell me. I'll fly out there and help you pick a place. But don't tell me my life is picture perfect because you don't know the half of it and I'm not in the mood to get into a pissing match with you right now. So back off."

Angela's voice softened. "I'm sorry. You're right, that was out of line. Is everything okay with you and Paul?"

"Yes…no…we're just going through a thing with Mona and money right now. I don't want to talk about it."

"Well, you knew what you were getting into when you married a man with a kid. It's not the best situation you know. Kids are hard. Believe me, I know."

I really hated it when people told me I should have known what I was getting into. First of all, how could anyone know that? Secondly, Mona was the exception to the rule. She deliberately made things harder than they had to be. I knew lots of women who were divorced with children and their kids visited their Dad and things were fine. Even Angela, for all of her selfishness, supported her daughter's relationship with Ed, her ex.

"Look, Sara, let me see how it goes for the next few weeks. Michelle will be home from college soon and she can help me a bit. Maybe after she goes back to school we can see how things are and then make a decision. How does that sound?"

"That sounds fine."

Paul and I had our dinner on the deck that night after all but instead of romance, we talked about Claudia. Paul reminisced about her baby days, how he couldn't believe she was ready for college.

"How does it feel to be old enough to have an eighteen year old daughter?" I asked him.

"Hey, if I'm old, so are you."

"Nope, she's not my kid and I'm your child bride." I was glad things were back to normal. I ached when Paul and I fought.

That night, I dreamed about the day that Mom had told us that Dad had died. It was a recurring nightmare. In my dream, just as Mom was telling us that Daddy had died, I hear him calling to me from the driveway. Mom grabs me just as I'm about to run out the door. I can see Daddy in his car with Eleanor. He looks at me, backs up, and drives away. No matter how hard I try to yell, no words come out. The dream always ended there.

I woke up in a sweat. Paul lay sleeping next to me, oblivious. His arm was thrown over his head and his eyes fluttered, dreaming. Jesse was curled up on the bed, snoring, while Toby slept on the rug on my side of the bed. I took comfort in my family and snuggled into Paul. He curved around me and we spooned. I held onto his hand and fell back into a more peaceful sleep.

The next afternoon, I was once again working in my office when I heard a car drive up. Toby was barking and clawing at the front door, a sign he recognized the sound of someone's brakes. I looked out the dining room window and saw Gregg's car in the driveway. I could see Carol sitting in the passenger seat but Gregg wasn't with her. I assumed he was in the garage, talking to Paul. Minutes later, I heard the car drive away and Paul came into the house, smiling.

"How would you like to go out to eat? Carol and Gregg are going to have dinner at the Lake House and invited us to join them." The Lake House was probably the nicest restaurant that we had in our little town. It had recently come under new management and Paul and I hadn't been there in a while. I thought Carol and Gregg eating there was unusual, though. There were so many nicer, pricier restaurants more to Carol's liking in Scottsdale where they lived. But I never refused a chance to eat out.

"Sure. Just give me a few minutes to freshen up."

Half an hour later, we walked into the Lake House. My eyes took a few minutes to adjust to the dim lighting. If menu prices were proportionate to the amount of lighting in the restaurant, tonight's dinner was going to be costly. The front of the restaurant was taken up by the bar, gleaming copper and polished wood. Several couples were gathered around it, obviously waiting for tables. I didn't see Carol or Gregg and wondered if they had been able to get a table. It looked like we were going to have to wait a while to be seated.

The young hostess smiled as Paul approached her.

"Yes, sir, may I help you?"

"We're supposed to be meeting some people here. The last name is Weber."

She looked down at her table outline. "Oh, yes, Dr. Weber and his wife are already seated. Follow me, please."

I smiled at the hostess' "Dr. Weber" remark. I was sure that was Carol's doing. Gregg had his doctorate in education but she always liked to imply that Gregg was a medical doctor. I wondered what she would have done if there was a medical emergency. I didn't think Gregg's dissertation on medieval literature would come in handy then. But it had obviously gotten us a good table.

Gregg waved as soon as he saw us. He was a smaller, slightly younger version of Paul. He and Carol made an unusual couple. He typified the absent-minded professor look. He didn't care what he wore, who his friends were. Carol, on the other hand, was always dressed impeccably and cared deeply about image.

"So glad you guys could make it." Gregg stood up and kissed me on the cheek. "Haven't seen you in ages, Sis. How's it going?"

"It's going great, Gregg. Hi, Carol. Thanks for inviting us."

Carol smiled and pulled out the chair next to her for me. "You're looking good. How is your business going?"

Carol's interest always put me on guard. I felt I was always fighting a battle between wanting to be close to her because she was my sister-in-law and feeling on edge because she was still Mona's best friend.

Gregg poured us some wine from the bottle already on the table. He raised his glass. "To us, to being together and being a family."

Paul looked at him. "How much of this have you had? You getting sentimental on me?"

"No, but I do have a reason for asking you here tonight. I have a proposition for you. Let's order and then we can talk about it."

Once the appetizers arrived, Gregg put his fork down and cleared his throat. "Okay, here's the deal. Mona called us last night." He put his hand up when he saw the reaction on Paul's face. "Hang on, let me finish. She told us about Claudia and this college thing. That Claudia wants to go away to an out of state university."

"It hasn't been definitely decided yet. It's kind of late in the year to be planning this anyway. Why was Mona talking to you about this?"

"Actually, she called to talk to me," Carol said. "And she

didn't call to tell me about college. We were just catching up with each other and the topic came up."

"And that's why I wanted to talk to you," Gregg said. "What if Claudia came out here and went to Arizona State University? I think I can help her get this done." Gregg smiled, obviously pleased with himself. Gregg taught English at the University. I knew if he was offering this, it was something he knew he could deliver.

I felt my mouth go dry and took a sip of wine. I just looked at Paul. I couldn't believe what I was hearing. I couldn't read the expression on Paul's face and he wasn't meeting my gaze, probably deliberately.

"I don't know. I don't know if Mona will want her that far away from her. That's a big step."

"She's fine with it," Carol said. "She and I have already discussed it and she thinks it could work. Especially if Claudia lives with you and Sara. That would keep expenses down and Claudia could apply for in-state tuition rates."

I felt the color rise in my cheeks. Carol and Mona had already discussed this. Of course, now it made sense. Dangle Claudia in front of Paul. Get what she wants. No matter what I thought.

Paul finally looked at me. "What do you think?"

Uh, let me think...NO! I took another sip of wine to stall. Maybe Claudia would refuse. One could only hope. And if Claudia were living here that meant dealing with Mona on an almost day-to-day basis. God help me!

I knew saying *What the hell are you all thinking?* was not the right answer. But my insides were churning. This morning when I woke up, everything was perfect, the sunshine, the dogs, my Paul... and now a mere twelve hours later the world was chaos. All of a sudden everyone had plans - plans for me, and my life, and my time, and my home. I could barely swallow my wine.

I looked Paul in the eye, hoping he could read my thoughts. "And this is a good idea because…"

Paul put his hand over mine and squeezed. "This will give me - us - the opportunity to get reacquainted with Claudia and rebuild our relationship. She's going to be grown and on her own pretty soon and this might be my last chance with her. And as Carol said, it will be a less expensive option."

It was obvious Paul didn't see the pitfalls I was seeing. I was still hoping he would know what this would mean to me, to us. "Well, off the top of my head, it sounds okay ... financially...." I let the rest of it linger, hoping Paul would get my meaning.

Paul looked back at Gregg. "Let me talk to Mona and Claudia about it some more and then we'll get back to you. And thanks, Gregg, I appreciate this."

Paul was hooked. Now if I objected, I was going to be the troublemaker. Great.

Gregg slapped Paul on the back. "No problem. That's what family is for."

Paul chatted for the rest of the meal, never noticing that I wasn't saying very much. I, on the other hand, was numb. I wanted to scream *Hell, no!* as loud as I could and run from the restaurant.

Chapter Five

The ride home was mercifully short. Paul chatted about the prospect of Claudia coming to live with us and never noticed that I had little to say about it. Frankly, I was surprised that Mona agreed to this new plan. I would have thought that having Claudia living with us and going to school out here would have been too threatening to her. However, I was not going to be the one to mention this to Paul. If Mona felt threatened, let her bring that up with Paul. He already hated her.

I made sure that Paul was asleep before I went to bed that night. I just couldn't handle any more discussions about Mona and Claudia and school. And I certainly was not feeling romantic. I didn't like the way my life seemed to be turning.

Paul called Claudia two nights later because, of course, she had not called him. It turned out she really didn't have a clear idea of what she wanted to do in college. She threw out things like journalism and business but the kid really didn't know what she wanted. She didn't have much enthusiasm for anything. She talked a lot about friends and what they were doing and seemed to just be going along with the idea of college because it was expected. However, it was obvious she wanted to go away somewhere.

Then, Paul suggested ASU.

"I don't know Dad. Mom mentioned that, too, but I really was thinking more like Boston or U of P."

"Do you know what you want to major in?"

"I was thinking journalism."

"ASU has a great school for that. And you could live here."

"At your house?"

"Sure, what's wrong with that?"

"I was planning on living in the dorm. I think that's better when you go to college."

"It's silly to pay for room and board when you have a perfectly good home right here. Besides, you have really left this to the last minute. I think we should see about getting you enrolled the first year and then we can go from there. Uncle Gregg is going to help us with that."

"Your father has a good point, Claudia. Let's at least consider this," Mona chimed in. She was listening in on the extension, as always. She sounded far too enthusiastic, if you asked me, too eager to work this out. It was totally out of character and my guard went up.

Paul left it that Claudia was going to think it over for a few days. She wanted to talk to her school guidance counselor and get her opinion about the college and then she and Mona would call us back. Nothing was worked out regarding financial arrangements. I felt Mona should be paying us child support now if Claudia came here to live but I didn't see that ever happening. I knew Paul would never ask for it. I wanted to suggest that Mona pay something toward tuition at least but Mr. "I don't want to rock the boat" might not agree to that, either.

I didn't say anything when Paul ended the call. Instead, I

51

went out to the deck and sat on the deck swing. Jesse trotted over and laid his soft head in my lap. Toby climbed onto the swing and nuzzled my hand. My kids. They would never ask for money for college. I absently stroked one and then the other while I thought of all the possible ways this could go. How would I deal with Mona in such a forced closeness? I could just see her calling all the time wanting to talk to "her baby". The thought made me shiver and, despite the warm night, I pulled my sweater closer.

Mona had tried to dictate what we did with Claudia when she was a little girl, when we had regular visitation, before they moved away. She had even insisted on inspecting Claudia's room in our house so that she could make sure everything met her standards before she would let her sleep over. What did she think we were going to do? Chain her in the basement, for God's sake? She was Paul's daughter, too. He wasn't going to do anything to hurt his own child.

Even now, all those years later, my jaw still clenched when I remembered how she had pranced through my house sticking her nose in all the rooms as she went by and making that snorting/sniffing sound she made when she was looking down her nose at someone. She had such an air of – I didn't know what to call it – entitlement. An "I'm better than you are" attitude. I always felt like dirt beneath her feet. I hated that she made me feel like that. I couldn't say anything to Paul about it without causing a fight. His attitude was just to tolerate her and get her out of the way as fast as possible. She got away with so much because of that.

But that was Mona. She was such a control freak. Well, maybe this time would be different. Claudia was almost an adult. Maybe Mona had mellowed.

Maybe pigs had learned to fly, too.

Paul had the good sense to leave me alone for a while. I heard him rummaging around, opening and closing cupboards. A few minutes later, he came out with two glasses of wine and sat beside me on the swing. Toby scooted over and snuggled between the two of us.

I took the glass that Paul offered me.

"Hey, don't look so worried," he said. "This just might work out after all."

I smiled and sipped and wondered if drinking heavily for the next four years would be a bad thing.

We had two nights of peace after that and I was able to lull myself into feeling good again. On the third night, we were snuggling on the sofa, watching TV, when the phone rang. I muted the volume on the TV while Paul got up to answer the phone. I could tell from his end of the conversation that it was Mona and quickly got up to join him in the kitchen. Paul clicked on the speakerphone as I walked in.

"...and good news, Paul. It looks like we are on target to get things done in time for the Fall semester. But Claudia wants to make sure this is what she really wants so we're going to come out there next month to look the place over."

My jaw dropped and I stared at Paul, eyes wide. He shrugged. This had surprised him as well. I shook my head No! but he put his hand up to silence me.

Mona kept up a steady chatter about how great this would be. She was going to see where Claudia was going to school. She had never been to Arizona but had heard so much about it and blah, blah, blah.

My mind was buzzing. This couldn't be happening. Then the hammer fell.

"It would mean a lot to me if I was able to see where Claudia would be staying. Claudia told me you want her at your house for the first semester at least. I think that's great but do you think I could be a part of this? I know you're going to laugh at me but this is my little girl, after all. I don't know, maybe I can help with decorating her room at your house? I would love to decorate my baby's room."

I couldn't believe my ears. It was like the old days all over again.

And what did my husband say about this? "That sounds like a great idea. I'm sure it will help the transition for both of you." I waved my arms in front of him. This was anything but a "great idea" but he was either ignoring me or pretending not to see.

They talked about airlines and possible dates and then Paul said, "Fine. Great. I look forward to hearing from you. Talk to you soon." And then they hung up. Just like old buddies.

I exploded.

"What the hell were you thinking?" I screamed. I'm sure the neighbors heard through the open kitchen window but I didn't care. "I would love to decorate my baby's room," I mimicked Mona's syrupy sweet voice. "Give me a fucking break."

Paul slammed his hand down on the kitchen counter. "I thought she was being very nice and very cooperative but as usual that's not good enough for you."

"Don't you go defending her to me." I was out of control and unable to stop. "Maybe you two should get back together and share your baby all you want. Is that what you want? Is it?" I threw the dish towel I had been twisting across the counter. "I can't take this anymore. I'm out of here."

I stomped off to the garage, slamming the door behind me. Paul hated when I slammed doors and I did it on purpose to aggravate him. Part of me was watching me from a distance and telling me I was being childish but I was too far gone to listen. I started the car and backed out of the garage. Paul came out to see what I was doing. Like an enraged teenager, I peeled out of the driveway and squealed into the street. I stuck my hand out the window as I drove away and gave him the finger.

I drove down to the town lake and parked in the lot overlooking the water. I watched the moon sparkle on the lake's surface and tried to calm myself. Shaking from anger, hurt, and frustration, I wondered how things had gone so wrong, so fast. A noose was tightening around my throat and Mona and Paul were both pulling on it.

I sensed Paul and I were headed down a dangerous path. He often accused me of making snowballs and then expecting him to throw them. But since Mona refused to deal with me...hell, she barely acknowledged my existence...how could I deal with her directly? I would have been more than happy to confront her on my own. Well, I said that in anger. I'm not sure I would have in person. But I had offered to write to her. Paul refused to allow that. He was afraid anything I wrote would certainly get taken the wrong way and also find its way into court. He was probably right but that didn't help my frustration. I expected him to stand up for us...for me. And he never did, not to my satisfaction. His need to get Mona off his back dictated how he reacted to her. He seemed more comfortable fighting with me afterwards than with her at any time.

I turned off the ignition and slammed the steering wheel. How could Paul not see what she was doing? How could he let her invade our life like this? There was no way I could work with Mona on this. It wasn't that I didn't want Claudia here. I did. I just wanted this to be our relationship with Claudia. Mine and Paul's. I wanted Mona to stay out of it.

I had tried so hard to make friends with Claudia in the early years.

"My Mommy loves Daddy and if you would leave, he could come home," Claudia said to me on one of our first visits together. She was only a little more than three years old at the time. Paul and I had taken her to a park in Philadelphia near our apartment. We were talking marriage but he had not told Claudia and certainly had not breathed a word to Mona. She still blamed me for their breakup.

I didn't know how to respond to Claudia's statement and I'm sure my mouth just hung open. Paul had gone for ice cream cones and I wished he would hurry back.

"Well, I'm sure your Mommy didn't say that," I finally

answered.

"Yes, she did. She told me."

Mona was being as difficult as possible with the divorce proceedings. She had been dragging her feet on the custody agreement, throwing all kinds of roadblocks in the way. At first, she refused to let Paul see Claudia unless it was in their old home that Mona now owned. "Claudia is far too young to be staying away from her mother. It would be too upsetting for her," she had told Paul.

Paul's attorney made it clear that Paul was not going to comply with that and that Mona had to let Claudia go with Paul to his home for visits. Then Mona objected to overnight visitation. That ploy failed, too.

So it was apparent that Mona's next trick was to tell Claudia stories in the hope of alienating her from Paul and me. Luckily, Paul arrived just then with ice cream cones for everyone. Mona was temporarily forgotten.

But peace was short-lived. When Mona heard that Paul and I were going to be married, she went crazy. She refused to let Claudia attend the wedding. She demanded to know details of the wedding that were none of her business. She even went so far as to tell Claudia that we wouldn't have time for her anymore because we were going to have babies now and they would replace her.

Right after our wedding, Mona started playing around with the visitation schedule more than ever. There were actually times when Mona flat out refused to let Paul exercise his court ordered time with Claudia. Paul's breaking point finally came the second year after we were married. We had just bought a home closer to Mona in the hopes that visitation would be easier. Mona had seen it as a threat and became more difficult, instead. That year, it was our turn to have Claudia for Easter. That meant, according to the order, Claudia was to arrive at our house the Saturday before, no later than 6 PM. Saturday morning Mona called. She told Paul in that smug voice of hers that I had come to hate, that her family was in town and Claudia needed to be there that night and most of the following day.

"After all," she said, "this is her family and she wants to play with her cousins." I didn't think it mattered to Claudia one way or the other. To a child, Easter was about the Easter Bunny and Easter baskets, not cousins. Paul felt helpless and something in him finally woke up after that. He found the resolve he needed and he decided to go for joint custody.

Mona, of course, objected. The day she received the court papers telling her what we were proposing, she called Paul on the phone and screamed at him that he was trying to take her child away from her. "This is all her doing. She just wants my baby. Tell her to have her own damn kids and leave mine alone. You weren't like this before you were married."

"No, this is about my time with my daughter, Mona. I love Claudia, too."

Mona then tried a different tactic. Sobbing, she said, "Why don't you and I meet to talk about this? Why don't we have dinner here in town this week? We can make arrangements between just the two of us. We don't need the lawyers."

Mona had tried to seduce Paul once, right after he had left her and he wasn't falling for that ploy again. "No, Mona, I'm not doing that. We need to have this worked out properly and I *am* going for joint custody. I'm Claudia's father. I have rights just like you do. You're not going to be calling the shots anymore."

Mona screamed "Fuck you!" and hung up.

A few weeks after Mona's phone call, we had a meeting of all parties and attorneys in our lawyer's office. I accompanied Paul to the meeting and our attorney asked me to sit in.

As soon as we were all seated, Mona piped up. "Why is *she* here? This doesn't concern her. Claudia is *my* child with Paul."

My face must have gone instantly to red because Frank, our attorney, put a hand on mine and just patted it, a signal to let him handle it.

"Ms. Weber, I asked Sara to sit in on this meeting. She's here to show her support of the proposed parenting custody plan and to give her input," he said. "Claudia is going to be spending time in her home under her supervision and I think it's imperative that we work together for Claudia's sake."

Mona opened her mouth to say something but her attorney cut her off. "Excellent point," he replied. "Now let's go over the holiday schedule, shall we?"

Mona kept quiet for the next few minutes until it came time to discuss the wording of the custody. She objected to joint physical custody and she absolutely refused to agree to the every other week schedule we were proposing. She said she wanted Claudia to spend the majority of her time living with her. "A child should be with her mother."

Frank pointed out that most custody case decisions were leaning toward both joint physical and legal custody unless one of the parents was unfit. Mona sniffed. "That's certainly a matter of opinion."

Frank ignored her and continued. "Because of the physical proximity of both parties, this will work out in the best interests of Claudia. It's important for her to have a relationship with both parents and since everyone lives so close, she can easily stay in her school district. The judge will not object and will more than likely grant Paul everything he has asked for. It's incumbent upon us to have everything hammered out so that all he has to do is sign it. We don't want any surprises."

Mona was unusually quiet for the rest of the meeting. I told Paul and Frank afterwards that I thought she had something up her sleeve. They both assured me I was reading too much into it.

"I hope I'm wrong but I have a bad feeling about this," I said.

Unfortunately, I was right. Within a week of that meeting, Mona was simply gone. Paul kept calling her house but never got an answer. On the third day, the line was disconnected. That's when we panicked. We drove to Mona's house. The place was dead silent. We looked in the windows. Nothing looked disturbed. Her furniture was still there. We called the school and they told us that Claudia was "out sick". We were baffled.

A week went by with no word. For the first time in my life, I saw my husband cry. Paul was heartbroken and there was nothing I could do. My hatred for Mona grew. How any mother could do this to her child just to get back at the father was something I couldn't understand. I was finally starting to see the depths that Mona would go to just to get back at Paul for having the nerve to leave her.

Finally, after about ten days, Paul got a call from his attorney. Apparently, Mona had notified her lawyer that she had moved to New Hampshire. And she was getting married! She had met a man while on one of her ski vacations and she had moved to be with him. He was a teacher and she was going to get a job selling real estate in the ski resort area. Since there was no provision in the current custody order forbidding her to leave the area, Mona had simply done what she wanted. She claimed this was a move that would make her life better and consequently better her child's life. She definitely sounded coached. I was convinced she was lying but she actually submitted proof of a marriage to the court during the subsequent custody hearing a couple of months later.

Our attorney told us we could fight and force her back to Pennsylvania, but Paul was reluctant to do that. In the end, they agreed on joint legal custody with Mona having primary physical custody and Paul getting longer periods of visitation because of the distance involved.

It soon became apparent that the joint custody agreement was nothing more than a joke to Mona. In court, she had

59

agreed to bear most of the burden of transporting Claudia to us since she was the one who had moved away. In reality, however, this gave Mona more control. Many an argument ensued over the next few years over travel arrangements.

Regardless of her motivation, Mona's marriage didn't last very long. A year later, she was divorced for a second time. She decided then she would go back to using Weber as her last name "because it would be easier on Claudia". The surprising thing was that she stayed in New Hampshire. Paul tried to maintain a long distance relationship with Claudia but the reality was we saw her less and less. No matter how we attempted to make a schedule for Claudia to visit, Mona managed to mess it up. Either she suddenly had plans that same weekend, or she was having company that Claudia "wanted" to be involved in, or school was a factor. It didn't matter as long as Paul lost out in the end. Eventually, Paul gave up. He knew it was just going to get worse the more he pushed it. So he resigned himself to accepting whatever crumbs of visitation Mona threw his way.

Life settled into a routine after that. Then, a few years later, Paul's mother died. We knew there was really nothing holding us to the East Coast any more. We had always wanted to move out of Pennsylvania and the time seemed right. Paul's brother had moved to Arizona years before after accepting a teaching position at Arizona State University. Paul and I had vacationed there many times. It seemed like home from the very first time we were there. I wasn't afraid to leave my mother. I knew Angela would be there for her.

So, several years ago, we sold our house, packed up our belongings and drove across the country. A week later, on a bright September morning, we walked into our Arizona home and never looked back.

As I sat in my car, I watched a couple walk out of the Lake House. I couldn't believe all that had happened since Gregg had laid out this horrible plan. I didn't see any way out of this for me. I was screwed. If I complained, I was the bad guy, the one who was making everyone else miserable. Now, even if Paul and I somehow made up and got beyond this and he called Mona back and told her something different from what they had already agreed to, Mona was going to know that I was behind it all. She'd know that she had gotten to me and that Paul didn't back me up with her unless we fought. Then I'd be in a worse position than ever.

I started mentally dividing up all the things in the house. I couldn't take this tug of war any more. They could all have each other. I was done with it. But I couldn't bear being without Paul. A tear slid down my cheek. Why did this have to be so hard?

I put my head down on the steering wheel and cried. I sobbed until my throat ached. Maybe my sister had been right when she warned me about marrying a divorced man. Paul just didn't have "baggage". He had steamer trunk loads full of crap leftover from his life with Mona. I had stupidly thought I could rise above it.

Chapter Six

I had met Paul a few weeks after I left Kevin. Paul was working as a drug representative for a pharmaceutical company in Philly. I was a nurse at one of the local hospitals. We were both attending a seminar on heart disease. I had just moved into my own apartment and had been cleaning and unpacking the entire two days prior to the conference. We were all sitting in a dark, warm auditorium and I was having trouble staying awake. The speaker had perfected the monotone and I kept nodding off to sleep. After one nod too many, I remember getting prodded in the elbow by the man sitting to my left.

"I'll bet they paid this guy a lot of money to stand up there and bore us and you're showing him no respect."

I jerked my head up, embarrassed. The man who had said these words was laughing, at my expense, and very pleased with himself. It was Paul. I didn't know who he was then but I recalled seeing him earlier that morning. I recognized him as the man in charge of one of the booths in the lobby. He had been talking with another male attendee before the session had started and I remembered thinking to myself then that he was rather attractive.

I figured him to be in his mid thirties. He was tall and thin, totally the opposite of Kevin. I had been admiring his cute rear end that morning while he chatted with his friend. He had been unconsciously running his hand through his hair while he talked. He also had a way of crinkling his eyes when he smiled that I found endearing. He smiled a lot. He had definitely looked like someone I wouldn't mind knowing better.

I guess I had been staring and admiring more than I thought because I suddenly felt very self-conscious to have him see me in such an embarrassing way. I had no idea I had been sitting next to him in the darkened auditorium.

I stammered something incoherent which just made those eyes crinkle again.

"Why don't we go outside and get some air?" Paul asked. "I'm about to fall asleep myself."

The two of us crawled over the rest of the people in our row and made our way outside. We exited to a courtyard of the hotel. Concrete benches were laid out around the perimeter. It was early October and the trees in the courtyard were turning beautiful colors of red, yellow, and gold. The air was cool but comfortable and had a wonderful smell to it.

Paul and I sat on one of the benches away from the entrance to the auditorium. I knew I wasn't doing anything wrong but I couldn't shake the feeling that I shouldn't be there with him. There was an attraction in the air that I couldn't ignore.

He pulled out a pack of cigarettes and offered me one.

"No, thanks," I said. "I don't smoke."

"I shouldn't either but I just can't break the habit. My name's Paul Weber, by the way."

"Hi, I'm Sara. Sara McDowell...I mean Cavaleri."

"Not sure who you are, 'Sara Sara McDowell I mean Cavaleri'?" Those eyes were crinkling again. I could see he liked to tease but he was also flirting.

"I'm in the process of getting divorced and I'm going back to my maiden name. I'm not used to it yet. It's been a while since I went by Cavaleri."

"Divorce, huh? That's too bad. I'm sorry to hear that. That must be hard."

"Yes, but it's been a long time coming. And it's a matter of safety, too. My husband drinks too much. Then he gets angry. And, well, you know how that goes."

Paul sensed my discomfort so he just nodded and changed the subject. "Do you work here in town? I don't remember seeing you at one of these things before." He took a drag on his cigarette and blew the smoke away from me.

"I'm a nurse at Jefferson. On the telemetry unit. I've been there about a year. You?"

"I'm a rep for Smith Kline. We do these seminars pretty regularly. Good marketing. I know most of the people here."

"Do you like it?"

"It's okay. The pay's great. I like the people I network with. I occasionally meet with the docs on your floor. I'm surprised I haven't seen you there before this. I would have remembered you." There was that smile again.

"I was working the afternoon shift until recently."

"Oh, that explains it."

We chatted back and forth for about ten minutes. The session must have broken right about then because a bunch of people came out and started milling around, smoking, drinking coffee, and talking.

The man I had noticed Paul with earlier that morning came over.

"Hey, I wondered where you had gone off to. Couldn't handle it, huh?" This guy was shorter than Paul with dark hair and brown eyes. It was obvious that he and Paul were good friends. Paul just smiled. I thought I sensed a little annoyance when he saw his friend but it might have been my imagination. "We better get into that luncheon if we want to get a table for the bunch of us." Obviously, there had been a few of them who had come together. Paul looked at me.

"Are you with anyone here, Sara?" he asked.

"No," I answered. "I came alone."

"Care to join us?"

"Sure, why not?" By now, I knew I really was attracted to this guy but I had a feeling I shouldn't be. He hadn't mentioned a wife and I didn't notice a ring but something was telling me not to go. Warning bells were going off in my head.

I didn't listen.

Lunch was animated,, to say the least. I sat between Paul and his friend whose name I learned was Ned. The rest of the group consisted of three other co-workers of Ned, all social workers, two women, and another man. The conversation was lively, mostly about work or the conference. It was obvious they had known each other for a long time. There was a lot of innuendo passed in that conversation – all of it went over my head.

It also became very obvious from the conversation that not only was Paul married but his wife was expecting a baby! I felt myself flush when I heard this and hoped no one had noticed. I was surprised at the depth of my disappointment. I had actually allowed myself to feel an attraction for this guy. Well, that was obviously going to go nowhere.

While we all walked back to the auditorium after lunch for the afternoon session, I was trying to think of a polite way to excuse myself from the group. I certainly didn't want to sit with Paul anymore. I felt very uncomfortable.

I held back as everyone filed into the auditorium.

"Aren't you coming?" Paul asked.

"I want to pop into the ladies room first," I said. I didn't dare sit next to Paul for the entire afternoon.

"Okay, see you inside." He went in with his friends.

I walked as quickly as I could to the lobby restroom. I

couldn't understand why I felt so guilty. Nothing had happened. But I had to be honest with myself. If the opportunity had presented itself, I'm not so sure how strong I would have been. I was attracted to Paul. There has always been a part of me that believed in instant attraction and soul-mates and all that, and looking back now, I think that's what was going on. I knew Paul was special. And I believed on some level he felt it, too.

I sat in one of the bathroom stalls until I was sure everyone had gone in. Then I crept into the auditorium quietly and took a seat in the back in one of the empty rows. I left before the end and went straight home.

My life soon became busy with all the details of my divorce. Kevin was not willing to be cooperative about the divorce even though I was not asking for much. He and I had often talked about divorce in those last few months but his ego was bruised that I had actually left him. My attorney kept pushing me to hold out for more support money but I knew this would aggravate Kevin more and I didn't want to prolong the inevitable. My cat, a few possessions, and my maiden name back…that was all I wanted. Luckily, we had no children so Kevin and I were free to go our separate ways as soon as the ink dried on the decree. That happened right before Christmas that year and life settled into a nice routine after that.

I had occasions to talk to Paul a few times after that initial meeting. Sometimes, he came by to see one of the attendings. He lingered after his meetings and we chatted. The conversations were stilted at first but it was no time before I was at ease with him again. I really liked this guy and it was hard to hide. Sometimes, his appointments were with someone on an entirely different floor but he made time to stop in on my unit and say hello. But this didn't happen often and his visits were never without a work-related excuse.

I also ran into him while I was Christmas shopping at

the local department store. He was with Mona buying presents. He said hello to me but she just nodded at me when he introduced us and then looked away and pretended to be looking at something on the counter while Paul and I chatted a little. She wasn't what I had imagined. I had pictured someone about my own height and blonde. Kind of cheerleader cute. Mona was a tall brunette. Attractive in a haughty kind of way. Or maybe it was just the fact that she didn't/wouldn't speak to me. Shadows of things to come. I remember noticing her pregnant belly and immediately felt uncomfortable. I made an excuse and hurried off.

Then, out of the blue Paul called me at work in February. It was late afternoon and I was just about to leave for the day when a co-worker handed me the phone.

"He says he wants to talk to you," she said. "Some guy named Paul."

I froze. There was no good reason I could think of for him to be calling me.

"Here, take it. I have to answer that bell." I took the phone from her and stared at it a second. I was tempted to hang it up and just pretend we got disconnected if it ever came up again but knew that wouldn't be right. Paul deserved better.

"Hello, this is Sara," I said a little too hesitantly.

"Hi, Sara," said that voice I knew. "This is Paul. I have a favor to ask. I hope it's all right." I could sense worry in Paul's voice.

"What is it?"

"My wife just had our baby. The baby's premature and very little and I was wondering if you could help me out."

"How?"

"Well, the doctors are telling us everything, I'm sure, but I was wondering if you could find out for me that she's really going to be all right. I'm not even sure what I mean but I'm so worried and scared..." I could hear his voice crack. This was not the call I had expected and my heart immediately went out to him.

"Where is she? The baby, I mean?"

"She's in the nursery here at Jeff. They have her in a special area for High Risk babies. I guess it's the High Risk Nursery. This just happened a few hours ago. I'm not sure of all the details. She's so little, Sara. I've never seen a baby that small before."

"Hang on a minute." While Paul had been talking, I had pulled up the Nursery census on the computer. There she was. Baby Girl Weber. Condition "Serious" but not critical. Our computer system was not that sophisticated back in those days so there wasn't much else there.

"Paul, I don't know anyone personally in Nursery but one of the girls I work with here has a friend there. I'll see what we can find out for you."

"Thanks, Sara, I appreciate this. Mona and I are so afraid. I hope you don't mind that I called you but you were the first person I thought of."

"Where can I reach you, Paul, if I find anything out? I see your home number on the computer screen here. Is it okay if I call you there?"

Paul seemed to hesitate for a minute. "Why don't you call me at work? I don't want to upset Mona. She's coming home tomorrow." Upset Mona? How would that upset Mona if I called with news about their baby? I didn't think I understood that reasoning but I didn't feel like I wanted to know the answer either, so I agreed. Paul gave me his work number. He thanked me again and hung up.

I must have been staring off into space for a few minutes thinking about what had just happened because the next thing I knew my co-worker had come back and was snapping her fingers in front of me and laughing.

"Hey, dream girl. Was that a good call? You have a dumb look on your face. Hot guy?"

"Huh? Uh, no...look, I'm outta here. See you tomorrow."

"Sure. Have a good one."

As it turned out, I was able to find out for Paul that baby Claudia was premature, little, and going to be fine once she gained a little weight. Lungs were good, heart was fine, all the necessary parts were in all the right places. I went over to the Nursery to take a peek at her before she went home. I knew I shouldn't but I was curious. I wanted to see what Paul's baby looked like. I felt guilty and couldn't even explain to myself why.

Little Claudia was adorable. For some strange reason, that made me sad. And jealous. I left quickly before I ran into Paul or Mona. There was no way I could have explained my presence there.

My friend's friend had been very helpful. I called Paul as he had asked and reassured him that his daughter was going to be everything that he and his wife hoped for.

Paul was grateful. That started our "talks" on the phone. At first, it was about the baby. Paul had lots of questions and fears and I was glad to be of help. Then the conversations took a more personal turn. Paul started calling me at home. We talked about anything and everything. Work. Friends. Our lives before we met.

I learned that Paul was from Pennsylvania, near Philadelphia. His father had died when he was in high school and his mother still lived in their home there. He hadn't known what he wanted to do with his life so he had joined the Army after high school. After his discharge from the Army, he decided to finish his education. His GI Bill helped him through school. I learned he wanted to leave his job. He really wanted to build houses. But he had responsibilities and didn't feel he could change jobs, especially now.

There was nothing sexual about our talks and Paul never asked me out but I could tell he wanted to and we could be more than just casual friends. There was more than just a little flirting. Inevitably, he started talking about his marriage. How unhappy he was, that he was trying to decide

69

what to do. That before Claudia came along, he had seriously considered divorcing Mona but now wasn't sure. I tried to be impartial all the while aching to hear him say that he wanted me, that we should run away together. Instead, I was just a good listener.

He didn't call often. He didn't usually have the opportunity to either be alone or have the free time. He could only call me from work and I had to be off from work and home to be able to take his call. But I found myself looking forward to his calls and although I kept telling myself I should put a stop to them, I seemed powerless to do that. Talking to him that way just aroused all the feelings I was trying hard to suppress. I found myself having fantasies of what it would have been like to be Claudia's mother and having Paul dote on us. Not safe fantasies at all. His calls made me sad more than anything else, dangling something in front of me that I couldn't have.

The next few months just dragged on. I worked, dated a little (all disasters), worked some more. Often, my mind drifted to thoughts of what Paul would be doing. I imagined his life with his baby. Claudia would be this old now, she would be doing that by now. I imagined Paul holding her, feeding her. I wondered what he and Mona were doing. Were things better? Were they worse? Was he just saying things were bad to get my sympathy? Was he just like all those other married guys you hear about who claimed to be misunderstood and under-appreciated, whose wives were cold fish in bed and they were staying just for the children. "Honest, my marriage is over. It's okay if we sleep together. She really doesn't care what I do."

It was also very strange that someone with whom I had not spent that much time could occupy so much of my mind. I told myself I was building a fantasy in my head because my real love life was a wasted desert. That might have been true, or it could have been what I had always suspected. That Paul and I were soul mates and my heart recognized him the minute we met. I know some people thought that was crazy but I believed it. I couldn't explain it any other way.

Then one day, I got "the call" from Paul. I'll never forget it. I was at home on a Saturday afternoon when the phone rang. I had been cleaning the apartment to loud Billy Joel music. Mr. Smudge, my old cat, was hiding under the bed until the nasty vacuum was put away. I almost didn't hear the phone ring. I grabbed it out of breath (I liked to dance sometimes while I dusted and vacuumed). Paul was the last person I expected to hear from since he always called from work during the week.

Huffing like an obscene caller, I quickly said "Hello".

"Hi, it's me," he said. "I really need to talk to you. Can we meet somewhere?"

I could feel the blood stop in its tracks in my veins. My mouth went dry. Something was telling me this was going to be BIG.

"Sure, I can meet you. Paul, can you tell me what this is about?" My stomach was flipping. I knew what I wanted to hear but was afraid to wish for it.

"I'm at a phone booth. I really don't want to talk about it here." I could tell from Paul's voice that he was really upset. Cars were rushing by in the distance on his end, making it difficult to hear him.

Before I could stop myself, I heard myself saying, "Paul, why don't you come here? I'll put some coffee on and we can talk."

Thirty minutes later, I opened my door to the man of my heart and my life has never been the same. Over the next hour or so, Paul poured out his soul, telling me all that had gone wrong in the last week and how he and Mona had finally agreed to split up. Actually, leaving was Paul's idea. I got the impression that Mona was alternating between being devastated and livid. He had already moved out and most of his things were in his old sedan outside my front door.

I couldn't believe what I was hearing. Paul and Mona

71

were going to get a divorce. The man whose voice sent chills up my spine was sitting in my kitchen, drinking coffee from my cup, telling me that he was soon going to be a free man. Mr. Smudge was circling his legs and purring. My romantic mind was telling me this was a good sign (although he was probably just grateful that the vacuum was put away).

A part of me was admiring this little domestic scene from afar. This was how I wanted my life to be. I wanted to reach across the table and touch Paul's hair. I wanted to kiss the worry off his forehead. I also wanted to do a lot more I wasn't willing to admit just then.

"What are you going to do?" was all I could say at the end of his story. "Where are you going to live?" Pick me! Pick me! My heart was screaming.

"I've already told Ned this might be coming and he said I can move in with him until I get it a little more together. Mona and I still have to work out the financial arrangements and I want to make sure that I can still keep seeing Claudia as much as I want to. There's so much to figure out. I'm still in shock over this. I think it's just starting to sink in." Paul put his head down on his arms. He looked devastated as the reality was starting to overtake him.

I moved my chair closer to him. "Paul, I don't know what to say. I'm here for you."

Did you ever just have a really clear idea of what was going to happen next and even though you knew it could possibly be a disaster you couldn't help but do it anyway? That's where I was at that point. Here was the man I had been dreaming about for so long, sitting in my kitchen, and telling me that he had just left his wife. I touched his hand then and knew I was signaling a turn in our relationship. He turned those crinkly eyes toward me with that look that melted me and it was all over.

Paul never did leave my apartment that day, or the next. In fact, he never moved in with Ned at all. I know it sounds crazy but it was what we felt we wanted to do. We were both in the mood to just do what felt right and damn the consequences. Paul made an initial arrangement to have Ned contact him if Mona ever called him there so that he could cover up that he was staying with me. He knew she would hit the ceiling if she found out.

Warning sirens were going off left and right in my head but I refused to listen. Instead, I focused on the moment and the moment included Paul living with me and us enjoying every minute of it.

My fantasy came to a screeching halt a couple of weeks later when Mona found out the truth and the roller coaster ride that we continued on to this day started. Our world was in chaos for a while but soon, the pieces weren't falling nearly as often and life entered into a semblance of what I considered normal.

Through it all, my sister told me time and again that I was being foolish.

As I sat there in my car, looking at the lake, I had to admit she was probably right. I knew my marriage was basically good and that Paul loved me. I certainly loved him but maybe that love just wasn't enough anymore.

When I felt I had no more tears in me, I put the car in gear and drove home. I expected to see Paul's rear end poking out from under the antique's hood again, signaling he was withdrawing from me. I parked my car next to the old Mercedes but there was no sign of him.

I walked slowly into the house, not sure what to expect. The house was quiet. I found Paul still in the kitchen where we had fought. He was sitting at the breakfast counter and the smell of fresh coffee was in the air. The look of relief when he saw me was obvious. Jesse was curled up at his feet and he raced toward me when he saw me, his tail wagging. I patted his head and felt comforted with him beside me. I still didn't know what to expect and stood in the middle of the room, my arms at my sides.

"Hi," was all I could manage.

Paul didn't look as angry as I expected. He put his coffee cup on the counter and walked over to me. Putting his arms around me, he said, "I've been worried sick about you. Where did you go?"

"Down to the lake. I needed to think."

"I did some thinking while you were out, too," he said. "I think I see what got you upset."

"You do?"

"I shouldn't have let Mona go on like that about making plans and decorating. You're right, I should have included you."

I hugged Paul. "That's all I wanted."

He hugged me back. "Next time, when it comes to stuff like that, she'll have to talk to you directly."

"She won't do that," I answered. I snuggled closer to Paul. I could smell his after-shave and my heart melted. Paul kissed the top of my head. All my anger was evaporating but I was still upset. I could feel a tear running down my cheek. Paul wiped it away with his finger.

"I hate it when we fight," he said. "I love you, sweetie. We're so good together. We can't let her come between us like this."

I mentally unpacked all the furniture and moved back in. God, how I loved this man. I looked up at Paul. "What are we going to do about all her plans? You know how I feel about this."

"We'll do it gradually but she's going to have to learn to deal with you, too. If this is going to work, it's time she started acknowledging you, don't you think?"

I looked up at Paul and smiled. "Paul," I said, "it's only been sixteen years. Give her time."

Paul hugged me again and offered me a cup of coffee.

I took a sip and decided to take advantage of Paul's new understanding. "So, we're agreed that Mona decorating a room in our house is just not an option. She can send Claudia a stuffed animal to put on her bed if she wants to contribute."

Paul nodded. "Sara, I really didn't think it was all that important. I thought it was an easy way to shut her up."

"You should be more worried about keeping me happy, not her," I said. But I knew why he did it. It was why he always did what he did when it came to Mona.

"I want us both to be happy, Sara…and Claudia, too. I just wish you could see it from my side more often instead of flying off the handle like that."

"Ok, truce. How about we both make more of an effort. Deal?" I raised my coffee cup.

"Deal."

We clinked mugs.

Then, it hit me. In all my anger over Mona's decorating plans, I had completely forgotten her other announcement. She and Claudia were coming out to Arizona in just a few weeks!

Chapter Seven

Icalled Carol the next day and we made plans to divide the visit as painlessly as possible. Carol was more than happy to entertain her friend. It was decided that Mona would stay with Carol and Claudia would divide her time between Carol's and our house. During a moment of insanity, I volunteered to make dinner for everyone one night while they were here.

I also promised Paul that I would try to be less sensitive concerning my insecurities about Mona. It wasn't fair to expect him to fight my battles for me. He said he had no problem with me talking to Mona directly about any issues I had. Just because she didn't want me to speak to her didn't mean that had to be the rule. Claudia was going to be living here now and it was time she got used to the idea that I existed. This was a big step for Paul and an even bigger one for me but I thought I was up to it.

My newfound resolve was put to the test that following weekend. I was home alone on Saturday evening. Paul was at a friend's house helping him work on his car. The phone rang and without thinking, I picked it up. I was expecting it to be Paul. Instead, it was Mona.

I think her throat closed up when she realized it was me because it took her a second to recover. I have to admit, my knees started to shake, too, when she finally spoke and I realized it was her but I was determined not to let it show. This was my first real test of the new me (I kept hearing my mother's voice in my head reassuring the five-year-old me whenever I was afraid of bugs: "They're a lot more scared of you, Sara, than you are of them.").

"Hello."

There was a short pause at the other end and then, "I need to speak to Paul."

No "Hello, Home-wrecker." Nothing.

I immediately felt my hands shake and I was angry with myself for feeling this way. Damn it, I was not going to allow her to do this to me.

"He's not here. Do you want to leave a message, Mona?"

"No, but there are some things I need to discuss with him before we come out there. I just need to speak to him about that. Have him call me."

Yes, sir. Anything you say, sir.

Then, I decided it was time. I took a big deep cleansing breath and forged ahead. It was now or never. I was afraid she was going to hang up then so I spoke up quickly.

"You can speak to me, Mona. Paul and I will be sharing all the decisions along with you. I can pass along any concerns you have to him." I had been practicing this line in the shower and I was anxious to see what her reaction would be.

"Look, I guess we need to get something straight right from the beginning. Just because you get to be a stepmother now doesn't give you any real power."

"I have always been Claudia's stepmother."

"That's not what I meant. I mean Claudia is going to be living there full time now."

"I understand that. That's why I have to be involved. You need to understand something…"

Mona was getting angry now. "No, *you* need to understand something. Claudia is *my* daughter and I say what happens to her."

"I didn't say Claudia wasn't your daughter, Mona. But she's Paul's daughter, too, and I'm Paul's wife, so what we decide affects both of us and we make our decisions together…as a couple."

I knew that was a dig but I had to do it. It felt good. I was getting heady with the progress I was making so far. By this time, I could tell Mona was boiling but controlling herself. I had to give her credit for that. This was probably more than we had ever spoken to each other in all the years I had known her. I didn't think she wanted me to know how much this was bothering her and I decided to take advantage of that.

"Mona, one more thing before we hang up…"

She sighed loudly. "What?"

"Paul tells me that you were planning on decorating Claudia's room for her while she's living here."

"Yes, we had talked about that." I detected a sneer in her answer. She emphasized the word *we*.

"I want to thank you for offering."

Mona hesitated for a fraction of a second, suspecting something, I'm sure. "You're welcome."

"…but that won't be necessary. I do all the decorating of our home. Claudia has stayed here before, you know, and we already have a bedroom set up for her. If she needs anything else, I'll let you know. I'll tell Paul you want him to call you. Good night, Mona." She sputtered something at that point but I just hung up.

My knees were like rubber but I was so proud of myself for getting through that. It was a small victory at best and I was sure there would be repercussions. I probably should have let her hang up first but I was all out of nerve at that point and couldn't handle any more. I didn't care.

I told Paul what happened when he came home and he didn't have any problem with anything I had said. He, too, thought he'd get some fallout from it but he didn't care, either. I was all through running from Mona.

Paul did call her the next afternoon. I guess she had had time to get her wits about her by then because she turned the whole conversation around.

"I'm sensing Sara has a problem with Claudia's living arrangements in your home. I hope it isn't going to cause a difficulty for you or Claudia. After all, it's only natural that I, as a mother, would want to have a part in my daughter's college life."

"There's no problem, Mona. I don't know what you're talking about."

"Well, Sara told me she is uncomfortable with me doing anything for Claudia while she is staying with you. She told me she doesn't want me helping you decorate her room, or anything like that."

"I see." Paul smiled at me and shook his finger at me.

Mona continued. "If Claudia were staying in a dorm room, I would have the joy of helping her to decorate and settle in. But, in the interest of peace, I'm going to take a step back and let Sara handle those details."

So, my good feelings didn't last too long. Mona had cleverly managed to make it my problem. The rule was: Mona was never wrong. But, at least I didn't have to deal with that issue again. I thought I had made a point with Mona that she understood.

And the information that she needed to talk to Paul about? She just wanted to let him know what time their plane arrived in Phoenix for their big weekend in two weeks. They would be arriving early that Saturday. Claudia had plans to see the campus on Monday and they would fly back on Tuesday morning so that Claudia didn't miss much school and "I have to work, too, you know". Yes, long-suffering

Mona had to work while I sat home all day and drank mint juleps.

Inwardly, I reminded myself to enjoy the time while I had the chance. The next four years were going be very tense.

I was sure of it.

Chapter Eight

The next two weeks flew by. Mona and I hadn't seen each other in person in many years. However, I had seen recent pictures of her. Carol and Gregg had gone back east just two years before. When they came back, I made it a point to ask to see their pictures, including those of the day that they had spent with Mona and Claudia. I had a morbid curiosity that would not be denied. So I knew Mona was still "not bad looking". That was as far as I would let my imagination take me when it came to categorizing the woman my husband used to sleep with.

I knew I wasn't fat by any stretch of the imagination but I had put on a few pounds over the years that I wouldn't have minded losing. I dieted for about a week but I was so nervous that just made me eat more. I prayed for a bad intestinal infection. That would have guaranteed a five pound weight loss but it didn't happen. Instead, I made myself feel better – and prettier – with a new outfit planned just for the day of "my dinner" and another one for the big first meeting at Carol's house on Saturday. I also got a haircut and had my nails done.

Our house was another matter. I scoured it from top to bottom. I put up new curtains in the kitchen. I vacuumed. I dusted under the refrigerator. I made lists. I crossed things off the lists. I made new lists. I even took poor Jesse and Toby to the groomer so they would look their best. I made myself sick with nervousness and anticipation. I doubled up on the herbal medications my gynecologist had given me to prevent my hot flashes, all the while thinking there wasn't enough black cohosh in the world to get me through this.

Paul just shook his head and laughed at me.

I talked with Carol the night before Mona and Claudia's arrival to go over the plans for the weekend. I knew Carol wanted to run the show as usual and, frankly, I didn't care. We confirmed that she would make dinner for them the first night. Paul and I would stop by for lunch but Carol wanted time for them to "settle in." Whatever. We would have Claudia at our house all day Sunday, all to ourselves, which would be nice. That would give Mona and Carol time to spend alone. Monday, Paul, Mona, and Claudia were going to the ASU campus (I volunteered not to go. It was better than being asked to stay home) and that night (gulp!) I was scheduled to have everyone at our house for dinner! That meant Mona, Claudia, Carol, and Gregg. I wondered if I would survive.

Mona and Claudia were scheduled to leave the next morning to go back home. Peace and sanity at last!

I knew I shouldn't be making such a big deal about everything but I was powerless to stop myself.

Angela called the evening before The Big Arrival. She was upset about Mom again. This time, it seemed to have been triggered by a strange phone message.

"After she heard this message," Angela said, "Mom got very upset and agitated. She was mumbling and pacing around the house. I tried to calm her down. I thought I did. I persuaded her to go in and take a nap. But when I checked her about a half hour later, she was gone!" I heard Angela's voice catch. I could only imagine the panic she must have felt. Angela may be hard to deal with at times, but I had to admit she was very good about taking care of our mother. I'm sure she was frantic when she saw that empty room. Angela's house was in a very nice residential area of Long Island but there were dangers all over, especially when you were a confused old woman.

"I couldn't imagine where Mom had gone," she continued. "She had never done anything like this before."

I couldn't stand the suspense anymore. I practically screamed into the phone. Sometimes, Angela loved the drama and drove me up the wall. "Angela, where is she now? Is she home?"

"Yes, she's back. I immediately searched the neighborhood and found her about fifteen minutes later. She was sitting at a bus stop, a few blocks away. There she was in her bathrobe and her fuzzy slippers. She had no idea why I was upset with her."

I had to agree with Angela this time. We couldn't close our eyes to this anymore. Mom needed more supervision and it was unfair for Angela to have to supply it. Besides, if something bad ever happened, Angela would feel extremely guilty and so would I.

We decided that Angela would install locks on the inside of her outside doors and she was going to have to hire a sitter to stay with Mom while she was at work. I said I would split the cost of that with her. Right after this visit with Mona and Claudia, we were going to have to look for a place for Mom to live permanently, someplace with twenty-four hour supervision.

"But, Angela, I don't have a clue how to go about doing that."

"I'll ask around and see what I can find out. One of my friends recently had to go through something like this with her father. Maybe she'll be able to help us."

"I promise I'll be out there as soon as I can. Just let me get through these next few days."

Angela actually seemed relieved and grateful. Then she told me about the phone message that had so upset Mom. She said she had come home from grocery shopping and, as usual, had Mom with her. The answering machine was blinking so she just played the messages as she always did, not thinking anything of the fact that Mom was standing right there in the kitchen with her. A male voice came on and identified himself as Eleanor Cavaleri's attorney!

"Can you imagine? Dad's wife's attorney calling," she said. "What could that possibly mean? What did he want?" She still didn't know because by the time Angela heard the message it was too late to call him at his office. Angela said Mom got upset right after that so we had to assume that hearing Eleanor's name really bothered her.

"And, Sara, I really can't deal with that right now. Whatever Eleanor wanted is low on my list of things to worry about, what with my business and taking care of Mom." I could sense Angela winding up for another speech about how busy her life was so I took the attorney's number and told Angela I would call him myself and get back to her about it. After I hung up the phone I stood there for a minute, trying to imagine what that call from Eleanor's lawyer could possibly mean. Maybe Eleanor had died and left us a bunch of money? It didn't seem likely but I couldn't think of anything else.

Then before I knew it, it was time for The Visit.

Paul and I had agreed that he would pick Mona and Claudia up from the airport and I would meet them later at Carol and Gregg's. I thought it would be less stressful for everyone concerned if I wasn't there when they first got in. I tried to banish the thoughts of my husband alone in our car with his ex-wife. Paul tried to make me feel better by promising to strap Mona to the roof rack.

"I'll settle for the back seat."

So, bright and early, Saturday morning, off Paul went. I busied myself making the lasagna platter that I planned to serve on Monday evening.

About three hours later, I parked my car in front of Carol's house and immediately my stomach started to do rolls. I took some deep breaths but they didn't do a thing to help. I resisted the urge to start the car up and drive home.

My feet felt like lead as I trudged up Carol's walkway. I stopped and stared at Paul's SUV parked in the driveway. I peered in the windows, searching for signs of the previous occupants. There was nothing inside that indicated that my nemesis had just ridden in our family vehicle. Scolding myself for being so petty, I stood in front of Carol's front door, my hand raised, indecisive. Should I knock or ring the bell? Paul and I had been to Gregg and Carol's many times. It wouldn't do if I acted like a stranger now. Besides, I wanted to give Mona the impression that I belonged. This was my territory. Carol was her friend but she was married to *my* husband's brother.

Then what? Should I shake Mona's hand? Should I just give her a warm hello? Welcome her to Arizona? Ask how her flight was? What if she didn't answer me?

Our interactions over the years had been rare and not once were they friendly. I couldn't imagine how they were going to be now that we would be forced to interact with each other in such close quarters. I was aware that Mona had hated me from the beginning and that hadn't changed. She usually refused to speak to me. Even if I asked her a direct question, she often pretended not to hear. The only times we had anything that resembled a conversation was when she called our home and I answered. Then, she would usually just ask me to put Paul or Claudia on, if Claudia was staying with us at the time. Even so, it sounded as if every word pained her. I didn't want to appear rude, though, by not acknowledging her. I felt that the next few minutes were going to set the tone for the next four years. Picturing her in

Carol's living room, mere feet away, made it hard to think.

I decided to try the door handle. It was unlocked. Opening the door slowly, I called out as I entered, "Hi, everyone."

Carol's entryway opened up into their living room, picture perfect. Muted desert colors, tiled floors, fresh flowers. I automatically started comparing Carol's room to my own "lived in" room, complete with its assortment of dog toys and dog beds. Carol's house didn't suffer from balls of dog hair, either.

But the room was silent and empty. I felt let down. I had finally gotten my courage up and there had been no one to witness it. I scanned the room and the dining room beyond, looking for traces of Mona and Claudia but saw nothing and assumed Carol must have put everything in the guest room. Then I heard laughter coming from the far end of the house. Of course! Everyone was in the family room. I should have thought of that. Carol and Gregg's house was enormous compared to ours and their family room was in the back of the house and overlooked their deck and pool. It had a wonderful view of the Arizona desert beyond.

I followed the sounds. With a stiff smile plastered to my face, I stood in the doorway of the family room and hoped I could catch Paul's eye quickly. I trusted he would rescue me before I had to open my mouth again.

Claudia was sitting on the sofa between Paul and Gregg. She had cut her hair since I had last seen her. A lock had fallen across her forehead and I was struck again by how much she looked like Paul, especially when she smiled.

Carol and Mona were sitting on the loveseat opposite them. Carol was wearing expensive-looking slacks and dripped gold jewelry. I would have felt overdressed but she pulled off the look flawlessly. I tried to look at Mona without staring. Her brown hair was longer than it was in the pictures I had seen. It brushed her shoulders and she had added some nice highlights (wish I had thought of that!). She hadn't gained any weight (darn!) and actually looked very trim. She was wearing a short skirt and high-heeled sandals. Paul had told me she thought her legs were her best feature (not information I really needed) and she had them crossed now. She had obviously gone to one of those spray-on tanning places. Well, maybe Mona wasn't as comfortable with herself as I was imagining. I was beginning to feel more brazen. She and Carol looked my way as soon as they heard me enter the room but said nothing.

Paul caught my eye and I waved to him. He immediately stood up and came over and kissed me hello. He took my elbow and guided me to his seat on the sofa.

"Want something to drink, Sara?"

"Ice tea would be nice. Thanks."

I said Hi to Claudia and Gregg as I sat down and then I turned to Carol and Mona. I knew I had to acknowledge the Mona-elephant in the room. I was not going to allow Mona to intimidate me. This was my turf, damn it.

"Hi, Carol. Hello, Mona. Welcome to Arizona. I hope you had a pleasant flight." My mouth was dry. It took everything I had to be polite to Mona. I felt a combination of fear and loathing. Here was the woman who would like nothing more than to see me fail as Paul's wife, who resented me in Claudia's life. Yet, in order for us to survive the next few hours, I had to pretend that all was well and we could get along.

I continued to look at Mona. Would she actually answer me or would she continue to deny I was even in the room? Mona's mouth moved as if she were about to actually say something but Carol cut her off. "Mona and I were just reminiscing about our last trip out to visit her. We met the most wonderful couple." She turned back to Mona. "What was the name of that restaurant we went to again?"

So that was how it was going to be. Carol was going to rescue her friend from the dreaded second wife, poor baby. Well, I couldn't blame her. Mona was her best friend and she probably felt this was the best way to handle it. We were all dancing the steps to this new waltz. I turned back to my sofa-mates.

"This is fun," I said to Paul through a clenched smile as he handed me a glass of ice tea. I took a sip and balanced the glass on my knee.

Paul took a seat on the floor at my feet since I was occupying his place on the sofa. He patted my knee. "Gregg and I were telling Claudia what she could expect the first year," he said. "She might even have Uncle Gregg as an instructor." He turned to Claudia and made a face. "But she's not sure she wants Uncle Greggie for a teacher."

"Dad!" Claudia giggled.

I hugged her. "It's so good to see you again. I love your hair like this. It's really cute."

"Thanks, Sara. It was Mom's suggestion."

"Well, she had a good idea."

Hear that, Mona? I'm not undermining your life with your daughter? Get the idea?

I wanted to cast a sideways glance at Mona but I was afraid she would catch me. Mercifully, Carol got up just then and went into the kitchen. Mona followed her. A few minutes later, Carol announced that lunch was ready.

Paul and I stayed through lunch, made idle talk around the table for a little bit and then my sweet husband said he had some things to work on and we left. Mona didn't say a word to me the entire time I was there although I caught her stealing glances my way several times because, honestly, I was doing the same thing. We were sizing each other up, trying to decide what kind of an enemy the other was going to make.

I'm sure she was just curious about me. I know I was about her. I often found myself wondering what Paul had seen in her. I used to try to imagine them being married to each other. When I was feeling low and insecure, that thought made me nauseous. I had tried picturing them in bed together. I wasn't happy about that thought but I knew they did it at least once. I mean there *was* Claudia. I wondered if that made me weird or perverted. Did Paul compare me to her when we made love? Was she better than me? Sexier than me? I reminded myself that he was with me now and unless I was really stupid, I knew he was happy. The evil part of me wondered if those same thoughts went through her head, too.

I was so glad I had made sure I was looking my best when I went over to Carol's that day. I knew I wasn't the most beautiful person in the world but I had to admit, I looked pretty good when I wanted to. And, yes, Mona was not ugly. But the years had taken their toll on her and she did look her age. She wore a look of disdain most of the time, as if everyone on the planet were beneath her. Maybe it made her feel more confident.

Carol got on my nerves that day, too. She seemed to be making a point of walking down memory lane with Mona all afternoon and it made me feel like a fifth wheel. If I heard one more time "Remember when we...blah, blah, blah", I was going to strangle her perfect little neck. My cheeks were sore from forcing a smile all afternoon.

Paul was very amorous in bed that night. He made love in a way that reminded me of our first time together. I didn't know if he was trying to erase a bad memory of Mona with a good one of us but I sure enjoyed myself.

I was initially reluctant to make love. Seeing Mona brought back my old insecurities of her nights as my husband's wife. I was actually thinking about them making love when Paul started kissing my neck.

"What are you thinking about?"

"Nothing," I lied.

His lips were working their way down. "Well, stop thinking about nothing."

I felt his hands on my thighs and moved toward him. "Whatever you say."

Afterwards, he fell asleep in my arms and I felt on top of the world. He was such a little boy sometimes, especially when he was sleeping. I stroked his hair and just watched him breathe.

Chapter Nine

S unday was rather anticlimactic. We picked Claudia up after Church in the morning and spent the day with her. Or rather, she spent the day with Paul. But I didn't mind. He needed that time with her. And it was good to see them together. I think Claudia, when left to her own devices, really liked her father.

After a light lunch, I asked Claudia to go into her room with me and go over what changes she wanted to make. I pulled out a catalog I had saved and showed her some comforters I thought she might like.

"You know, I really had my heart set on living in the dorm."

"Claudia, I know that but it really isn't financially feasible right now. Why don't we see how this works out for this year and maybe you can qualify for some funding for next year."

"Is that because Mom won't be paying you any child support?"

I was taken aback by this and didn't respond. As it was,

in order for Claudia to get the in-state tuition rates, we would have to claim her as a dependent on our income taxes. Mona pitched a fit when Paul told her that. The agreement they finally came to was that we would claim her on our income taxes, Mona and Paul would split the cost of college tuition after loans and grants, and we wouldn't ask Mona for any other money to support Claudia staying with us. But the first year was going to be especially hard since we didn't think we would get any financial aid for Claudia, at least for the first semester. Obviously, Mona had shared this with Claudia.

"Claudia, why don't we leave the finances to your Dad, Mom and me? It's not something you need to worry about. You just worry about your classes and boys." Claudia dropped the subject.

Later that day, Paul mentioned getting a job to Claudia.

"A job? Dad, I'm not going to have time for a job."

"Sure you will. You're going to need spending money. Where did you think that was going to come from?"

Claudia looked at him. "Well, you, of course."

"Really? I don't think so. Do you have a job now?"

"Well, yeah. But that's because Mom is single. You have Sara."

I looked at Paul. His eyes told me to keep quiet. I left the room and silently wished him luck.

Monday was the day that Mona, Paul, and Claudia were to tour Arizona State's campus. They had arranged to spend some time with students and a couple of the teachers and then were to meet Gregg and have lunch in the school cafeteria. I knew they were going to. What I didn't know was that Carol met them as well. I didn't find out until after Mona went back to New Hampshire. Paul let it slip one evening during dinner.

We had been discussing things to do when Claudia moved here. She was going to have a few days before classes officially started and I thought we should do a fun, family outing in celebration of this new chapter in her life. Paul mentioned that Carol had suggested a weekend trip up to the Grand Canyon.

"When did she mention that?" I asked.

"The day we had lunch at the coll –" Paul suddenly realized his blunder and stopped, fork in mid-air.

"Carol was at lunch that day and you didn't tell me? Who invited her? Mona?"

"I honestly don't know, Sara. All I know was that she was already there when we arrived at Gregg's office. I had nothing to do with it. It was a surprise to me, too. There was no time to invite you by that time. I didn't tell you because I didn't want to hurt your feelings."

Paul was right. There was nothing he could have done about it and it would have looked strange if he had. It was silly of me to get upset over it. If this whole arrangement was going to work at all, I was going to have to develop a tougher skin when it came to Mona.

Anyway, the rest of the day at ASU had apparently gone smoothly. Claudia declared the college acceptable. After my discussion with her the day before, I had half expected her to say she didn't like the school because she wasn't staying in a dorm. I thought she might make a play for another school entirely. But she surprised me. The die was cast.

Then came my big dinner. The weather was beautiful. The air was clean and clear. Spring is perfect weather in Arizona. Not too hot but warm enough to wear short sleeves and keep the windows open. Our house looked fabulous. There wasn't a speck of dust anywhere. Paul had cleaned the walkway that led to our front door and I had hung a new dried flower wreath on it. I knew we would be spending all our time in the living room and the dining room so I took special pains to make sure those rooms shone. The furniture was all polished. I even burned a little incense earlier in the day to make sure there was no "doggie smell". Of course, I noticed every little pull and scuff on our furniture but I

93

hoped no one would notice. Besides, there hadn't been time to buy new (I checked!).

I was a nervous wreck all evening. Whatever had possessed me to agree to do this was beyond me. I was obviously some sort of masochist. How stupid would someone have to be to invite her own husband's ex-wife to dinner? I guess I had this compulsion to show how good I could be in this situation but I would never do it again. It was bad enough having Mona under my roof. Serving her dinner was going above and beyond. It was the guest list from hell.

When the doorbell rang, I thought my heart would explode in my chest. I took deep breaths and kept telling myself I could get through this. It was only going to be for a few hours. How bad could it be?

Mona no sooner walked into the foyer and I knew how bad it could be. It was "The Inspection" all over again. She still had that pinched pained expression on her face that I remembered the first – and only – time she had been allowed to come into my home. It was as if she were afraid to breathe the same air as me. She had been so comfortable and almost giddy in Carol's home. In mine, she made it look like she was about to have major surgery without the benefit of anesthesia. It gave me a perverted sense of satisfaction. Maybe she was as uncomfortable as I was.

Paul escorted everyone into the living room. Mona was rather quiet at first, looking around, and probably mentally adding up the cost of everything in sight. Gregg, Carol, and Claudia said "Hello" to me and Gregg gave me a hug.

The dogs were out on the deck, peering in through the sliding glass doors. As soon as the doorbell had rung, they started to bark. They continued to bark when they recognized Gregg and Carol, but now in anticipation of games with Uncle Gregg.

Mona looked at my boys and said to Paul "Oh, you have dogs" in the same way one would say, "Oh, you have weeping infected sores." Paul just smiled and gave me the eye, afraid I was going to say something. I didn't. I knew how much he wanted this evening to go well. I just let it pass, thankful the boys were outside, away from Mona. Frankly, I wished I were with them.

Claudia volunteered to help me set the table. As I walked into the kitchen, out of the corner of my eye, I saw Carol sit on the loveseat and watched as Mona sat right next to her, for safety, I'm sure. That made me feel better. Mona was as insecure as I was.

Paul and Gregg sat opposite them on the sofa and talked to each other. It looked like some adolescent party where all the girls and boys lined up on opposite ends of the room, afraid someone would approach them.

I passed the appetizer tray around a couple of times and Mona helped herself without saying a word to me. She was in my home but I was still invisible. That woman was amazing.

Carol wasn't much better although she did tell me that the house looked very nice. Then she turned to Mona. "Paul has done a lot of work on this house."

"Really? Well, I'm not surprised. He always was very good about working around the house. He made so many improvements to that house we had. Paul, remember when we had that leak in the bedroom ceiling and we had to sleep in the guest room all week?" I just rolled my eyes and retreated to the kitchen. I was not going to stand there and listen to her go down memory lane, especially if it involved memories of sleeping with my husband.

Then dinner was ready. I stood in the doorway of the dining room, feeling like the butler when I called everyone in. There was an awkward moment when everyone jockeyed for seats at the dinner table. I sat at the foot of the table and Paul sat at the head. That left two seats on either side.

Claudia looked at me, then her father, unsure what to do.

"Claudia, sit next to your Dad," I said, pointing to a chair on his left. I immediately sensed Mona tense up when she realized that if she wanted to sit next to Claudia she was going to have to sit next to me. Carol stepped in at that point and suggested to Mona that she sit on Paul's other side. Gregg sat between Claudia and me on the one side and Carol sat between Mona and me on the other side. I wasn't happy about that but the alternative would have been to sit next to Mona and that didn't feel good, either. I guess I hadn't thought this through when I suggested dinner. Of course, that meant Paul and Mona holding hands when we all said "Grace" before dinner. After that was over, I smirked at Paul from across the table. He just raised an eyebrow at me, all the while looking like Mr. Spock from *Star Trek*.

Dinner went fairly well since everyone had their mouth full most of the time. Gregg was trying too hard to make small talk and told me several times that dinner was delicious. I think Carol kicked him at one point because he stopped almost in mid-sentence once and didn't bring it up again after that.

I served cheesecake for dessert that I had bought at our local Italian bakery. Mona must have seen the box in the kitchen.

After taking just a small mouthful, she said, "This is the best part of the meal" and actually turned to me. "Did you make this yourself, Sara?"

"No."

Mona just smiled. "Well, it's excellent."

There was dead silence after that. I thought I heard crickets in the distance. Paul asked Claudia some stupid question to change the subject but what Mona had done wasn't lost on anyone. I don't know why I was the one who felt embarrassed. She was the one who was rude.

After dinner, everyone seemed more than happy to leave. I said good-bye quickly and retreated into the kitchen to clean up. I really didn't care if I should have played hostess and walked them all out to the car. At that point, I was just glad to see them go. I didn't know what I expected to happen by having them all there. Was Mona going to say what a fool she'd been all these years to resent me? Were we all going to sit down like old friends and plan outings together?

I guess the only thing I accomplished was that I showed Claudia I could try for her sake to be friends and if her mother refused to accept my olive branch, I wasn't responsible. Hopefully, the next few years would bring very few instances when we would have to share the same oxygen together.

Paul came into the kitchen after they drove away and hugged me from behind. I was furiously feeding the remains of dinner to the garbage disposal.

"Hey, that was a good meal. Don't throw it away like that."

I just kept shoving food down the hole. "Mona didn't seem to think so. She preferred the cheesecake." I shoved the last of the lasagna into the disposal and turned on the switch. When the last of the meal was gone, I turned it off and turned to Paul. "I don't want anything to remind me of this night. Tell me about this evening in painful detail next time I get another stupid idea."

"Come on, Sara. It wasn't so bad."

"Wasn't so bad? Were you even in the same room as the rest of us?" I narrowed my eyes at him. "And did you wash your hands?"

Paul gave me a confused look.

"Don't touch me with hands that held hers." I smiled. "Did you enjoy the hand holding?"

Paul's eyes crinkled up just the way I liked them. "You didn't see what she was doing under the table. Mm-mm."

I hit him with the dish towel. "Get out of here and go scrub yourself with a brush before you come into my bed, Mister."

When I crawled under the covers later that night, exhausted and drained, Paul smelled of fresh soap and had my favorite lavender candle burning on the nightstand. It

97

didn't take a genius to figure out what was on his mind. I was starting to get a little concerned why he was so loving this particular weekend that Mona was visiting but a few seconds of cuddling put that all out of my mind. Paul's kisses and caresses soon made all traces of that horrible evening disappear in a flash. As I climbed on top of my husband, I couldn't help but feel a sense of satisfaction that I was the one he was with and obviously wanted.

Chapter Ten

Mona and Claudia went back to New Hampshire the next morning as planned. Paul and I drove them to the airport. Carol begged off saying she had an important meeting at work that she couldn't miss. Frankly, I was surprised by that. I had thought she would have wanted to accompany her friend and spare her the misery of being in the same car as me.

Mona was very quiet on the ride to Sky Harbor International but Claudia chattered on as only a teenager can do and made the ride fairly pleasant. Because of all the post-9/11 security at the airport, we couldn't walk with them to the gate so we just dropped them off at curbside check-in. I was hesitant to hug Claudia in front of her mother so I just hung back while Paul gave her a hug and a kiss.

Back in the car, Paul turned to me. "What is it with that Cheshire grin? Are you that happy to see them go?"

"Yes."

Paul just shook his head, probably wishing he had never married anyone and started the car. For my part, I just hoped we wouldn't be hearing too much from Mona and her daughter until it was time for Claudia to move in.

Life was actually calm for the next few weeks. Angela had decided that Mom was less agitated and was easier to handle. Having Michelle home for the summer helped. Angela relaxed a bit and asked that we put off deciding about placing Mom. She just couldn't bear the thought of doing it yet. I knew we needed to make plans because this calm was going to end suddenly but Angela had a Scarlett O'Hara approach to some things. She was even better than Paul was at it. I didn't push it. I made my own small plan of attack in my head.

1. Fly out to New York
2. Find a group home for Mom
3. Handle guilt
4. Move Mom into said home
5. Handle more guilt
6. Handle drama from Angela
7. Quickly fly back home
8. Drink heavily

I knew it was only a matter of time before I would be heading out there but I wanted to enjoy this respite in the meantime.

And I was busy with my work. For some reason, I suddenly had a bunch of new cases. As a legal nurse consultant working from home, I often had to go into the office for some face-to-face contact with either the paralegals or the attorneys. I enjoyed the contact. It was nice to be able to work at home in my pajamas if I chose to, but it was also nice to get dressed up, grab my briefcase and play business woman for a while.

I arrived at the office on Monday morning, a few weeks after the Mona dinner. Since I didn't have an office at the law firm anymore, I usually just took whatever room was free if I needed to do any work while I was there. That morning, I only needed to meet with Judy to go over the details of an expert who was going to testify the following week for our side.

I told Dorothy the receptionist I was there for my appointment and took a seat in the waiting room. It was a small but pleasant room. Jeff wanted to give his clients a feeling that the company was successful but didn't waste profits on trappings. Wide windows looked out onto the courtyard that often reminded me of Carol's deck, minus the pool. A fountain bubbled in the center and birds were at its edge, drinking. In the distance was a clear view of the mountains. The sofa I was sitting on was covered in floral chintz. It made me feel as if I were in the living room of an old friend. I could only imagine the anguish of some of the clients when they first arrived at the office and the overall ambience was meant to put them at ease. It certainly worked on me that morning. I read an issue of a gardening magazine until Dorothy told me that Judy was off the phone and I could go in now.

By the time I walked down the hallway and arrived at Judy's office, she was on the phone again. Papers were lying in multiple piles all over the floor, her favored filing system. She was getting Ted Concetti ready for a product liability case involving a baby car seat and had a demo of the offending carrier sitting on the only chair in her office. Her flyaway hair was barely kept off her face with a couple of combs, the phone was cradled between her shoulder and ear, and she was typing at her computer while she talked to whoever was on the other end. She smiled at me when I walked in and motioned for me to remove the baby seat and put it on the floor. I did and sat. She held up a finger to tell me she would be with me soon.

She nodded while she talked on the phone. "Uh, huh. I see. Ok, well, let me know as soon as he comes in. I really need to talk with him today. Thanks." She hung up and turned to me.

"That was about my contact in the manufacturing plant. Looks like we may have some good info. Maybe we can force a settlement and avoid a trial."

I had worked on that case for them. It involved allegations of damage done to a two year old because of the malfunction of the car seat during a rollover accident. "Good. I hate Ted when he's in trial mode. No one is happy those two weeks."

Judy nodded. "Tell me about it. Sphincter Boy makes everyone crazy with his constant worrying about every detail. But I guess that's why he wins so many cases. But enough about that - how are you doing? Last time we talked, you were still fuming over your husband's ex. Is she still giving you problems?" Judy enjoyed my stories about Mona as much as I enjoyed her dating fiascos.

"No, things are quiet for now. She's back in New Hampshire, tending to her cauldron. I'm hoping we won't hear too much from them until it gets closer to the time for Claudia to move out here. Looks like I have a reprieve for a few months anyway."

"How's that sexy husband of yours? If you ever get tired of him, I'll gladly take him off your hands."

"Thanks, I'll keep that in mind. You know you could find someone of your own to pester." Despite all her dating, Judy couldn't seem to find anyone who met her standards. Frankly, I thought she was just looking for excuses not to get tied down with anyone again.

"Nah - too much trouble. I'll just take your leftovers. I know you broke him in already. Say, speaking of husbands, have you heard from your stepmother's lawyer?"

Judy had a very circular way of thinking sometimes and it took me a moment to focus. I had forgotten all about calling Eleanor's attorney in the heat of the Mona/Claudia visit until Angela brought it up a week after they had left. Apparently, she had received another message on her machine. Luckily, Mom hadn't heard that one. What could Eleanor possibly want with us after all this time? Maybe her estate was leaving us some effects from Dad.

"No, as a matter of fact, I haven't. I called him a couple of weeks after Mona left and he was on vacation. Now he's back but I just keep missing him. It's frustrating and I'm getting more and more curious. I can't imagine what he wants."

"Well, why don't we finish up what we need to do here today and then you can call him again before you leave. I'm curious about what he wants, too."

We talked about the expert for the next fifteen minutes. I had found some articles he had authored that bolstered our position in our case and I wanted to make sure that Judy was aware of them. I had prepared a list of the articles with some summaries and she looked it over. "This is really good, Sara. I sure wish you worked back here in the office again.

I wrinkled my nose. "I don't think so, Judy. I really like working from home. I'm too spoiled to go back to a 9-5 grind. I don't think Tanya would like to see me back here, either." Tanya was the other paralegal and she and I had locked horns from my first day at the firm.

"I think you underestimate Tanya. She's really a good kid deep down and now that she got married she's a different person." Judy lowered her voice. "They're trying for a baby so she's getting it on a regular basis. It's really improved her mood."

I had to laugh. "Thank you for putting that picture in my head. Not one I wanted, though."

Judy put my report on top of one of her piles. "Well, I think we're done here. Now for you." She held out the receiver to her phone. "No time like the present. Wanna try Stepmom's lawyer now?"

It took me a minute to realize who she was talking about. It had been a while since I thought of Eleanor as my stepmother. I stared at the phone she held out. I was really afraid to turn this rock over. There was no telling what was underneath.

I hesitated. A part of me had been glad that Mr. Brumley had been so unavailable. It was the perfect excuse for not dealing with all of this. That part of my life was so well sealed over; I didn't want to disturb it. Every time I thought about his call, my stomach flipped. Like it did now.

The phone was still in Judy's hand, dangling. She sighed. "Sara, give me the number, I'll dial it for you."

I gave her the number. By now, I knew it by heart.

Judy dialed and handed me the receiver across her desk. "It's ringing," she said.

I reached across her desk and took the receiver, stretching the cord across Judy's pile of papers. In seconds, I heard the familiar answer of the receptionist.

"Hawkins and Brumley."

I felt my throat tighten. "Mr. Brumley, please."

"Whom shall I say is calling?"

"Sara Weber. I'm returning his call."

"Just a moment."

I was on hold for a few seconds while classical music played in the background. I barely had time to catch my breath when I heard a deep voice. "Hi, Mrs. Weber. So glad we've finally been able to connect. I've gotten your messages. I apologize for not getting back to you before now. "

"Uh, yes, well, as I mentioned in my message, I'm calling for my sister Angela. It seems there was a message a few weeks back for her to call you. You said you represented our stepmother Eleanor Cavaleri."

"Yes, that's right. Eleanor asked me to get in touch with you and your sister. Your sister's number was the only one we had."

My mind was now buzzing furiously. Eleanor wanted him to contact us? Eleanor wasn't dead? And how did he find Angela?

"Mr. Brumley, you seem to have me at a disadvantage. I have no idea why you're calling me or how you knew to contact me or my sister."

"I'm sorry, let me fill you in. I was hired by your father and stepmother to find you and your sister. Now that your father is deceased, your stepmother wanted to make sure that you got your inheritance. I had a private investigator look for both of you because your father and stepmother didn't have much information to go on. We were able to locate your sister because apparently she set up her business in her maiden name after her divorce. Then you called me."

"Wait. Slow down. I don't understand. An inheritance from my father?" I saw Judy's eyebrows go up. "I'm very confused. You said my father hired you? How can that be? This isn't making sense. My father died a long time ago. What are you talking about?"

"I don't know what you mean." Mr. Brumley cleared his throat. He obviously sensed a problem. "Your father died just a few months ago."

"What?" I screamed into the poor man's ear. "I'm sorry, just hold on a second." The phone shook in my hand and I suddenly found it hard to breathe. I took the phone away from my ear and stared at Judy. Sensing my anxiety, she came around from behind her desk and put her hand on my shoulder. I instinctively grabbed for it. My heart was pounding inside my chest. I was glad I was still sitting down. I put the receiver back to my ear.

"Mr. Brumley, tell me again when my father died. I have been under the impression my father died years ago."

Mr. Brumley's voice softened. "Mrs. Weber, I don't know what's going on here. I don't have all the details and, frankly, I don't want to pry. Why don't I have your stepmother get in touch with you? I know there have been some family difficulties from what she's told me. What I can tell you is this: your father died late last year and he has left you and your sister some money and Eleanor wants to make

105

sure that you get it."

Tears were streaming down my face. The room felt like it was closing in on me. I couldn't catch my breath and I struggled to find my voice.

"No...uh...let me call her. I don't think I'm ready to talk to her right now. Is there some way I can reach her?"

"I'll get in touch with her. If it's all right with her, I'll have my secretary call you with a number where you can reach her. Why don't you call me again after you speak with her?"

I nodded and then realized that he couldn't see me. "Okay. Thank you."

"I'm sorry to tell you this news in this manner."

"I understand. It's not your fault. Thank you again."

He clicked off.

I just stared at Judy for a moment afraid to voice what I had just heard. She took my hand in hers and reached across her desk to hang up the phone. She never let go of my hand and I squeezed it.

"It's okay. Sara, breathe. Can I get you anything? Water? Soda?"

I shook my head. I suddenly felt very ill and put my head down on her desk. The realization of what all of this meant was gradually sinking in. Daddy didn't die all those years ago as Mom had told us.

How could this have happened? Did Eleanor tell Mom that Dad had died to keep him from us? That seemed like the likeliest thing. But that couldn't be. Dad wouldn't have gone along with that and how would that have worked anyway?

Did Mom lie to us? Why? Why would she have done that? And to her own child? How could she have gotten away with it?

Maybe Dad was in on this? Did he ask to be torn from our lives like that? Why hadn't he come forward?

I had no answers and my head was beginning to hurt from thinking about it. I looked up at Judy and just said, "My father has been alive all these years and just died a few months ago. I don't know anything else. I'm going to have to talk to my stepmother to find out more." I just let the rest hang in the air. What the hell was Eleanor going to tell me?

Judy tried to hug me but I shrugged her off. "I'm okay," I said. I stood up quickly, almost knocking over the chair. "I have to go. I can't stay here. I'll call you." I practically ran out of the office and to my car. I had trouble getting the key into the lock, I was shaking so much. I slid in behind the steering wheel and just clung to it. The tears finally came in big sobs. I thought I was going to be sick.

I needed someone's shoulder to cry on. I needed Paul. I felt alone and frightened. I was a little girl again, sitting in my mother's living room and she was telling me that my father had died. I could hear my sister's sobs and could feel the tightness in my chest I had felt then, just as I did now. I always had thought it strange that Mom had never cried or even looked sad when she had told us. I just thought it was because she hated him so much and maybe was even glad that he was dead. Then Eleanor didn't have him, either. Or maybe she was in shock over losing a man she still loved...or at least still wanted. Maybe she was scared, wondering how she was going to support herself and us. I'm sure it wasn't easy to make ends meet, even with child support.

Now I knew that had been a lie. Whose lie, I didn't know. Regardless, this was serious. The only way to get any answers was to talk to Eleanor and hope she could shed some light on all this. Then I thought of Mom and Angela. How in the world was I going to explain this to Angela? And how could I face my mother after this? If she had believed that Dad had died all those years ago, I didn't dare tell her otherwise. I had no idea what the shock would do to her in her present condition. And if the lie had been hers...I just couldn't believe that she would have done that. No matter what I felt about my mother, I knew in my heart that even she wouldn't do something like that.

Slowly, the tears subsided. I started the car and drove home, barely conscious of how I got there. I pulled into my driveway, amazed that it took so little time.

The dogs jumped all over me when I walked in from the garage. I patted them absently and let them out into the back yard. It would be a while before Paul came home. I had to somehow get through the next few hours and get my bearings. Working on my cases would be useless. I was really having trouble concentrating. I needed something physical to relieve my stress. The idea of baking bread and kneading some dough into submission suddenly seemed very appealing.

When Paul came home that evening, there was no dinner ready to eat but there were three loaves of freshly baked bread. He looked at me and the bread lined up on the countertop and immediately knew something was wrong.

"Did Mona call?" was all he came up with.

Chapter Eleven

I had to smile. Leave it to Paul to think of Mona when things were going wrong. The man finally was learning. Too bad he was wrong this time. I opened my mouth to speak but literally did not know where to begin. I just stood there for a few seconds hoping something would fly into my head. Finally all I could come up with was "You're not going to believe what happened to me today."

My voice caught at that moment. I just stood there, afraid if I said another word I would start to cry again.

Paul hugged me. "Hey, what is it?"

I held on to him for all I was worth. My body trembled. Then I could no longer hold it in and the tears came.

Paul held me and smoothed my hair.

"Hey, Sara, it's ok. You can tell me. What happened? Did you have an accident?"

I shook my head. Taking a deep breath, I figured I would just plunge in. There was no easy way to say this and at least here was someone who would understand, who would know what this information meant to me, who could hopefully help me make some sense of it.

"I finally got hold of Eleanor's lawyer today."

"Sara, you're shaking. What is it, honey?" I could tell by the look on Paul's face that this wasn't what he had expected. His brows screwed up as he tried to understand why this would have gotten me so upset. "And...."

"And he told me that he was calling because Eleanor wanted to get in touch with me and Angela to give us some money that our father left us." I looked up into Paul's sweet face. The tears continued to roll down my cheeks. "Paul, he died just a few months ago. My father didn't die when I was a kid like I thought, at all. Something really strange is going on and I'm not sure what it is. I'm almost afraid to find out but I know I have to. All I know is this can't be good."

Shock and confusion registered on Paul's face.

"You're kidding," he said as he pulled me toward him. "No wonder you're so upset." He held me tight against him. "It's going to be all right, Baby. I'm here. We'll get through this together."

I buried my head in his chest. His shirt smelled of his Paul-smell and I found it comforting. I hugged him back. "Thank you."

Later, we heated up some leftover chicken and ate in front of the TV in the living room. I told Paul I really didn't want to talk about my father so he tried to distract me by making small talk about work and the dogs, but my mind was obviously elsewhere. My thoughts just kept coming back to how my father managed to stay out of my life for so long and what could possibly have happened to cause that.

Paul finally sighed and said, "So, then I told the job foreman that he was fired. Then, I set his hair on fire."

I looked at him blankly. "Huh? You what?"

"Sara, it's obvious you're thinking about your father. Why are we trying so hard to avoid it? Have you told Angela?"

Angela! I hadn't even thought to call her. Probably just

110

as well. Angela wouldn't handle news like this well. "No. I don't know what to say. I think I need a better idea of what's going on first. I can't explain something I don't understand myself. You know how Angela gets."

Paul nodded and smiled. "Angela gets a little intense sometimes."

I smiled back. It felt good. "You think?"

Paul stabbed another piece of chicken. "What I don't get is how whoever did this pulled it off. Your father had to have known something was up when he didn't see you guys. I sure as hell would have noticed if I wasn't seeing Claudia. It must have been him. I hate to say this but it sounds like he wanted out of child support to me."

I had never even considered this and I stopped, chicken halfway to my mouth. It made sense. Why hadn't I thought of it before? My father wasn't the victim. He was the one who had left. It would make sense he would want to sever all ties and save some money for his new family. This inheritance was probably the result of a guilty conscience.

I could feel myself getting angry. My father had been alive all this time and never got in touch with me.

He never called.

He never wrote.

It had been so easy to think of my mother as the bad guy...or even Eleanor. It was obvious now. It had to have been my father all along. The bastard!

I put my fork down. Eating was going to be impossible. "Paul, I need to walk. I can't do this right now. Please. I need to think. Give me a few minutes, okay? I just need to get out of here."

I grabbed my house keys and walked out the front door.

I had no special direction in mind. I just walked up our street and around the corner. I usually loved looking at the neighbors' yards, sometimes getting ideas for our own. But I didn't notice yards that night. All I could do was replay in my mind that afternoon when my mother had told Angela

111

and me that our father had died. Everything I had tried to bury from earlier in the day came bubbling back up.

I was afraid to hear the truth from Eleanor. I wasn't even sure Eleanor's version *was* the truth but I knew I had to hear it. By the third block, I had resolved that one way or the other, I was going to meet Eleanor and hear her out. Whether I told Angela - or my mother, for that matter – ahead of time, I hadn't decided yet.

Before I knew it, I reached our driveway again. The night air was still warm. I smelled a barbecue in someone's yard. All the birds had roosted for the night and the bats were out, darting around for bugs. I wrapped my arms around myself and stared at our home. This home had been my haven. Now, I felt invaded. First by Mona and now by the thoughts of my father's deception. Soon, Claudia would be living here and things could only get worse.

I sighed and walked in the door.

Chapter Twelve

Over the next few days, I tried to make peace with my life. I was not going to let the news about my father control me. He was gone. Someone had obviously done something horrible to separate him from my sister and me all those years but ruminating about it was going to get me nowhere. I was definitely going to have to bury this for a while. I decided that I was going to meet Eleanor face to face whenever I went back to New York to help Angela. I didn't want to hear anything over the phone. It was too easy to lie that way. I wanted the truth, finally. This was going to be very difficult to explain to Angela. But I was not going to ruin the life I had now by what someone had or hadn't done over thirty years ago. Life was going to have to move forward, Daddy or no Daddy. Eleanor and whatever stories she had to tell me were going to have to wait.

I went back to the law office the following week and met with Judy to discuss our cases. I worked at home. I cooked. I shopped. I played with the dogs. I was a wife to my husband and life was good again. I called Angela and told her that I had spoken to the attorney and we were apparently going to come into some money. I didn't tell her the circumstances because I hadn't absorbed it all yet myself. And surprisingly, Angela didn't seem interested. She was content to let me handle it and just tell her the outcome.

Mr. Brumley's secretary called a few days after my conversation with him and gave me Eleanor's phone number. "It's her understanding that you will call her," she said.

"Thanks, I will." When was another story. I had to come to terms with this and adjust to her in my own way and in my own time.

Mona called a few times to discuss arrangements for Claudia but was surprisingly civil and stuck to the details of the move and Claudia's registration needs.

Angela placed Mom in an adult daycare facility and she seemed to be responding to the structure.

I was able to lull myself into feeling that life was settling back into a routine. For the next few weeks, things seemed normal again.

Then in mid-August, Claudia moved in. She was arriving the week before classes were scheduled to start. I was glad. I was looking forward to spending some time with her so that we could bond a little more. Those first few days were probably going to set the tone of how the next four years were going to go and I wanted us all to get off on the right foot.

The week before Claudia arrived, several large boxes appeared behind my front door. It looked as though Claudia had packed every single piece of clothing she owned and shipped it out to us. I wasn't sure if I should unpack it or not. Would she consider that an invasion of her privacy? I decided to leave it in the boxes and just put them in her room. She and I could put everything away together when she got here.

Claudia's flight was due to arrive around three in the afternoon on a Wednesday, the second week in August. Paul and I had decided to take the rest of the week off to be with her. A few days prior to that, I scrubbed her room from top to bottom. The room itself was bright and cheery and had a window that faced the street. The street was quiet and her room had a wonderful view of the birdfeeder. It was adjacent to my office so I knew firsthand how pleasant it could be. I packed up all the things I had been storing in there and somehow found room for them elsewhere in the house. I loved our little Arizona house but one thing it lacked was storage space.

I shampooed the rug, dusted, and polished all the furniture. The bed frame was the first one Paul and I had owned as a couple and I treasured it. He had made the headboard for me from an old antique wooden valance that he had found in the attic of the house we had rented in Philadelphia. Paul and I now slept in a new king sized bed (we needed the extra room for "the boys", after all) but I still loved this smaller headboard and refused to get rid of it.

The bed linen was clean but plain. I had thought Claudia and I would go shopping and buy some new things for her room in the days before classes started. We could do those mother and daughter things I imagined mothers and daughters did when a child went to college.

Since security measures prevented us from meeting Claudia at the gate, Paul and I waited in the common area set aside for incoming flights. I had bought a magazine to read while we waited but I flipped through it aimlessly, barely seeing what was on the pages. My mind was racing.

I couldn't believe that within minutes, my husband's daughter by another woman was going to be living in my home twenty four hours a day, seven days a week for the next four years. I was torn between being excited and being scared out of my mind. Sure, Claudia had stayed with us before for stretches of time but never for more than a couple of weeks. Rarely, when she was younger, after Mona had moved them to New Hampshire, she even stayed for a month at a time during the summer. But she had been much younger then and far easier to entertain. I really wasn't sure what to do with a teenager. Heck, she was barely even that, anymore. Claudia was a young woman now, almost a stranger. I cringed when I thought about the months – make that years – that loomed ahead.

I didn't miss the irony, either. When I was Claudia's age, I would have given anything to have a relationship with my father. Now, knowing he had actually been alive then made it all the more poignant and heart-rending. Here was Claudia, within a plane's ride away from her father and the distance in some ways was almost as great. Mona's interference, whether out of her own fear of losing Claudia to Paul or her own anger at Paul for leaving her, made the result all the same. Claudia barely had more of a father than I did. But at least she was going to get a chance. I envied her. All my chances were gone.

Paul spotted Claudia first, coming down the walkway toward us. She had a small carry-on bag slung over her shoulder as well as her purse and looked tired. As she got closer, I noticed she also had a new stuffed animal that she had tried to shove into her large shoulder bag. Mona! She had struck again. I could imagine her trying to give Claudia that animal at the airport. Claudia would have been embarrassed but Mona would have wanted her to have something "from her Mommy". A little flag to wave when she showed up at our door. "See, I'm the real mother. I'm still here. I'll always be here." Maybe I gave Mona too much credit. But, come on, Claudia obviously didn't need one more thing to carry. It was a blatant attempt to mark Claudia as hers.

Within minutes, Claudia was right there in front of us. Paul hugged her. Claudia smiled weakly. My heart went out to her. I was going through a life change but so was she. I hugged her, too. "I'm so glad you're here," I said and surprised myself that I actually meant it.

116

Claudia fell asleep in the back seat of the car on the way home. It was mid-afternoon for us but early evening for her with the time change and she had been traveling all day. The poor thing was worn out.

We spent the evening quietly, letting Claudia ease into living with us slowly. None of us knew quite what to expect. This was very different from the visits we had had over the years. Claudia was going to be calling our home her home for the next four years. I still shook my head in amazement every time I thought about Mona agreeing to this. Claudia must have put up quite a fight to go away to school and Mona must have wanted to look like Mother of the Year to consent to this. Knowing how much Mona loved her child - or at least was possessive of her – this was totally out of character for her. Something told me to be wary, that Mona had to be getting something out of this, too, or she wouldn't have agreed to it. But for the life of me, I couldn't imagine what it was. Regardless, this was our life with Claudia now. I was finally going to stretch those maternal muscles I had dreamed about for so long.

Claudia and Paul went for a walk after supper. I stayed back and gave them some time alone. Paul was like a little kid, giddy with excitement. Whatever anxiety lay ahead in dealing with Mona and having a teenager living under our roof, it was worth it seeing the look on Paul's face. He finally had his little girl back after all these years.

Thursday they drove around town. Paul showed Claudia where everything was so that she wouldn't feel so lost. He had bought a little second hand car for her to use to get around in. He had wanted to get something "cool" but could only find a little compact sedan that was in the price range we could afford. I could tell by the look on Claudia's face that she was less than pleased with it. It didn't meet her standards, I guess. Poor Paul. I knew he was disappointed. He had expected a little more enthusiasm from her. However, he covered it well.

117

Mona called two times the first two days, Wednesday evening and again Thursday afternoon. Wednesday's call had been short. Exhausted, Claudia only gave her one-word answers. She stood in the kitchen talking while I cooked. I clanked a few utensils for Mona's benefit. I secretly hoped Mona would hear how well things were going.

When she called Thursday, Claudia was out driving with Paul. The disappointment was obvious in Mona's voice.

"Have her call me as soon as she gets in," she said.

"Is something wrong?" I asked. What could possibly have happened since you called her less than twenty-four hours ago, I wanted to ask.

"No, nothing's wrong. I just need to talk to my daughter." Then she hung up.

I made a face at the phone as I placed it back in its cradle. This was going to be a long four years. I was going to have to try harder to be patient with Mona.

An hour later, Paul and Claudia returned. I hugged them both. Claudia's hug back was limp, at best. I wondered if she had been given instructions by Mona. Then I dismissed that as silly. That might have worked if Claudia were a child but she was essentially an adult now. No matter what Mona had said, Claudia could think for herself and we did have a relationship of sorts that had built up over the years. Certainly, that counted for something.

"Your mom called while you were out. She wants you to call her."

Claudia nodded. "I'm going to call her from my room." She said this to Paul.

And she left.

I looked at Paul. It was obvious even to him that Claudia was holding me at arm's length and every time Mona inserted herself, the distance between Claudia and me widened.

Paul shrugged. "Give her time. She's tired and I'm sure she's going through a lot."

I ached to hear what was going on in that conversation. I imagined all sorts of things, all of them stressful. I imagined Mona drilling her about every detail in our home. Those old feelings of Claudia's youth came back. I pushed them away.

Friday morning over breakfast, I asked Claudia if she wanted to go shopping. Paul had decided to go to work that day, after all. He thought if he weren't around, perhaps Claudia would open up to me.

"I thought we would go get some new things for your room today," I said. "Maybe some sheets, a new comforter. A pony. Whatever you'd like."

Claudia actually smiled at me. "No, that's okay. My room is fine. If I need anything, I'll get it later."

This was going to be harder than I thought.

"I'm going to drive down to school today," Claudia continued. "I need to finalize registration, get my books, and figure out where everything is. I thought it would make Monday easier."

I smiled. She was her father's daughter, all right. That was exactly the thing Paul would have done.

"I have a surprise for you." I opened the kitchen drawer and pulled out the cell phone that Paul and I had purchased for Claudia. "We thought you'd like to have this. In case you get lost. To call your friends. Whatever. It shares minutes with Paul and me but we don't use ours much." I handed the phone to her.

"Cool." This was the first sign of excitement I had seen since she arrived. Claudia flipped the phone open.

"Here, this is your number." I gave her one of my business cards with her new phone number written on the back.

"Thanks, Sara. This is great." She gave me a quick hug as she got up to leave. "I'm going to go into Tempe now. I don't know when I'll be back." She turned and waved the phone in the air. "I'll call you," she said with the biggest smile I had seen since she arrived.

Within minutes, she was out the door and gone. I heard her car drive away and cringed a little. Claudia drove a little too fast for my liking. But I was encouraged with our little exchange. Maybe once Claudia settled in, things would work out after all. Mona would get used to Claudia being here. Claudia would bond with her father. She might even accept me more and we would develop our own special relationship.

Chapter Thirteen

The phone rang as I was clearing away the dishes. Assuming it was Judy calling to ask a question about a case, I didn't check the caller ID before answering.

"Sara, Mom's getting bad." It was Angela, her voice strained. "She's talking to herself a lot and even getting angry with me. Yesterday, she tried to hit me for the first time when I was getting her dressed. The people at the daycare say she's getting harder for them to handle, too. Things are getting worse instead of better. I think she's going downhill again."

"What do you want to do?" I dreaded hearing the answer.

"Well, I'm thinking about this winter. What if she gets out again? What if she gets more violent? I can't do this, Sara. Michelle is back at school and I'm all alone. You have to come out here and help me." Angela sounded as if she was going to cry and my heart ached for her. She needed me and it was time I helped her.

"You're right, of course. I should be there with you for

this."

Angela was quiet for a minute, probably expecting an argument from me. But I knew she was right. Mom was clearly deteriorating and it was wrong for Angela to have to go through this alone.

"I'll see what I can do about making a plane reservation and getting out there as soon as I can. Angela, you know it's probably time to place her. It's really what's best for her now. You can't keep doing this. This stress isn't good for you, either."

She sighed. "You're right. But placing her feels so final. I feel like I've failed her."

"Are you kidding me? You've done more for her than most daughters would. And you have to think of Michelle, too. This is taking a terrible toll on you. Michelle needs you, more than Mom." My heart went out to her. Despite our differences, my sister had always done what she could to provide a safe and loving home for our mother. Whatever her reasons were for doing it, she had been the good daughter, something I had to admit I was unwilling to be. My feelings for my mother ran too deep to allow me to get past them. I still blamed her for driving Daddy off. I was not looking forward to this visit for many reasons but resigned myself to its inevitability.

"You're right. When Michelle is here, I feel like I'm neglecting her. She's really good about helping me but I need time with her before she's all grown up and gone, too."

"I'll call the airline today and see what I can arrange. I'll call you tonight with my flight information."

"Thank you, Sara. I'll feel better when you're here."

After I hung up with Angela, I stood in the kitchen, phone in hand. It was finally time to call Eleanor. I retrieved the number Mr. Brumley's secretary had given me and dialed. The phone rang a few times and just when I was about to give up, Eleanor answered. Her soft "Hello" placed me on a path I knew was going to be difficult. I was finally going to learn the truth about my childhood. How ironic it was going to happen at a time when I was putting my childhood behind me forever. I was placing my own mother in a home from which she would never come out alive. I had become a parent to my parent. At a time when I should be feeling sad and reflective, I was feeling angry and resentful.

I really had no idea who to blame for my feelings. A father who had dropped out of my life? A stepmother who had maneuvered him away from me? An unhappy mother who had pushed everyone away?

I wanted to feel loving and concerned for my mother. She was going to be going through a very difficult time. I felt it was my job to be there for her and Angela. Now, faced with going to New York and meeting Eleanor and getting the true story finally, I knew it was time to put everything in perspective and let little Sara grow up.

But I wasn't quite as ready as I thought I was.

I hung up the phone on Eleanor's second "Hello".

I was able to get a flight out for the following Friday, leaving me a week to get myself prepared for what lay ahead. I did some paperwork, called Judy to let her know that I would be going out of town for a few days and put some chicken in the crock-pot for supper.

Claudia called as promised around two in the afternoon and told me that she had met some fellow students and would be having dinner with them at a place near the campus. My gut told me to tell her to come home instead but I didn't feel as if I had the right, so I agreed. I kept imagining Claudia telling me that she was eighteen and she could do what she wanted, that I wasn't her mother. I didn't want to go there, at least not so soon after her arrival.

Claudia came home around seven just as I was clearing the dishes from dinner. Paul was at the kitchen table balancing our checkbook. Claudia yelled a loud "Hi, I'm here!" as she hurried to her room.

I looked over at Paul and saw the scowl on his face. He

sighed and followed Claudia to her room. I followed him but kept a safe distance. I didn't want to look like I was interfering or that we were ganging up on Claudia.

"I had wanted us to have dinner together tonight, Claudia."

"I'm sorry, Dad, but I was with some friends and I was having such a good time. Besides, I called and told Sara. She didn't have a problem with it." Thanks, Claudia, blame the stepmother.

"I understand that but you have obligations here, too. Where are you going now?" Claudia was pulling clothes out of her dresser drawers.

"I'm meeting some people."

"I'm not happy with you leaving again. I had thought we would spend the evening together."

Way to go, Paul. I was shocked how ineffective he sounded. Heck, I would have gone out, too, if he approached me like that.

"Dad." Claudia dragged the word out in a whine. "Come on. Don't be like that. Be happy that I'm making friends."

"Who are these people?"

"You don't know them."

"That's my point, Claudia. I'm concerned who you're hanging out with."

"They're classmates, okay? I have to go. I'm going to be late." She gently pushed Paul out of the room and started to close the door. "I have to change my clothes."

Within minutes, she was gone again.

Paul and I were back in the kitchen and the sound of Claudia's screeching wheels had just died down. I looked at my husband. He just shook his head. "It will get better," he said. "She's just staking out her territory. When classes start, she won't have time for all this."

"I hope you're right. I wasn't expecting this kind of behavior at all."

Paul didn't answer. He went back to balancing his

checkbook. I thought I heard his head burrowing into the sand. Half an hour later, he closed the checkbook and said "I'm going for a walk. Want to come?"

"Sure, let's take the boys."

We walked. We talked. We avoided talking about Claudia. When we came home, Paul suggested we sit on the deck and look at the stars. He poured us some wine and we snuggled together on the swing. He kissed the top of my head. He held my hands in his and kissed them.

"I love you so much, you know that?"

I was beginning to think Claudia being out of the house was a good thing. At least, we had the place to ourselves.

We made the most of it.

We saw little of Claudia the rest of the weekend. I had never thought of Claudia as being a party girl. She had never come across that way during our short visits together and Mona had certainly never mentioned it as a problem. But she definitely seemed to be into partying that weekend with her new friends. It made me uncomfortable to see her gone so much without knowing where she was. Paul seemed resigned to it.

It became more and more apparent that his way of not-approaching Mona was going to spill over into his way of not-dealing/parenting with Claudia. Someone was going to have to step in soon if she continued this after classes started. I knew that someone was going to have to be me and that would drive one more wedge between us. I envisioned phone calls from Mona, too, chastising me for attempting to parent "her baby".

However, for the time being, Mona's calls slowed down and I was grateful for that. Maybe she was calling Claudia on her cell and we didn't know it. That was fine with me. I enjoyed not having to cringe every time the phone rang.

Sunday night I took the opportunity to talk with Claudia about the weather that was expected for the following day. She was going to be heading out for classes during rush hour and thunderstorms were predicted for most of the day. I wasn't sure she was up to the challenge. Even after driving in Arizona for years, I still hated driving in the thunderstorms. It was the tail end of our monsoon season but the local storms were sometimes still quick and deadly. Paul and I loved to watch them from the safety of our deck. But navigating the flash flood areas was a hassle we both liked to avoid. The lawmakers took these storms seriously, too. They had enacted a "Stupid Motorist Law" which allowed them to charge the stranded driver if rescue teams had to be used to pluck them from a flooded wash. I didn't want to see my stepdaughter being pulled from the roof of her car on the six o'clock news. I also didn't want to have to pay for the pleasure, either.

Claudia brushed me off when I tried to explain all this to her. I probably should have waited until Paul was with me to bring it up but he was out walking the dogs and Claudia was about to go off to bed. I didn't want to lose my opportunity.

"I'm a good driver. Why do you keep telling me what to do? I've driven in the rain before, you know. They have rain in New Hampshire."

I ignored the jab. "I didn't say you weren't a good driver, Claudia." Although I begged to differ with her. "All I'm trying to say is that the storms here in Arizona can be dangerous and I want you to be careful. This is the desert. The streets and washes flood quickly when it rains. You have to be prepared or you can get stuck. The streets get very slick, too. It's easy to have an accident if you aren't aware."

"Okay, storms, rain, danger, floods. Got it." She rolled her eyes at me. "You're taking this mothering thing way too seriously."

I wondered if that was how Claudia felt or if Mona had made that comment in the past. It sure sounded like Mona to me.

"Fine, Claudia. That's all I asked. Just be careful."

By the time Paul came back, Claudia was in her room. I

didn't even mention our conversation to him. What was the point?

Paul was already up and gone by the time I came out of the shower the following morning. I expected to hear Claudia up, too, but the house was eerily quiet. Had she left already? Eager to get to classes?

I showered and dressed and was pouring myself a cup of coffee in the kitchen when she swirled into the room, book bag slung over her shoulder, short hair a wet cap around her head.

"Oops, overslept a little," she said.

She grabbed a bagel from off the counter and stuck it into her mouth.

"Fee oo ater," was all I heard. She waved and was out the door. Seconds later, I heard her car speed away.

I looked at Jesse. "Well, that was fun." He wagged his tail and begged for a dog biscuit.

I had a meeting later that morning with Judy and Jeff to discuss how my cases were going to be handled while I was in New York and tried to put Claudia out of my mind for the rest of the day. Not my daughter, not my problem. If she wound up on the news tonight, so be it. Paul was going to have to deal with it, sooner or later. I knew I wasn't going to follow through on that but it would help me get through the rest of the day thinking that I wasn't responsible.

After our meeting, Judy and I went out to lunch a couple of blocks away at a Mexican restaurant. While we waited for our food to arrive, she filled me in on her date from Saturday night.

"I think I really like this guy, Sara." She was actually blushing. "He brought me flowers."

"Married?" I couldn't resist the jab.

She shook her head, her mouth full of salsa and chips. "'Divorced."

I rolled my eyes. "Haven't you learned from my life? Is his ex-wife alive?" She nodded. "Kids?" She nodded again

127

and held up two fingers.

"Fool." I slapped her on the top of her head. "You're in for it now."

"No, it's not like that. They all get along. The kids are teenagers, boys, and he says he gets along with their mother. They've been divorced for five years. Mom and the boys live in Sedona. He gets the kids once a month." Judy was trying so hard to convince me this was going to be all right. I wondered if this was the conversation she had had with herself.

"Well, I guess not everyone is like Mona. Where did you guys go on Saturday?"

"We went down to Tempe. We had dinner at a Chinese restaurant on University and then went to one of the bars down there. It was crowded though. I forgot all the college kids are back."

"You might have seen my stepdaughter down there and didn't even know it. I think she lived in one of those bars all weekend."

Judy gave me a quizzical look. By this time, our food had arrived and she was shoving refried beans into her mouth.

"We didn't see much of Princess Claudia this weekend. She has friends now." I made brackets in the air when I said the word "friends". "And liked their company better than ours, I guess. Paul is hoping she'll settle down when she has homework to do. I'm not so sure."

"Isn't stepmotherhood fun?" Judy was enjoying this at my expense.

"Choke on a burrito and die."

Claudia surprised me and came home for dinner that night.

And the next.

Maybe Paul was going to be right after all.

I had just come in from grocery shopping. It was five o'clock Wednesday evening and I was running late. I knew

Paul would be home within the hour and I hadn't even started dinner. I dumped mail and groceries on the kitchen counter and saw the blinking light on the answering machine. I hit the button and listened while I let the dogs out the back door. The little mechanical voice told me I had two messages. The first one was Mona.

"Hi, Claudia, honey. This is Mom. Give me a call when you get this. I tried your cell but it was turned off."

Well, my suspicions had been right. We had gotten a reprieve from Mona because we were now subsidizing her calls to Claudia's cell phone. Oh, well, I guessed it was worth it.

The second call was from Claudia. "Sara, this is Claudia. Look, I'm going out to dinner with some friends from class and then we're going to go to the library and work on a project. Don't wait up for me."

Don't wait up for her? What kind of "project" took that amount of time? When was she planning on getting in? I didn't like the sounds of this at all. I picked up the phone and dialed her number. All I got was her voice mail. I assumed her phone was still off and wondered why she was doing that. She probably didn't want to hear me or Paul telling her to get her butt home. I could feel myself frowning.

Paul and I stayed up as late as we could. I felt my eyes closing while I watched the ten o'clock news. By ten-thirty, I knew I wasn't going to make it much longer.

"Paul, I have to go to bed. I'm beat. Are you going to stay up?"

"Let me try her phone again." He went into the kitchen and came back seconds later.

"Still no answer?"

He shook his head. "You go to bed. I'm going to sit here and read a bit. I really want to talk to her when she gets in."

I went to bed then but was unable to get to sleep. Part of me kept listening for the garage door, signaling Claudia's return. Jesse fell asleep at the foot of my bed and I found his

129

snoring reassuring but Toby was out in the living room with Paul. Of the two dogs, Toby has always been the protective one. He must have sensed that all was not right.

After an hour, I heard the whine of the garage door gears and soon the opening of the laundry room door. Claudia was home. I strained my ears to hear what was going on. Should I go out there? Should I let Paul handle this on his own?

I heard muffled talking and could make out Paul's voice but couldn't hear any discernable words. I couldn't hear Claudia at all. Finally, it got quiet. Then I heard Claudia's bedroom door slam.

Paul came to bed. He punched his pillow a few times and rolled onto his side. I couldn't take it anymore and sat up.

"Well?"

"What?"

"What did she say? What did you say? What was resolved?"

"It's okay, Sara. I told her we were worried and she promised to come home early next time and to keep her phone on. It's not a problem. Go to sleep."

"I heard her door slam."

Silence from Paul. A few seconds, then - "She was drinking. A lot. I think she was drunk."

I reached out for Paul, found his hand, and squeezed it. "Paul, I get the feeling there have been some things that Mona hasn't told you."

"I was thinking the same thing. I'm going to call her tomorrow."

We snuggled a little then and I felt Paul relax and doze off. I, on the other hand, laid there thinking of all the possible things that Mona could have withheld from us.

Paul made the call the following evening. Claudia was in her room studying. We broke with procedure. Paul took the kitchen phone out on to the deck so that Claudia wouldn't hear him and I had an extension phone. Mona immediately got on the defensive as soon as Paul explained the phone arrangement to her.

"What's going on? Why are you ganging up on me like this? Has something happened to Claudia?"

"No one's ganging up on you, Mona. And Claudia's fine. She's in her room studying. I just wanted to talk to you without Claudia here so that we could get some things cleared up. And this was the best way to do it. Now, can we get past this, please? I think it's important that we talk about this."

Mona sighed, loudly. Something told me she knew what was coming. "All right. What is it?"

Paul took a breath. I knew he was dreading this. "Was Claudia having any kind of trouble before she came out here?"

"What kind of trouble?" Mona wasn't going to make this easy. And evasion was her middle name.

"Was she giving you a hard time about following rules? Staying out late? Running with a bad crowd? That kind of thing?"

"Well, I don't know what you mean by a bad crowd. Claudia is a good girl and I was doing the best that I could. It isn't easy raising a child all by yourself and working full time."

Mona loved to play the "poor me" role. We had heard this speech on more than one occasion: "Pity me. I was left all alone to raise my child with no support and no help." I could see Paul's face getting tight.

"Mona, let's not go down that road right now, okay? I'm trying to help Claudia. This isn't about you. And I'm not accusing you of anything. I'm worried, that's all."

Mona sighed again and then made that condescending snorting noise she was famous for. I knew Paul was trying to placate her to get her to be honest with him. The question was if she was going to take the bait.

"Well ..." Mona was obviously trying to decide if she was going to say something or not. "There was one thing...."

"Mona, if you know something that can help us help Claudia, now is the time to say it."

"She had been staying out a little later than I would have liked the last few months and she did seem to be neglecting her studies a little but I just chalked it up to her trying to find her own way. You know, she's getting older and she wants to be independent."

"Mona, this is important. Was she drinking?"

Mona cleared her throat. I found myself holding my breath. Come on, Mona, spit it out.

"A little. But she promised me it wouldn't happen again."

"What wouldn't happen again?" Paul ran his hand through his hair. If Mona had been standing in front of him, I think he would have strangled her at that point. But losing his cool was only going to shut her down. The key was to keep her talking.

"Well, right after the holidays last year, she got into a little bit of trouble with her driving." She stopped.

Paul's eyes were getting larger the more frustrated he was getting. "And..."

"And she was drinking and driving and got stopped by the police." This last was said as fast as she could. She was probably thinking if she said it really fast it would go away.

"And you didn't think you needed to tell me this?" Paul had now lost all control and was yelling into the phone. I motioned for him to calm down and he gave me a dirty look.

"Don't scream at me, Mister. This is exactly why I don't tell you everything. Besides, I handled it."

"You handled it. How did you handle it?"

"I got her a lawyer and she only had to do community service."

"Wait a minute. You got her a lawyer? Why did she need a lawyer?"

Mona was obviously starting to feel more comfortable now. Her tone had gone from anxious back to her normal condescending one. "I told you. Weren't you listening? She got stopped by the police so she had to go to court."

"She was charged with drunken driving?"

"Well, we got the charges changed to something less."

"What were they changed to?"

"Look, it was a while ago. I don't remember it all. Ask Claudia if you want all the details." Mona was obviously all through with being afraid ...and divulging any more information.

Paul sighed. "You know, Mona, I'm getting a little tired of you withholding information from me. It would have been very helpful if I had known this before Claudia came out here to live."

"Why? Would you have refused to let her live with you and your perfect wife if you had known? Maybe that's why I don't tell you things. You're so judgmental. Claudia doesn't need that. She needs someone to love her and accept her. It's important..."

"Stop. Just stop right there. I don't need you lecturing me. I'll handle it from here. Thank you for your information."

"Fine." She hung up.

Paul looked at me for a few seconds without saying anything. Then, "Do you believe this?"

"Don't ask me. I'm still basking at being called 'perfect'."

Paul gave me another dirty look. "Sara, this isn't the time for jokes."

I ran my hand through his hair. "I was just trying to get you to smile. I know you're upset. I am, too. But we'll figure this out. Maybe it's a good thing we got Claudia away from Mona. Maybe we can help her. Maybe this all happened for a reason."

Paul gave me one of his "don't tell me your metaphysical crap" looks.

"I just meant that I think we'll be good for Claudia.

You'll be good for Claudia. Mona was teaching her how to get away with things and not be responsible. Now's your chance to make a difference in Claudia's life. Isn't that why you wanted her out here?"

"You're right. It's just..." he got up and started pacing around the deck. "I just had no idea things were this much out of control. It's like I don't even know these people. Mona, Claudia...they live in their own made-up world. Claudia is turning out just like her mother and I don't know if there's anything I can do about it."

"Maybe not, but you have to try."

"You're right but I think I'll have to tread lightly. Claudia is not going to accept what I have to say right now."

And you hate confrontation, I felt like saying. But instead, said, "She's going to be defensive, too. Don't think for a minute that Mona isn't calling her right now and telling her what just happened here."

It was obvious from the look on Paul's face that he hadn't even thought of that. "Drinking. Stopped by the police, for God's sake." He slapped the railing on the deck. "Shit," he shook his head. "Why does it have to be so complicated?"

I wanted to say "Because you married a wacko bitch" but refrained.

We walked back into the kitchen.

"Are you going to say anything to her tonight?" I wasn't happy about all this drama the night before I was scheduled to leave for New York. I had planned to spend some quiet time with my husband before going off to face my own freak show with my mother and Angela, and possibly my stepmother's attorney and my stepmother herself. But thanks to Mona, that wasn't to be.

"No, I've had enough for tonight. It can wait until tomorrow." Paul pulled me to him and hugged me hard. He sighed and I sensed a change in his mood. "I don't want to talk about Claudia or Mona or anything else right now. My wife is going to be gone for a few days and I'm going to miss her." He put his hand under my chin and tilted my head up to his. His kiss was soft. "Why don't you and I go into our room, close the door, and see what comes up?"

"You silver tongued devil, you."

Early the next morning, I sat in the kitchen with Paul. Our plan had been to have breakfast together as a family before I left but Claudia was sleeping in and refused to get up when Paul knocked on her door.

"Your stepmother is leaving soon," he said to the closed door.

"Wish her a good flight for me," she mumbled back.

Claudia was probably feeling hung over and deserved it. My own stomach was doing cartwheels. All I could get down was coffee. Paul made himself toast.

"You have all the phone numbers, right?" I asked him.

"Sara, relax. We'll be okay. You just worry about what you need to do. Call me. You have your cell phone, right?" I nodded between sips. "It will be okay, sweetie." Paul gave me a hug and that made me want to cry. But I didn't want him to remember me that way in case the plane went down, so I just hugged him back and gave a weak smile in return.

I had refused a ride to the airport from Paul. He needed to be here with Claudia. I had called for a cab and soon we heard a horn beep outside, signaling the taxi's arrival. I hugged Paul again. I hugged both of the dogs who wagged their tails at me, totally oblivious to my concerns.

"Take care of my babies," I said. I buried my nose in their fur inhaling their doggie smell.

Paul carried my suitcase out to the cab for me. "What are you taking to New York? Bricks? You'd better tip this guy good. He's gonna need it for his hernia operation."

Another hug, another kiss, a wave good-bye and I was off, tears streaming down my face, wondering what the heck the next few days would bring.

Chapter Fourteen

My sister lived in a large ranch house in North Merrick, Long Island, the same house she had shared with her husband Ed while they were married. He gave her the house as part of the divorce settlement, something she had argued for in the best interests of Michelle. Angela had insisted that she didn't want Michelle to change school districts and be "disrupted". The fact that Michelle was only six years old at the time and had attended school for all of three months was something that she overlooked, I guess.

Frankly, I think Ed would have agreed to anything to get the divorce. The marriage hadn't been a happy one for years from what my sister told me. They had put up a blissful front for friends and relatives but I heard from my sister that all was not happy in Angela-land for a long time.

Ed was a successful antique dealer. He was often away on buying trips and he and Angela didn't see eye to eye on many things. When she found him cheating with his secretary, she threw him out. His guilty conscience got the best of him and Angela got the best of everything else, as a result. However, to hear her tell it she was barely breaking even every month. How she scraped by on her child support, alimony, and her housecleaning business was anybody's guess. Angela was a successful business woman who ran her own company and I always thought she should have had more self-respect, or at least shut up about her problems. Maybe she just reminded me too much of Mona and I wanted...or expected... more than that.

The plane ride across the country wasn't bad despite my nervousness at flying alone. I busied myself with listing what I wanted to accomplish while I was in New York.

1. Visit nursing homes with Angela
2. Choose one
3. Call Eleanor
4. Meet with Eleanor
5. Meet with Eleanor's attorney
6. Move Mom into nursing home
7. Talk to Angela about Dad and whatever I learned from Eleanor

I knew that last item was going to be very difficult and I wanted to put that one off as long as possible. I tried watching the in-flight movie but got bored and dozed off a little. I dreamed I was back in New York living with Kevin and Dad came to visit me. He was laughing about how he had fooled us all along and was actually living just blocks away from me. I awoke with a start when the captain came on telling us we were beginning our descent.

After retrieving my luggage from the carousel, I rented a car for the drive to Angela's house. Traffic was picking up and it slowed me down but I didn't care. Unlike Paul, I didn't mind long drives and this one gave me a chance to prepare myself for what I feared I was going to face. I hadn't seen my mother or Angela in quite a while and I felt as if I were going to see strangers.

Angela lived on a very nice residential street. The homes were large, the lawns green and lush. The air was warm, the flowers plentiful and colorful. So different from Arizona. In some ways, the whole scene seemed idyllic, far from what I was feeling.

As I pulled into Angela's driveway, I saw her and an old woman sitting in lawn chairs in the front yard. I recognized Angela immediately. She had changed very little in the years since I had seen her. Her dark hair was chin length with no hints of gray. She had always been a fashionable dresser and today was no exception. She was wearing shorts and a top. Both looked expensive and showed off her slim figure.

I looked at the old woman sitting next to her and, at first, thought Angela had company. Then I realized with a start that I was looking at my mother! How she had aged! Her gray hair had lost its luster. Her eyes stared off into a land where no one lived. Her hands trembled in her lap. I couldn't believe the changes I saw. Angela had been right. We needed to do something and fast.

My sister got up as I pulled in and parked in the driveway.

"Hey, you." She hugged me as soon as I exited the car. "So good to see you. I've missed you." Her hug lingered more than I expected and I sensed she was really feeling overwhelmed by all of this. She took my hand and led me over to Mom.

"Mom, look who's here."

I knelt down and said, "Hi, Mom."

My mother looked at me, patted me on the head, and smiled. "You're a nice girl," she said.

Angela squeezed my shoulder. "See? I wasn't exaggerating."

I shook my head and wiped a tear from my cheek.

"Why don't we all go inside?" Angela took my mother's hand and led her into the house like a child. She settled Mom in front of the TV and then showed me to my room. I looked around the house as we walked to the back where the guest room was. Angela had exquisite taste even if it ran to places I wouldn't go. The house was loaded with antiques, many that she had acquired while married to Ed. It displayed a hominess I didn't expect from Angela. She came across as cold and aloof but her house was warm and inviting.

My room was done in soft blues and greens and was a tribute to Angela's talents. If she ever got tired of managing her cleaning business, she could easily have hired herself out as a decorator. She helped me put my things away, making small talk about Michelle and Ed's new wife. I felt she was trying very hard to put off talking about what had become of our mother and I let her. There was plenty of time after Mom went to bed.

Dinner was awkward. Mom ate her food without saying a word. Angela fluttered nervously. I swallowed my food but tasted none of it. I was just so overwhelmed with what I was seeing. My mother had transformed into a small graying child. It made what I knew I had to eventually tell Angela all the more difficult.

We watched some television after dinner and when Mom started to doze off on the sofa, Angela suggested she should go to bed. She got up obediently and walked down the hallway toward her room, without so much as a glance in my direction. Angela noticed the hurt on my face.

"Don't take it personally, Sara. She has quiet days like this. Tomorrow she may turn into a chatterbox and chew your ear off. I'd better go supervise. Be back in a minute."

After Angela settled Mom in, she and I sat up in the living room and shared a bottle of wine. I filled her in on how it was going – or not going – with Claudia. Angela talked about her business. She was doing quite well and I told her how happy I was for her. Angela found a lot of satisfaction in her work. She had a neighbor that she paid so she could make her appointments if they fell outside of the

139

day care hours and Angela stayed home at night with Mom. Not much of a life but Angela seemed content. We talked about the kind of place we could put Mom in. Angela had gotten a couple of references and she suggested that we go the next day and look them over.

I decided now was the time to tell Angela about my phone conversation with Mr. Brumley, our stepmom's attorney. When I got to the part about Dad dying just months previously, Angela's eyes grew wide.

"You're kidding me. You must have misunderstood. I distinctly remember Mom telling us about Dad when I was what? Ten?"

I shook my head. "I'm afraid it's true. I'm having trouble understanding this, too. I have no idea what this means. I think the only way we're going to find out is if we talk to Eleanor. Apparently, she lives around here somewhere."

Angela frowned and started waving her hands as if she were swatting flies. "I don't want anything to do with that attorney or with Eleanor. That's something you're going to have to handle." She took our now empty wineglasses and walked into the kitchen.

I followed her. My instinct was to say "Angela, this woman that you take such loving care of may be the one who lied to us" but I didn't.

"Angela, don't you want to know the truth?"

"The truth? The truth is we grew up without a father. Regardless of who's to blame, you're telling me now that Daddy was alive. That means someone lied to us. Yes, I realize that could have been Mom but we don't know that and how can we trust Eleanor to tell us the truth? She's going to tell us whatever makes her look good. The bottom line is Daddy was alive and he chose not to tell us. He could have contacted us so many times and he didn't. All that does is make me angry."

I tried to say something but she waved me off.

"He left us money. Fine, he should. It's the least he could

140

do after abandoning us like he did. Maybe he thought that would make it all better. But he was wrong and so is Eleanor. I'll gladly spend his money but I'll be damned if I'm going to play nice with his wife, too."

She put her wine glass in the sink and turned to me. "All I want is a check. I don't care what Eleanor has to say. Don't ask me to go with you. I won't. I'm going to bed. See you in the morning."

I stood in the empty kitchen. The hall clock ticked and I could hear Angela brushing her teeth in the bathroom. Just like that, she had dismissed any notion of knowing more. Her life was moving on and she didn't want it fouled with stories about fathers and mothers and second wives. That was not the reaction I had expected. Surprise, certainly. Tears, maybe. Anger definitely. But Angela had thrown up a wall to even being told what had happened. Was she that afraid of what she would find out? Doubt started to replace my resolve. Maybe I was foolish for wanting to know the truth, too. Maybe a part of me agreed with Angela. After all, I had been reluctant to contact Eleanor myself. What did that tell me?

And Eleanor had made no effort to reach me, either. I suddenly realized what a minefield I might be walking into. I had just assumed that Eleanor would welcome contact from me but what if that wasn't the case? What if she had been the one to wrench Daddy from us? What if my mother had been right about her all along? Maybe Angela's approach was the best one, after all. The easiest thing to do was just to meet with Brumley, collect our checks, and go back to life as we knew it. What was to be gained by delving into the past now?

But I knew I would never be satisfied if I did that. I would always wonder what I might have learned if I had talked to Eleanor. Even if all I got was her version of things, I could still sift through it all and come to my own conclusions. There was a big hole in my life and she was the

141

only one who could patch it up for me.

I needed to call Eleanor and finally find out what she knew. I needed to fill in the missing pieces. I went into my room so Angela wouldn't hear me and dug my cell phone out of my purse. I dialed Eleanor's number, hoping it wasn't too late at night to be calling. I had no idea what time she went to bed. This time I answered when she said "Hello."

"Eleanor?"

"Yes? Who is this?"

My throat was dry. "Eleanor, I'm sorry to be bothering you so late but this is Sara...Peter's daughter. Your attorney said I could call you."

There was a short pause during which I had the strongest impulse to hang up. Then, "Sara! Oh, my goodness. I never really expected you to call me. No. It's not too late. I was just watching some TV. I have trouble sleeping lately and I'm spending way too much time in front of this silly thing. Wait a minute. Let me turn it down so I can hear you better."

I heard her put the phone down, the noise in the background disappeared, and then she was back on the phone again.

"So, Sara, we finally get to talk after all these years. I have to say, I'm surprised. I'm pleased, too, but I really didn't think you or your sister would ever change your minds and call me."

That struck me as an odd thing to say but I ignored it. I couldn't believe how alert Eleanor sounded. After spending all evening with my mother, I guess I had assumed she would sound frail and feeble-minded. Then I remembered that she was much younger than Mom. Something else she had hated about Eleanor.

"Eleanor, I'm in New York visiting my sister. I was wondering if you and I could get together to talk. From what Mr. Brumley said, it sounds like there are some things to clear up."

Eleanor hesitated again. When she answered, her voice

142

was a little more reserved. "Yes, I guess there are. I wasn't expecting to hear that you were in New York, though. My attorney told me you lived in Arizona."

My paranoia kicked into gear. Was Eleanor saying she didn't want to meet me?

"Yes, I do, but I figured as long as I was here anyway, it would be easier to meet in person rather than discuss things over the phone. I'm sure this seems unexpected. Maybe I should have called sooner but...if you don't want to...."

"No, no, that's not what I meant at all. I think you're right. We should meet. It will be a lot easier in person. And I would like to see you, Sara. Would you like to come here?"

"Your house?" I couldn't imagine myself going to the house she had shared with Daddy. It was too much, too soon. I didn't think I could handle it. Besides, I remembered how Jeffrey always wanted to quiz deponents in his office conference room, how much he liked what he called "the home court advantage." But having Eleanor meet me in Angela's house wasn't an option.

Eleanor sensed my hesitation. "We could meet somewhere else, if you'd rather."

"How about someplace convenient for both of us? Where do you live? I'm staying with my sister on Long Island right now, in North Merrick."

"Oh, all right, if that's what you want. I live in Hempstead. Very near to you, actually. There is a wonderful little shopping center near here in Bellmore on Monroe Avenue called The Belle Commons. Are you familiar with it?"

"No, but I'm sure I can find it."

"Well, there's a little shop in there called *The English Rose*. They serve tea and lunch. I know the owner. Why don't we meet there and we can catch up?"

"I'll find it. When do you want to meet?"

"I think the sooner the better, don't you? How about tomorrow? My social calendar isn't too full these days." She chuckled.

Things were moving rather fast but there was no point in waiting. "Tomorrow is okay but it will have to be later in the day. I have some appointments in the morning."

"That's fine, Sara. We can have a late lunch together, my treat. How about two o'clock? Just ask for me when you come in. I'll have a table reserved."

I was too nervous to sleep after that and sat up for a while going over all the possible scenarios for tomorrow. What a day it was shaping up to be. First, nursing home interviews for my mother in the morning and then meeting my stepmother in the afternoon. I suddenly wished I had another glass of wine.

I barely remembered Eleanor from my youth. All I could picture was a short woman, brown hair, glasses. Not much to go on. It had been over thirty years. I wondered how she would look, what I would say, what she would say. Not to mention how I would feel.

Something Eleanor had said on the phone came back to me and I realized it had been nagging at me ever since. *"I really didn't think you or your sister would ever change your minds."*

I had no idea what that meant. Changed our minds from what?

I called Paul. He had fallen asleep watching TV in our bedroom. I filled him in on my mother and Eleanor. He said he missed me, that everything would turn out all right. I asked about Claudia. He said she was okay. She was asleep in her room. Yes, Mona had called but he didn't talk to her. He said he just gave the phone to Claudia. That struck me as odd. Up until I had left, Mona had called for Claudia on her cell. Now, I'm gone one day and she was calling the house. Did she know I was gone? I was sure Claudia had told her. I couldn't help but read into this change. Obviously, she was taking advantage of the fact that I was out of the house. I didn't dare mention this to Paul but I was determined to get home as soon as possible. I had visions of Mona flying out to Arizona in my absence.

Paul sounded tired.

"I love you, sweetie," I said. "Go back to sleep."

Chapter Fifteen

Angela had found two nursing homes for us to look at the next day. The first one was a couple of towns over. The woman who introduced herself to us as "Susie, the case manager" was a little too cheery for my taste.

She dragged us around the premises pointing out all the happy residents and speaking to them as if they were five years old. I felt like I was placing my child in kindergarten. She showed us dining rooms covered with construction paper pictures. We were guided through bedrooms made up to look like little girls and boys lived in them, stuffed animals all over. But it was clean and the residents looked well cared for. The people who worked there seemed to genuinely care for the men and women who were staying there. I had to keep telling myself to look at this place through Mom's eyes. She would probably respond well to their brand of attention.

The next place was entirely different. It had the feel of a hospital. Antiseptic smells everywhere. Old people with blank look, riding the halls in their wheelchairs. I had the odd sensation that they were all just sitting around, waiting for death. It broke my heart. I could not imagine relegating my own mother to a place like that.

Angela and I drove home in silence, overwhelmed by what we had seen. I had thought we would stop somewhere to get a bite to eat. I wanted to give Angela a break, give her some time just for herself. I was starting to get a full grasp of just how much she had really sacrificed to take care of our mother and I was feeling really bad that I hadn't done my share. But after the last nursing home she said she just wanted to go home. I had to agree. I wasn't in a very social mood, either. We were both drained emotionally.

We were barely inside the house when Mom ran up to us. Her fists were balled up and she was visibly shaking. "Where were you?" she demanded from Angela.

"Mom, I told you Sara and I had to go out for a little while. Did you have your nap yet?" Angela looked to Clara, the neighbor who had stayed with Mom while we were gone. Clara shook her head as warning.

Mom pointed a bony finger at Clara. "She was stealing all the money I had in my room. I saw her."

Clara smiled. "Now Helen, I told you there was no money there." She looked at Angela as if to say that this was not the first time they had gone over this.

"Don't you lie to me. I saw you!" Helen shook her fist in Clara's face.

I stepped forward, afraid Mom was going to hit Clara but Angela put a hand on my shoulder. "Let me handle this," she whispered.

Angela took my mother's hand. "It's ok, Mom. Clara will give it back. Won't you, Clara?" She looked at Clara, pleading with her eyes for her to go along with the story. But it was obvious Clara didn't like being called a thief, even by an old crazy lady.

"Angela, there was no money there. Honestly. I wouldn't

147

steal from you."

"Maybe you made a mistake, Clara. Maybe you thought it was yours. Right?"

Clara sighed. "Yes, that's right. I'll give it back. I'm sorry." She grabbed her purse from the living room sofa. "I guess I'd better be going." Clara practically ran from the living room and out the front door.

"Well, that's a sitter I'll never see again. Thanks, Mom."

But Mom didn't even hear Angela. She was looking out the window at the car in the driveway. "Who's here? I don't recognize that car."

"Mom, that's Sara's car. Remember? She came to see us? See?" Angela pointed to me.

I looked at my mother. "Hi, Mom. Remember me?" *Please remember me.*

"Sara? When did you get here?" Mom stroked my hair. I could feel the tremor in her hand and my heart ached. The look in her eyes brought me back to my youth and I thought I would cry. I held my mother's frail hand and I looked at Angela. I didn't know how she did this day after day. I was gaining a new respect for my sister.

"Why don't you take a nap, Mom? You look tired." Angela led her into her bedroom. Napping seemed to be Angela's answer to all our mother's problems but I couldn't say that I blamed her. I could have used one myself.

While Angela settled Mom in her room, I freshened up in preparation for my visit with Eleanor. As the hour for our appointment grew closer, I was getting more and more nervous. I was more than tempted to call Eleanor and just cancel the whole thing. Brumley could mail us our checks and we could all go back to living in our protected worlds. Angela had made some good points last night. There wasn't any good reason to know the truth now. What was to be gained? Dad was dead. Mom was living death. Angela and I had survived this long. Raking up the past was only going to cause hurt and heartache for both of us. But I knew in my heart I would never be satisfied until I knew everything, good and bad. That was just how I was wired. If Angela wanted to stick her fingers in her ears and yell "Na Na Na –I can't hear you," I could live with that. Besides, after her outburst last night, I knew forcing her to do more than that would only have led to more harsh words. I was nervous enough about meeting my stepmother without an ugly scene with Angela just before it. I was going to do this all by myself.

I took one last look in the mirror, sighed a heavy sigh, and went back out to the kitchen. Angela was pouring herself a glass of ice tea.

"I think I'm going to go shopping for a bit. It helps me to clear my head. Do you mind?"

"No, why should I mind? I think we both need a little break after this day."

"Can you give me directions to The Belle Commons in Bellmore?"

Angela shot me with a look that told me she suspected something. "Why do you want to go all the way out there? There are plenty of shopping centers close by."

"Someone told me about a tea shop that was there and I wanted to bring something back for a paralegal I work with. She's crazy about anything that has to do with tea." It surprised me how easily the lie came out.

I don't know if Angela believed that one or not but she looked up the tea shop for me and gave me directions. I told her I would call her if I was going to be late for dinner.

As I drove through the streets of Bellmore, I couldn't help but imagine that my father might have driven down these very same streets just months before. The feeling was unsettling.

I found the teashop easily and was actually a few minutes early. I parked the car and sat at the wheel a minute, trying to quiet the tap dance that was going on in my stomach. My inclination was to put the car in drive and speed out of the

149

mall and back to Angela but I took a deep breath, locked the car, and entered *The English Rose*.

The door jingled as I pushed it open. Soft music was playing and I felt myself relax a little. The store was divided into two sections. The front half was filled with shelves and tables full of what Paul often referred to as "crafty crap." Teapots, Victorian dolls, lace tablecloths, and other assorted items seemed to be everywhere. There was an island in the center of the store where a woman was ringing up a customer. The back half was cut off from the rest of the shop with a few tri-fold screens, hand stenciled with ivy. I could see that there were tables beyond the screens and assumed that was the tearoom.

I approached the island and waited for the woman to finish with her customer. She handed change to the woman. "Thank you for stopping in. Next time you will have to stay for tea." She turned to me. "Can I help you?"

My mouth went dry and I could hear the blood rushing in my ears. I swallowed hard. This had to be the biggest mistake of my life. What was I thinking? What was I going to say to this stranger?

But something about the shopkeeper made me stop for a second. Her eyes had a familiarity to them.

"I'm supposed to meet someone here. Her name is Eleanor Cavaleri. My name is ...."

"Sara," she finished for me.

I was taken aback at her casual mention of my name. It must have shown on my face.

"It's OK, Sara. Eleanor and I know each other really well. She told me she was waiting for you. I'm Maria, by the way. I own this shop." She extended her hand and I shook it. I was thrown off by her unexpected friendliness. The whole situation was becoming more and more overwhelming. "Let me take you to Eleanor. Follow me."

I followed Maria past the folding screens to the tearoom. A few of the tables were occupied. Women chatted and silverware clinked as we walked by the tables. Maria took me to a table in the far left corner. A woman with short brown hair sat with her back to the wall and she was anxiously watching the entrance to the tea room. Her eyes got a little wider when she saw Maria and realized that we were headed her way. I don't know why, maybe because of my own mother, but I was expecting to see a little bent-up old lady. I was not prepared for the woman who was now rising to greet me. I had heard over and over from my mother how Dad had dumped her for a younger woman but it didn't make much of an impression on me when I was fourteen and my stepmother was in her late twenties. Hell, she was ancient to my teenage mind back then. Now, however, the age difference hit me with a start when I realized I was being greeted by a very good-looking woman who I estimated to be in her early sixties, at the very most. The light in her eyes when she looked up at me told me there wasn't a hint of senility in her head. Her hair was softly curled and she was dressed in brown slacks and a summer weight white sweater. Her trim figure was obvious. I couldn't help but think about her and Dad as lovers and I could feel myself blushing. Dad had done well for himself.

She smiled as we approached. "Sara?" She held out both of her hands to me.

I didn't know if I was expected to hug her or not. I felt uncomfortable doing so, especially in front of Maria. Instead, I took both of her hands in mine and said, "It's so nice to finally meet you."

"Yes, it is. Here. Have a seat." She motioned to the other chair and then looked at Maria. "Maria, will you bring Sara some tea? And we're ready for our lunch now, too." To me, "What kind of tea would you like?"

"I don't know. Anything. Earl Grey is fine."

Maria hurried off and Eleanor stared at me for a couple of seconds. She shook her head. "You look so much like your father. The last time I saw you, you were just starting to

151

get into those awkward teenage years. Now, look at you. You're a grown woman." She sighed. "It just reminds me all over again what we've missed all these years."

"I don't remember too much of those days. I don't think I would have recognized you, either." I was confused about the missed time remark. I played with the silverware, praying for a speedy delivery of tea.

"How is your sister? And your Mom?"

"Angela's good. She has a daughter now. Michelle. Mom...Mom is okay. Getting older."

"Aren't we all?"

I smiled. What can you say to that?

Maria mercifully returned then with my tea and a tray of finger sandwiches. After she served us, she patted Eleanor on her shoulder and said she would be back to check on us in a little while.

"Try these sandwiches, Sara. They're delicious."

"Sounds like you know this place quite well."

Eleanor smiled. "Yes, I do. The owner and I are very close and I come here a lot. These salmon sandwiches are my favorite." She took a bite and then looked right at me. "But the food isn't why we're here today, is it?" She hesitated for a moment. "I have to tell you. I was surprised when Mr. Brumley told me you wanted to speak to me. I really expected that you and Angela would just accept the money and go on with your lives."

Again Eleanor was referring to rejection. I didn't know what to say to that so I just kept quiet. Eleanor looked at me, waiting for a response, though. Maybe it was my imagination, but I was beginning to sense that there was something, not quite hostility but more than displeasure, just below the surface.

She finally looked away and took a sip of her tea. "Tell me about you. Are you married? My attorney tells me your last name is Weber now."

"Yes, I'm married. My husband owns a construction

152

company in Arizona."

"Arizona. My, so far away. And you? What do you do? Do you have any children?"

Maybe I should have been put off by all the questions but I tried to imagine myself in Eleanor's place. If I were seeing Claudia after many years of separation, I might be saying and asking the same things.

"I'm a nurse, a legal nurse consultant. I work with attorneys on their medical cases. It's my own business."

"Your own business? That's impressive. But you always were the ambitious one. And so smart, too. I'm glad to see you did so well." She took a sip of her tea. "You didn't mention children...?"

I always hated when people asked me about that. As if not having children was some kind of failing. And it always reminded me of my miscarriages. Opening that wound all over again. One that wasn't probably ever going to heal.

"No, we tried. It just didn't work out. I have a stepdaughter, though. Paul was married before."

Eleanor nodded. "A stepdaughter - life is funny, isn't it?" She took another sip of tea, probably regretting that she had asked. I knew I was. She played with the silverware.

I wondered where this meeting was going. It certainly was not what I had expected. I had thought I would be meeting a sweet old lady who would tell me all about my father. I wasn't prepared for this woman who seemed to be holding all the cards and telling me nothing. Part of me wanted to just grab her and ask "Why did my mother tell me my father died when I was fourteen? What happened?" but I didn't. I was afraid of what I would hear and I wasn't sure I would get the truth. I thought it best to just see where Eleanor would take this.

A few seconds went by. I was getting more and more uncomfortable. Our table seemed so quiet compared to the others around us. Everyone seemed to be chattering away and having a good time, except me and Eleanor. I was tempted to just get up, say, "Thanks for meeting with me but, I'm sorry. I have to go." I pictured myself just walking out of there without a glance back. Angela had been right. This had been a horrible mistake.

But I didn't budge. Instead, I sat there, waiting for Eleanor to make the next move. I couldn't help but notice her rings as she toyed with her spoon. She wore a plain gold wedding band on her left ring finger with a band of diamonds next to it. On her right hand was a large cocktail ring of rubies and diamonds. I thought again of the money my father had left us.

"Sara, I should be honest with you. I probably know more about your family than you obviously know about me. Your father and I hired a private detective to track you and your sister down."

Now we were getting somewhere! "I know. Mr. Brumley told me."

"I know this must be very difficult for you. I know it is for me. I understand from Mr. Brumley that he was the one to tell you that your father died just last year. Apparently, you were under the impression that he had died some years ago. I'm sorry you had to find out that way. I don't quite understand the confusion."

I felt my stomach tighten. I thought about the day when Mom told us Daddy had died. Was that where the lies had started? Did my mother make that up to keep Daddy away from us? Or did Daddy somehow concoct that story to keep us away from him? Neither alternative made complete sense but I knew somewhere in there was the truth. And how could Eleanor not have known about any of it?

That would have been the perfect time to tell Eleanor about that day and see what she said but how would I know it was the truth? Maybe my years working with lawyers had jaded me, but I couldn't help but think that the only way I was going to find out what really happened was to let Eleanor do the talking.

"I think it would be best if we went to see Mr. Brumley first and get the will out of the way," she continued. "Maybe we can piece this all together after that, you and I. What about Angela? I'm assuming she knows about all this?"

"The will...that sounds fine. Angela knows about the will and about Daddy. But she...she's very busy with her daughter and her business. She asked me to handle everything for her." No need for Eleanor to know Angela's true feelings and I certainly wasn't going to let her know how bad off Mom was. At least, not until I knew more about all the missing pieces to this story.

"Oh." Eleanor was obviously disappointed. "I had hoped to meet her, too." She sighed. "Well, everyone has to deal with this in their own way. I suppose we can handle this without her. I'll let Mr. Brumley know and see what has to be done."

I had planned to ask Eleanor more questions about my father. What had he been like? How had he died? Did he ever talk about me? But the words kept dying in my throat. A slight buzzing started in my head. The desire to run out of the room was overwhelming. I needed to get out of there. I wanted to go home...not to my sister's. I wanted to be home in Arizona, with Paul, and my dogs, and my cacti. Anywhere but here. This was wrong.

Maria mercifully came by then. "Everything ok? Anyone need anything?" She looked at Eleanor.

Eleanor smiled. "I'm fine, dear. How about you, Sara? More tea?"

The buzzing in my head was getting louder and I needed to escape. I saw my chance. "No, I'm fine. Actually, I should be getting back."

"So soon?" Eleanor started to reach for my hand but I slid it back and pretended to fumble for my purse. "I understand." She looked at Maria. "We won't need anything else. Thanks, dear."

Maria smiled at Eleanor and again squeezed her

shoulder. Eleanor reached up and tapped her hand. The friendship between the two was palpable.

I reached into my purse and pulled out my business card case. "Eleanor, I hate to have to leave so soon but I really need to go. Why don't you get in touch with your attorney and call me?" I gave her my card. "Call me on my cell. The number's on the card. Thank you for lunch."

I stood up, not knowing what was expected at that point. Should I hug her? Offer to walk her to her car? Run screaming from the room?

Eleanor toyed with the card I had given her. "I think I'm going to sit here and have a little more tea," she said. She looked at me and gave me a little smile. "It was nice meeting you, Sara. I hope we get to see more of each other."

"Me, too." I was sure neither of us meant it.

I tried to walk calmly back to my car. Once I was behind the wheel, I drove to another part of the lot and parked again. My hands were shaking uncontrollably and I needed time to calm my nerves but I didn't want to run the risk of running into Eleanor leaving the tearoom. I certainly didn't want her to see me sitting in my car, falling apart. The pounding in my head was so loud. I put my head down on the steering wheel and tried to get my heart to quiet down. I took some deep breaths. Then I checked my watch. I had been with Eleanor barely thirty minutes. I decided to call Paul. I needed to hear his voice if only for a minute. I called his cell but only got his voice mail.

"Hi, hon. It's just me. I just met with Eleanor and needed to hear your voice. I think meeting her was a big mistake. Call me when you can. Love you."

Chapter Sixteen

Angela's house was quiet when I got back. Both she and Mom were napping. I went into my room and I booted up my laptop, hoping to do some work but my mind kept going over my meeting with Eleanor. I had hoped for answers but all I had were more questions.

I walked out to Angela's back yard and sat in one of her lawn chairs. Listening to the birds feast in the feeders calmed me a bit. Why had I been so afraid to confront Eleanor? I should have just asked her what had happened. Yet, the question had frozen in my throat. Maybe a part of me knew what the answer was all along. Somehow, my mother had engineered that separation from my father and he had gone along with it. Eleanor probably knew about it, too. As always, everyone was dancing around the truth. Paul did it with Mona. Maybe it was a divorced father thing. Story of my life. If I had heard Paul say "I don't want to rock the boat" once, I had heard him say it a hundred times. Maybe my father had done the same thing.

But to allow my mother to erase him from our lives in that crazy way was more than over the top.

Maybe he didn't know she had done that. But how could she have pulled it off?

The more I thought about everything, the more confused I was getting. It looked as if I was going to have to swallow my fear and ask Eleanor some important questions.

Some day.

The thought of actually talking to her about it made my heart beat faster all over again. The chirping of my cell phone disrupted my daydreams. Could it be Eleanor already?

"Hello?"

"Mrs. Weber?"

"Yes." I didn't recognize the female voice.

"This is Dolores, Mr. Brumley's secretary. I'm calling to let you know that Mrs. Cavaleri has made an appointment for you to meet with Mr. Brumley and her tomorrow morning to go over the details of the will. I know it's a Sunday and I'm sorry for this short notice but she said you would be leaving soon. He can see you at ten o'clock. Can you be here then?"

"Yes, I can. I'll need directions."

"Certainly. Do you have a pen handy?"

"Hold on, please, while I walk back into the house."

We hung up after she gave me directions to the office just as Angela came into the kitchen to make dinner. She saw me disconnect my phone and place it on the counter but didn't say a word about it.

"When did you get back?"

"A little while ago."

"Enjoy your visit with Eleanor?"

The look on my face must have told her how surprised I was that she knew.

"I'm angry, Sara, not stupid. I figured you would try to meet up with her while you were here." Angela took a bag of potatoes from the pantry and started peeling them over the sink. "What's she like?" Ah, she was curious, after all.

"Older. Pretty. Not what I expected. A little aloof. She seemed to think we didn't want anything to do with her...or Dad, I guess."

"Did she know...you know, what Mom told us?"

"Some of it but I had the impression that this was new information. She got it from her lawyer."

"Did you ask her about that?"

"I wanted to but the words just wouldn't come out."

"Wasn't as easy as you thought it would be, was it?"

"No."

Angela gave me a smug look.

"Okay, you were right...sort of. But the other thing is I wanted to see what she would say. See if she would slip and tell me what really happened. If I told her what Mom told us, it would have been too easy for her just to say it was all Mom. What if it wasn't? What if it was Dad? I could see her protecting him now that he's gone. Make him the poor suffering father and Mom the bad guy."

"What difference does it make now?"

"I don't know. Maybe none. I just want to know, that's all."

I told her about the appointment with the lawyer the next day. As I expected, she refused to go.

"I meant what I said before. I don't want to hear anything either of them has to say. What good will it do to drag it all up now? It won't bring Daddy back and I'm not going to turn my back on Mom now, no matter what she did."

I had to agree with her. Maybe I needed to re-think my own plan for the next day.

Dinner with Mom and Angela was a repeat of the night before. I wondered how Angela did this, day after day. She didn't seem to notice. I helped her clear the table and then begged off and went to my room. I told her I had some work to do but I just wanted to be alone.

I called Paul again. The connection was very bad. They were having a thunderstorm in Phoenix. I was upset to be missing it. I used to love to sit on our deck with the dogs and Paul and watch the light show. The more violent the storm, the better we liked it. As best I could, I told Paul about my meeting with Eleanor. He listened but I could tell he was distracted.

"How's it going with Claudia? Any more blow up?"

He sighed. "It's not going well. Maybe she needs a mother's touch. She was out most of the day. Then she was late getting home. She hardly talks to me. I have no idea what's going on. I don't know. She just doesn't seem all that interested."

I heard distant warning bells in my head.

"When are you coming home?" Paul asked. My heart ached for him. He sounded so lost.

"Well, tomorrow morning I'm meeting with Eleanor's attorney. I'll know more after that. Angela and I found a nursing home that might be okay to place Mom in but we have to talk about it some more and I think I'd like to go back and look at it again. My flight back is scheduled for Tuesday."

"Okay, I miss you, baby. Call me tomorrow night."

"I will."

The next day, true to her word, I couldn't convince Angela to go with me to meet Mr. Brumley. She wouldn't talk about it in front of Mom for fear of upsetting her at the mere mention of Eleanor. All Angela said when I left was, "Bring home a bag of money."

The plan was for me to meet Eleanor at her attorney's office at ten o'clock. His office was very near where I had met Eleanor the day before. As I pulled my car into the parking lot, I saw Eleanor getting out of her car as well. I was struck again by how young she looked compared to Mom. She waved when she saw me and we walked into the small one story office building together. Eleanor seemed subdued this morning. I imagined it was hard for her to be dealing with anything concerned with Daddy's death.

The lobby of the building was small. Several doors opened onto it and Eleanor steered me to the far right corner. "Hawkins and Brumley, PC" was written on the glass front in gold letters.

"David's office is in here," she said as she opened the door.

The office was quiet. The chair behind the receptionist's desk was empty but I could hear someone rustling papers in a back room.

"I'll be right out," a male voice called out.

We took a seat on the leather sofa in the waiting area. A few minutes later, David Brumley walked out. He was tall, and dressed in a very expensive three-piece suit. I figured him to be about sixty-five years old.

"Eleanor, how are you?"

He extended his hand to Eleanor and she took it in both of hers.

"Thank you for meeting us on such short notice," she said.

"No problem. You know I promised you and Peter I would do whatever it took."

He turned to me. "You must be Sara." He offered his hand to me. I nodded as I shook hands with him. His handshake was firm. "Let's go back to my office, shall we?"

We followed him down a long hallway to a large office that overlooked a small flower garden. Eleanor and I sat in deep upholstered chairs in front of his desk. David – as he asked to be called – took a seat behind his expansive desk. I noticed some pictures of laughing teenagers on the credenza behind him. They appeared to be a little younger than Claudia, probably his grandchildren.

David cleared his throat, opened a folder, and looked straight at me with clear blue eyes. I had the impression he had been in this position often. Helping families go over the leavings of their relatives, calming shattered nerves, smoothing over hostilities.

"I didn't know your father very well, Sara, but I understand that he was a wonderful man. Our office was only brought into the picture at the end to set up his estate right before his death. And then to find you and your sister. I understand that there had been some family problems years ago," he nodded at Eleanor, "and I know that you and your sister were estranged from your father. Eleanor and your father didn't go into details with me so I have no idea what happened. And it's not important that I know any of that now. I just want to tell you that your father was kind and gentle and everyone here had the utmost respect for him. I'm sorry to be meeting with you under these circumstances. That being said, I want to go over with you what your father has left you."

Over the next half hour, he walked me through the trust funds that Angela and I were now owners of. Actually, he just went over mine. However, he told me that an identical fund had been set up for Angela. He needed to meet with her. I told him she wasn't ready. He said that was fine, she could have an attorney contact him and they would handle everything.

I had trouble reconciling the man I knew as my father with the man David was describing. Apparently, Peter Cavaleri had gone on to develop a very successful contracting business. He had also invested in real estate and, apparently, had done quite well. I couldn't stop myself from imagining what my life would have been like had Daddy been in it. I guess once free of my mother – and us – he was able to become the man he wanted to be.

My head was spinning when I walked out of there. I was a very rich woman. I wavered between being excited over having this new financial freedom with being angry with my father all over again for hiding so much from me.

Eleanor walked me back to my car. "Do you feel up to having a cup of coffee or something?"

I felt sorry for her. This must have been hard for her, too, but I really needed to be alone right now. "I'm sorry, Eleanor. I can't. I'm leaving soon and I have to get back and pack." It was a lie and she probably sensed that but didn't let on. "Maybe next time I'm in town we can get together again."

Eleanor nodded. "I'm sure this has been all very overwhelming."

Was that relief I saw in her eyes?

We said our good-byes, promised to keep in touch and I was soon on my way back to Angela and Mom, back to the way things were.

Chapter Seventeen

I wanted to go home. I needed Paul.

Instead, I had lunch with Angela and Mom. Angela seemed tense and even snapped at Mom a couple of times, something I had not seen her do before. After lunch, she settled Mom in the backyard and she and I escaped to the kitchen. We could see Mom from the kitchen window but could talk without her overhearing us. Angela was indifferent to most of the details.

"What's the bottom line? What do we get?"

Angela's eyes grew wide when I told her the amount. She whistled. "I had no idea Dad had done so well. If he left that portion to us, Eleanor must be swimming in it." I hadn't thought of that. No wonder she dressed so well.

Angela thought for a moment. "Let's do this," she said. "Mom seems a little better this week. Let's hold off just one more time before we place her. Let's go look at that first place again this afternoon and make what pre-arrangements we need to. Then, you can go back home. We'll get all this money stuff straightened out and then in a couple of months, if Mom is no better, we can place her in the nursing home. I'm just not ready to do that yet. And this money that Dad left us will help us pay for a sitter."

I resented Angela making plans for how we were going to spend this money. I could easily see how families were torn apart by wills and inheritances. But what she said made sense. I was too tired and worn out from the past couple of days' events to argue. How much could a sitter cost anyway? Besides, it made me feel less guilty about leaving Angela to take care of Mom while I went back to Arizona...to my own problems.

It was more than ironic that Dad's money was going to help us take care of his ex-wife. I wondered what he would have thought if he knew.

Angela was able to convince Clara to sit with Mom again while we went to look at the first nursing home we had seen the day before. It didn't look any better to me that day than it did the day before but Angela seemed to think it would work when the time came. I just went along with her. As long as she was happy with it, I didn't have the energy to argue. We toured again and filled out some paperwork to leave for the social worker when she came in the following day.

Afterwards, Angela and I stopped at a little coffee shop. We sipped lattes and laughed. I told her about Tanya and Judy. She told stories about her clients. It was nice to spend some time with her just like the old days. So much had happened since we were little kids huddled under a blanket together while Mom and Dad fought.

On the drive back home, Angela squeezed my hand. "Thanks for doing this with me. I know you didn't want to."

I squeezed back. "You're welcome. It's the least I could do. You've done a fantastic job of taking care of Mom and I've been no help at all. I'm sorry about that."

Angela patted my hand before returning it to the steering wheel. "Don't worry about that. It just made sense for me to do it. You have other things to take care of. I don't mind. It fills my day. And it's really not that bad."

We traveled in silence for the rest of the trip back home.

Mom was sleeping when we got home. Angela thanked Clara who looked happy to be leaving. The rest of the evening went smoothly. Mom seemed more alert and all three of us watched television after dinner. I put thoughts of nursing homes and stepmothers and wills out of my mind and just enjoyed the interlude with my sister and mother.

After Mom went to bed, I called Paul on his cell phone and got his voice mail. I tried the house and got the answering machine. I thought that was strange but hoped that it meant that he and Claudia were out somewhere having a good time. With the time change, I figured it was about seven o'clock back home. Maybe they just went out to dinner.

I went to bed. The day after tomorrow I was flying back home and I couldn't wait. The sooner, the better. I needed to put all of this behind me and get back to my life, my dogs, my home, even Claudia and Mona. It all seemed tame after the last few days. I fell asleep and dreamed of my father. He was holding me and telling me how much he had missed me. But I was having trouble hearing him over the noise of his ringing cell phone.

On the third ring, I woke up and realized it was my phone ringing on the bedside table. I flipped it open and heard Paul calling my name before I even said Hello.

"Sara? Sara? Are you there? It's Paul." I heard a catch in his voice and immediately knew something was wrong. I tried to wipe the cobwebs from my head quickly. "There's been an accident."

I was instantly awake now, my heart racing. I felt panic start to rise. "What's happened? Are you all right?"

"I'm fine. It's not me. It's Claudia. There was a bad storm tonight and she had an accident with her car. We're at the hospital. She broke her leg. And she might have a head injury."

I cringed. I knew from my nursing experience that closed head injuries could be very bad.

"Have you contacted Mona?"

"Yes, I called her and she's on her way. She should be here in the morning."

My heart broke hearing the worry in Paul's voice. I wished I could be there with him and hold him, tell him everything was going to be okay. The truth was, I didn't know that but this was one of those times when lying was totally acceptable, even expected. "Paul, she's going to be okay. Claudia's young. She'll pull through. Who's her doctor?"

Paul mentioned the name of an orthopedic surgeon I knew who was excellent. He was also waiting for the neurologist to come in. Claudia was in radiology and would be seen as soon as the films were read.

"She's in good hands, baby. But how are you doing?"

"I'm a wreck, but I'll be all right. It's Claudia I'm worried about. I saw her for a few minutes before they rushed her off to X-Ray. She looked awful, Sara. So bruised and beat up. And she's still dazed. I just need you here, Sara. Part of me wants to be angry with Claudia and part of me feels like it's my fault."

"Your fault? How could this be your fault? Was she drinking, Paul?"

He hesitated. "I don't know. They took blood. I guess we'll find out. She went to the library at the University with friends. I should have made her come right home after that. I knew the storms were predicted. I shouldn't have let her drive on a day like this. Mona was furious when I told her what had happened."

"Forget Mona, will you? She's just upset. It's not your fault and don't let her blame you. This isn't going to help anyone right now, least of all Claudia. Just be there for her. Let the doctors do their job and then you'll know more."

"OK, I'll call you back as soon as I hear anything."

"Please, don't forget. I'll be waiting. I love you."

"Me, too." He hung up.

There was no going back to sleep now. I got up and made myself a cup of tea. I sat in Angela's living room in her rocking chair and listened to the hall clock ticking. I kept willing Paul to call me back with good news. An hour later, my phone finally rang.

"Both doctors saw her. She's stable now but we won't know anything more until the morning. They took her to the ICU."

"Ok, you need to go home and get some sleep now. Did you call Mona back?"

"Yes, I just got off the phone with her. I'm going to pick her up at the airport in the morning."

I felt myself tense up. He had already called her before he called me. I knew it was her daughter but I resented her hold on Paul right now.

"Ok, Babe, go home. Hug the dogs. Get some sleep and call me in the morning after you pick Mona up. Good night. I love you. It's going to be okay."

"I hope so."

I went back to bed, tossed and turned, unable to get Mona out of my head and out of our car. I fell asleep holding my cell phone.

Angela woke me up when she got up to make us all breakfast. After I told her what had happened, she hugged me. It was then that I finally felt safe enough to cry. She hugged me harder and smoothed my hair.

"It's going to be all right. Do you want to go back to Arizona today?"

I nodded. It felt good to lean on Angela.

"Why don't we see what kind of flight arrangements we can make."

We called the airline but as it turned out there wasn't a flight available until the next day anyway. I already had reservations for a flight out that day so there was nothing to gain. I was doomed to staying another day and letting my imagination get the better of me.

I waited for Paul to call me all morning. Finally, I could wait no longer and called his cell phone but all I got was his voice mail. Angela suggested we go for a drive to get our minds off things. There was a Farmer's Market nearby. She said Mom liked to walk around there and it would do us all good to get out.

We spent a couple of hours at the Farmer's Market. Angela had been right. Mom seemed to perk up and really enjoyed getting out of the house. I, on the other hand, kept watching the time and trying to imagine if Mona had landed in Arizona yet and what she and Paul might be doing.

Paul called me as we drove home. He didn't want to stay on the phone long. He and Mona were waiting for visiting hours to start again in the ICU and they were trying to catch Claudia's surgeon. We barely said a few words to each other when he rushed off the phone again. He had spotted the doctor and Mona was motioning for him to come over. He promised me he'd call later.

It wasn't until that night that he called. He still seemed distracted but he was alone this time. He was calling from the ICU Waiting Room. Mona had gone in to see Claudia and he was going in as soon as she came out. Claudia was still very much out of it but seemed a little more alert. At least the news was better and I could sense some relief in Paul's voice. I told him what time my plane was due in the next day.

"I...I'm not sure it's a good idea if I come get you. I'm afraid to leave the hospital for too long."

I sighed. "I understand. How about I grab a cab home, drop off my stuff, and then meet you at the hospital?"

Paul hesitated. "Why don't you call me on my cell when you get home?" By that, I assumed he meant to see if it was going to be all right with Mona.

Once again, I held back but inwardly I promised myself

169

that I was not going to allow Mona to dictate if I could be with my own husband at a time like this. I agreed to call but I knew in my heart I was not going to stay home.

I slept fitfully that night dreaming about hospitals and confrontations with Mona.

Chapter Eighteen

My flight home was in the afternoon. A layover in Dallas gave me time to think. Too much time. I didn't know what was bothering me more: my fears for Claudia or my fears at the thought of Paul being alone with Mona.

I had trouble sorting out my feelings. I was worried about Claudia but more because she was Paul's daughter and he was worried about her. I had never developed maternal feelings about her. I never really had a proper opportunity to bond with her. I was too busy trying to help Paul counteract the Mona attacks. Besides, how much of a relationship could I build on a few days a year? Nevertheless, I still didn't want to see her hurt. I knew if she were hurt, Paul was hurt and I certainly didn't want that.

I told the picture of Paul having romantic drinks with Mona to leave my head. Thinking romantic thoughts about Paul and Mona was ridiculous. Paul hated even talking to Mona on the phone. Why would he entertain any amorous notions about her now just because they were being thrown together? It was Mona I didn't trust. Her attempts to seduce Paul after the divorce and the fact that she still blamed me for everything, even after all the time that had passed, made me distrust her. She might not really want Paul back but if she could break us up and make both of us pay for what we did to her (in her mind), I was sure she would jump at the chance. I knew my thoughts weren't rational, certainly not while Claudia was so ill, but my heart wasn't always a logical organ.

I called Paul on his cell and got his voice mail again. I was starting to hate that message. More than likely, he was visiting Claudia in the ICU. I knew they asked people to turn cell phones off in there. But I hated not being able to talk to him. I left him a short message telling him where I was and that I loved him.

The flight from Dallas to Phoenix was very turbulent, much like my mind. The closer I got to home the more apprehensive I was getting. I kept running all possible scenarios through my mind:

1. Claudia hanging on to life and begging her parents to get back together so that she could get well. They do.

2. Claudia dying and Paul and I going to the funeral. Mona banning me from the funeral. Paul leaving me outside and going in alone.

3. Mona crying outside the Intensive Care Unit. I console her. She sees me for the compassionate person that I am. We bond. All is well.

By the time I landed, I was a nervous wreck. I took a cab back to the house. The dogs were overjoyed to see me. I scratched them behind their ears but Toby wanted more than that so I knelt down and buried my nose in his fur. He wagged his tail and licked my face. I wished everyone were this easily pleased. God, it was so good to be home.

I found a note from Gregg on the kitchen counter telling Paul that he had fed the dogs their supper. Underneath it was a previous note saying he had fed them breakfast. I was beginning to wonder if Paul had come home at all last night. Had Claudia gotten worse? I walked through the house, the dogs following behind me, tails wagging. In light of the past few days, it was comforting to look at familiar things.

I plopped my suitcase on our bed and changed my clothes. I grabbed a cookie and chomped on it while I walked the dogs in the back yard. As soon as we came back into the kitchen, I called Paul as I had promised him but got his voice mail again. I took that as a sign that I should just drive over there.

The trip to the hospital was a blur. I was worried about Claudia. I was worried about Paul. I was worried how I was going to do what was best for Paul and Claudia and still be civil with Mona. She was difficult on a good day. I couldn't imagine how she was going to be when she was distraught.

I parked in the visitor's lot at Scottsdale Community Hospital and looked around for Paul's car but didn't see it. I hurried into the lobby and quickly found the patient information desk. The smiling receptionist directed me to the ICU waiting room on the fifth floor. The elevator stopped at every floor and I cursed it every time the door opened and no one got on.

Signs easily led me to the ICU waiting room but it was empty when I arrived. A television mounted on the wall was tuned to the local news with the sound turned off. There was a desk marked Information on the far wall but no one was seated at it. I paced for a few seconds until a Candy Striper arrived. She smiled at me as she sat down and motioned for me to approach her.

"Can I help you?"

"Yes, you can. My name is Sara Weber and I would like to know if you have any information on the condition of Claudia Weber." She gave me a look that implied that she didn't know if she could or should give me any information. With all the new regulations regarding patient privacy, I understood her reluctance. "It's okay. I'm her stepmother.

173

Paul Weber is her father – my husband – and he's probably in there with her right now."

She gave me a vacant smile and checked her clipboard. "Claudia Weber. Here she is. Yes, you're right. Her parents are in with her now. But that's all I can tell you. You can speak to them when they come back out. Only two people can visit at one time."

"Thanks." I sat and stewed. I tried to lip read the TV but got nowhere and gave up. I flipped through an old magazine but couldn't concentrate. Time dragged.

Finally, Paul came out. He smiled when he saw me.

I went over to him and hugged him. "I tried to call you but I couldn't get through."

"That's okay. I'm glad you're here," he said.

"How is she?"

"The same. She opened her eyes before for a minute."

"Did she recognize you?"

"Yeah, she seemed to."

"Good. That's good."

The ICU doors swung open and Mona strode out. I caught a flicker of annoyance when she saw me but she recovered well and smiled. The cynic in me assumed it was more for Paul's benefit than mine. She didn't say anything to me but looked right at Paul.

"I'd like to go back to Carol's now. We should probably let Claudia rest for a while. The nurses will contact us if they need us." In other words, don't visit her, Sara.

Paul nodded. "That's probably a good idea," he said. I wanted to scream. I had just gotten there. Hello, did anybody see me here?

Paul looked at me. "I'm going to drive Mona back to Carol's and then I'll meet you home. You drove here, right?"

"Yes. But I thought I would take a peek at Claudia before I left."

Paul opened his mouth to speak but Mona answered before he could get a word out. "She's sleeping. I don't want

174

her disturbed."

I felt Paul's grip on my arm tighten, sign language for "Don't say anything". I turned to Paul instead. "Maybe tomorrow, then. Do you want me to make you something to eat?"

"No, I already had something in the cafeteria with Mona."

He hugged me briefly and stiffly. I couldn't dismiss the thought that he was uncomfortable showing me affection in front of Mona. "See you at home, Sara."

Then he and Mona were gone. I was left alone in the waiting room. I felt embarrassed in front of the goofy Candy Striper. It was obvious I had just been dismissed.

The walk back to my car was long. There was the smell of threatening rain in the air and the sky was becoming dark. I hoped the storm would hold off until both Paul and I were safely home.

I sighed as I put my key in the ignition. I wanted to see this from Paul's point of view, I really did, but I was feeling both deflated and confused. His only child was in the hospital and wounded. Her future was unclear. Nevertheless, I had gone through a lot this week, too. My whole life had changed and I needed my best friend, my husband, to talk to.

The house was empty when I got home except for the two dogs. I wandered around in a fog. I checked the answering machine to see if there were any messages and noticed the message light was blinking. It was my sister, just sending me a get-well wish for Claudia. Out of force of habit, I rewound the machine to make sure that the disk was empty in preparation for any new messages. I hit the play button again by accident and immediately felt my blood rush when I heard Mona's voice.

"Oh, Paul," it was obvious that she was crying, "I know you were just here but I wanted to tell you what's been in my heart. What I'm afraid to say to your face. I've missed you so much all these years. So many times, I've wished things could have been different. This is a horrible thing that has happened to us but maybe it was meant to bring us closer, to a better place. Something good has to come out of this."

She must have left that when Paul had come home to change clothes or walk the dogs, hoping to catch him. I could feel the heat rise in my face. How dare she leave something like that, to my husband, on my answering machine! Some part of her had to know that I might hear it. I paced the kitchen and played the message again. It sounded even worse the second time.

Maybe it meant nothing. Maybe it was just her way of reaching out and wanting to talk to the father of her child who was so hurt right now. However, all I heard was another woman trying to get close to my husband. I wanted to throw up. It didn't help that Paul took over an hour to come home. My mind played horrible games with me in the interim.

Chapter Nineteen

The storm started in earnest while I waited for Paul. Lightning flashed and thunder cracked overhead. The wind whipped the trees and I watched as the large saguaro outside my kitchen window swayed. I alternated between worrying about Paul driving home in the rain and being angry that he was so late and still with Mona.

By the time Paul came home, I was in a foul mood. I had opened a bottle of wine and had had a glass. He was barely in the door when I yelled, "I see Mona left you an amorous little message."

Paul looked as if someone had just slapped him. "What are you talking about?"

"I heard the message she left for you about how she wanted to be closer to you and she hoped that Claudia's accident would help do that."

"Oh, shit." Paul ran his hand through his rain-soaked hair. We were both standing in the kitchen. "I meant to erase that."

"I'm sure you did."

"Look, Sara, don't go off on this. It's nothing. She's just upset. Let it go. I don't need this right now."

The time that I waited for Paul to come home had just given my emotions a chance to churn and grow and there was no stopping them now that they were released.

"I don't need this, either. Neither of us does. But it's so like Mona to use a horrible accident to do something so devious."

"Devious? I don't believe I'm hearing this. My daughter is in critical condition in the ICU and you're worried about my ex-wife? Are you for real?" He slammed his hand on the countertop. Toby ran behind my legs for cover. "I knew you'd do this."

"Is that why you meant to erase it? So I wouldn't hear Mona say she wants you back?"

"She didn't say she wants me back. She just wants us to get along. I knew you would blow this out of proportion."

I couldn't believe how naïve Paul was being. How could he possibly think that "I've missed you all these years. So many times, I've wished things could have been different" meant that Mona wanted us all to get along?

I started to say something but Paul put his hand up to stop me. "Don't say another word. I don't want to do this. I'm exhausted and I'm soaking wet. I'm getting out of these clothes and then I'm going to bed. I'll see you in the morning."

And he was gone. He didn't even ask me about my trip. I knew I would have trouble sleeping and, frankly, I wasn't in the mood to slide into bed next to Paul. I poured myself another glass of wine and sat on the deck for a while and watched the storm. Toby jumped on the glider with me and the two of us rocked and listened to the thunder. The storm passed quickly and soon it was just us and the crickets. The night jasmine was in bloom and I inhaled deeply. The now quiet night was a welcome change from all that had happened in the last few days. When I finally went to bed, Paul's snoring assured me the rest of the night would be uneventful.

He seemed to be in a better mood the next morning. I was having a cup of coffee when he walked in, smelling fresh from his shower. He hugged me and gave me a kiss on my cheek.

"Let's start over, okay?" he said. "We were both tired and stressed out last night. We said some things that I know we're sorry for. I apologize, Sara. I want us to be there for each other, ok?"

I melted. I loved this man, after all, and the last thing I wanted to do was make his life miserable. I wanted to be his refuge, not the place he least wanted to be.

"I know, hon. I'm sorry, too. Tell me what happened yesterday."

Paul went over what the doctors had told him and Mona. Claudia's leg was broken in two places and would need to be pinned in order to set properly. However, it was expected to heal after that without any complications. There would be therapy and rehab but the result was expected to be a good one. The head injury was what was causing the worry. Claudia was lucky to be alive. Of course, she hadn't been buckled in and she appeared to have a concussion. How this would affect her was still unknown. The plan was to observe her for the next few days...and pray. Her leg surgery might have to be placed on hold until the head injury was better evaluated. I could easily understand why everyone was so upset. Paul certainly didn't need me to add to this.

I hugged him again. The intensity of his hug back told me I was being very foolish to think that Mona could ever come between us.

"How was your trip?" he asked when he finally let me go.

I told him about my first meeting with my stepmother and about the trips to the nursing homes with Angela.

179

"But Angela still wants to wait a little more before we place Mom. We both know once we do she's never going to come home again. It's hard to finally face that, especially for Angela. She's built her whole life around taking care of Mom. It's going to be a big change for her."

I deliberately left out the meeting with my father's attorney. I still hadn't absorbed the full impact myself and I wasn't ready to discuss it yet. Not right now, with Mona still on Arizona soil. Paul didn't even ask. I chalked it up to his preoccupation with Claudia and was grateful. I needed more time to think.

Then I said what had been running around my mind since that meeting in the ICU waiting room. "Paul, I want to visit Claudia. Is that going to be a problem?" I didn't want to come right out and say that I didn't think Mona wanted me there and risk another fight.

Paul sighed. "Look, I know Mona feels threatened by you. That hasn't changed just because Claudia's hurt. And I know this is a problem. But now isn't the time to make a stand. Can you understand that? I want you there but I just don't have the energy right now to play buffer between you and Mona. Maybe you should wait until Claudia's out of the ICU or at least until she's had her surgery."

"Can I at least come to the waiting room with you?"

"I'd rather you didn't."

I could feel the anger rising in my gut but held it in check. These next few days were going to be more difficult than I had imagined.

"I understand," I said, even though I really didn't. If it were me, I would want Paul there no matter what. I tried to imagine myself in Paul's place. If my ex-husband were trying to shut my spouse out, I certainly wouldn't let him. But Paul and I differed in that respect. Where I sometimes sought out conflict, Paul ran from it at all costs.

Paul must have read the expression on my face. "I know it makes you feel bad," he said. "Please just bear with it for a

180

while. For me. I appreciate whatever you can do to help but the biggest thing you can do right now is stay away from Mona and give her space. This is her child that's hurt right now and it will make my life a lot easier if I'm not running interference between the two of you. Yes, I know what you think you heard last night but it's not that at all. Believe me. I wouldn't allow that."

I sighed. What could I say?

"Okay, I'll back off. Just please know that it's not what I want to do. And when Claudia is transferred to a regular floor bed, I do intend to visit her. She's your child, too. And she's my stepdaughter. She lives here now, for God's sake. This is crazy." I could feel myself getting worked up again.

"Go. Go see your daughter. I'll be here when you get back."

I tried to distract myself with cleaning the house while Paul was gone. After about an hour of dusting and vacuuming, I decided there had to be an easier way to pass the time. I thought I would catch up with the gossip at work and dialed Judy at work.

"Hey, you're back," she said. "How did it go?"

I suddenly realized how much I needed to talk to someone who wasn't directly involved in all of this.

"Jude, you're not going to believe the last few days. How about meeting me for lunch?"

"Sure, just give me a chance to clear up a few things." We made plans to meet in another hour at a restaurant in Old Scottsdale.

Paul called me while I got ready to meet Judy and informed me that Claudia was headed into surgery. Dr. Kaufman was going to perform an internal pinning of her femur. I told him to call me when she was in the recovery room.

"Think you can handle Mona for the next few hours?" I teased him.

"Actually, Gregg is here with me. I think we're going to go shopping in Home Depot across the street while we wait."

181

"Sounds like a good idea." I figured Carol was there, too. Actually, that was a good thing. Mona needed someone in her corner right now and who better than Carol? Besides, if Carol was there, Mona was less likely to lean on Paul.

"Have fun with Judy," Paul said when I told him where I was headed. "Have a Margarita for me."

Judy was already seated at a table in the restaurant when I got there. She had a lemonade and a half-eaten plate of onion rings in front of her. I ordered an ice tea from the waitress who seemed to pop out of nowhere. As soon as she was gone, Judy pounced. "So, tell me. How did the trip go? Did you see your stepmother?"

"You know the trip wasn't for me to see Eleanor. I went there to take care of my mother."

"Yeah, yeah. Of course, you did and a fine job, I'm sure. Now, spill. What was she like?"

I had to laugh. Judy was so predictable. I told her about my meeting with Eleanor at the tearoom and about the attorney. When I got to the part about the trust fund, her eyes widened.

"You're kidding me! What did Paul say when you told him?"

"I didn't."

"What? Why?"

"There's been a complication."

Judy stopped in mid-onion ring. "Don't tell me...Mona. It has to be."

"Kind of." I told her about Claudia and her accident and that Mona was back in town. When I got to the part about Paul asking me to stay away from the hospital, she almost choked. "You can't be serious. He actually asked you to stay away from poor little Mona?"

Hearing Judy say it that way made me defensive about Paul. "It's not like that, Judy. It really just makes it easier for him. That's why I'm doing it."

"I'll bet it makes it easier for her, too. That'll be the day when I let some ex hang around my guy for hours on end and I'm not there."

At that point, I decided not to mention Mona's phone message. Judy would have thought I'd really lost my mind. Instead, I steered the conversation back to work. I had had enough of Mona for one day.

Judy told me about the new associate, Scott Something. Apparently, he had recently moved to Arizona from the Midwest and was the talk of the office...well, the girls anyway. Scott was around forty-five years old and recently divorced and very good looking, according to Judy. Despite her questionable taste in men when it came to their commitment phobias, Judy had a good eye for judging the opposite sex when it came to looks. If Judy said he was good-looking, he was definitely good-looking. The secretaries were taken in by his dark hair and green eyes, and so was Judy, from the sound of it. However, he seemed to be totally oblivious of the stir he was causing. That meant Judy was going to see him as a challenge. I smiled. He had no idea what he was in for.

"He has an ex somewhere but no one knows much else about him."

"Judy, I have every confidence you will know it all very soon."

"You think you know me so well."

"Yes, I do. Which reminds me, how's your boyfriend? The one who brings you flowers?"

"Oh, him. I'm not seeing him anymore."

"What happened?"

She told me and that took up the rest of our lunchtime together. Mona and my troubles were forgotten.

We did a little shopping afterwards before Judy had to get back to the office.

"You need to practice, now that you're rich," she said.

Paul called me while we were walking around, told me Claudia was out of surgery and headed to the Recovery

Room. He sounded relieved. He said he was going to stay until she was back in ICU and then would come home. Carol was going to stay with Mona.

Thank you, God.

Chapter Twenty

The next few days were a blur of half-eaten meals and Paul running back and forth to the hospital. Claudia stayed in ICU through the weekend and part of the following week. The night before she was to be transferred out to the regular floor, Paul told me what the plan was that he and Mona had made. She was going to stay on indefinitely and live with Carol until Claudia was discharged. Any rehab would probably be done back in New Hampshire.

College was definitely on hold right now. I ached to know what that meant for us. Was Claudia going to come back the next year? What about support? It was obvious that Claudia was going to need special services, at least for a little while. How was Mona going to manage with Claudia home and still be able to work? Frankly, it scared me but I was very reluctant to bring all of that up with Paul. I would just have to wait and see what happened - something I wasn't good at.

The day Claudia was transferred, I went out and bought her a teddy bear and a card. I was going to visit her finally.

I told Paul my plans over breakfast the next morning.

He sipped coffee while he went over a bid he was submitting that day and frowned as soon as I mentioned visiting Claudia.

"Don't you think she wants to see me?"

"Sure, she does."

"Well, then, she's going to wonder why I'm ignoring her if I don't show up soon."

Paul just shook his head. "Ok, but if this backfires, you're on your own. I'm not fighting this one for you."

That afternoon, as I parked the car in the hospital lot, his words came back to me. I wondered if this really was the right thing to do or was I just making a point? No matter, I was here now and I wasn't backing out. I got off the elevator at Scottsdale Community's second floor. The sights and smells brought me back to when I used to work there. As I walked over to the Nurses Station, I recognized the girl sitting behind the desk as the unit clerk who worked there when I still paced those halls.

"Hey, Steph. How are you doing?"

Stephanie looked up and smiled when she saw me. "Sara! Wow, it's been a while. How are you? Still working with those bad lawyers?"

I smiled. "Yup. That's me. The caped crusader. Say, listen, I understand my stepdaughter is on this floor. She was recently transferred from ICU. Claudia Weber. Can you tell me what room she's in?"

"I'm sorry to hear that. Let me look." Stephanie looked at her computer screen and tapped a few keys. Suddenly, her face clouded over and she frowned.

I started to panic. Don't tell me something bad had happened already. "What's the matter?"

Stephanie stumbled over her words. "Well, maybe this is just from the ICU and hasn't been changed yet. Sometimes, there are special rules up there that we don't have down here but it looks like you're not supposed to visit her, Sara."

I ran around behind her desk to see for myself. Stephanie pointed to the line she was referring to. "See. It says right here. 'Mother and father only to visit'."

I could feel the heat rising in my face. Another hot flash, courtesy of Mona.

"Let me talk to the Charge Nurse," Steph said. "Maybe it was a mistake." Stephanie was trying to make me feel better but I was embarrassed and just wanted to escape.

"No, that's no mistake." Stephanie looked at me oddly. "Look, don't bother the Charge Nurse. I don't want to cause any trouble. I'll have Paul look into it." Besides, how humiliating that would be to have my friends know that I was banned by my husband's ex-wife. "Just see that she gets this, would you?" I handed Stephanie the teddy bear and card.

"Sure, why don't you call back later? I'll see what I can find out for you." She noticed the look of discomfort on my face. "Don't worry. I'll be discreet."

"Thanks, Steph, I appreciate it."

I drove home in tears. I couldn't believe what Mona was doing and how blind Paul was being to the whole thing. I felt as if we had regressed to the early years of my marriage and Mona was back to her old tricks. Actually, she probably never stopped. She had just had fewer and fewer opportunities to practice them. Now, on my turf, she was enjoying herself.

By the time I got home, I had made up my mind I was going to detach from this whole situation. If Mona didn't want me around her precious daughter, so be it. In fact, maybe we were going to have to re-think this whole college thing. Granted, it might be a moot point now with Claudia's injuries but I was going to be dammed if I was going to be treated like this in my home, in my own town. Mona was going too far and this had gone on too long.

The phone rang just as I walked in the door while I was still in the middle of my peppy self-talk. I quickly checked caller ID and saw that it was the office of Thompson and Concetti. I figured it was probably Judy and picked up the receiver. "Hello, this is Sara."

"Sara? Hi, this is Scott. Scott Carter from the office." Ah, the Scott Something Judy had mentioned. She was right about him. Even his voice sounded sexy. Judy had said she thought he was in his mid-forties but his voice sounded much younger. "Is this a bad time? Looks like we're going to be working on a case together and I have some questions. Is now okay?"

I was glad for the distraction. "Yes, this is a good time. What can I do for you?"

Over the next few minutes, we talked about hysterectomies and complications. He talked about operating rooms and surgeons and I was reminded of Mona again. I found my mind wandering back to my experience that afternoon at the Nurses Station and I was having trouble concentrating. Finally, I stopped him. "I'm sorry, Scott. Maybe this is a bad time after all."

"All right. I could call back. When would be a good time?"

"Actually, things are kind of crazy here right now."

"Anything I can do to help?"

"No, it's just family stuff. Look, maybe I should come in and talk to you about this. I have to pick up the records from you anyway. That way we can talk in peace and there won't be any distractions. Will that work for you?"

"Sure. How about some time tomorrow. Say ten?"

"Fine. I'll see you then."

Paul walked in from work a little while later and before he had his coat off I told him I had gone to see Claudia. "Really? Mona didn't mention it." He obviously had stopped off at the hospital before he came home.

"Maybe that's because she had me banned from your

188

daughter's hospital room."

"What are you talking about? You're not banned."

"And I quote 'Mother and father only to visit'. That's what I was told today when I asked what her room number was. Someone I used to work with had to tell me I wasn't wanted. You could at least have warned me."

"There has to be a mistake." Paul picked up the phone and dialed.

I assumed he was calling the front desk at the hospital. I was stunned when I heard him say "Mona?" when someone answered. I didn't want him discussing this with her. I grabbed for the phone but he held me at arm's length.

"Oh, hi, Carol. It's Paul. Put Mona on, will you?"

I wanted to scream. Carol was there and I had been told to leave? What the hell was going on? By this time, Mona had gotten on the other end.

"Yeah, Mona, it's me. I just have a quick question. Sara tells me that she was there to see Claudia today and she was turned away. Something about not being on some kind of list. There's no list, is there?"

I couldn't hear what Mona was saying but I was sure it was a lie. She needed to look good in front of Paul. Paul was nodding while he talked. "That's what I thought. Sure, no problem. I'll tell her." Paul hung up and turned to me. Was it my imagination or was there a look of satisfaction on his face? "Mona says that it was probably something the staff put on the record when Claudia was in the ICU. She knew nothing about it but she'll make sure it's taken off."

"But Carol could visit?"

"Sara, don't start. I'm sure Carol just walked in with Mona. No one was going to question Mona. She's the – "

" – the mother," I finished for him in a singsong way. "Yeah, I know. I get that rammed down my throat a lot these days."

"Look, Mona had no way of knowing you were there. Stop looking for trouble. Come on, I'm tired. The last week

189

has finally caught up with me. I just want to get a little something to eat and then go to bed."

"I didn't make dinner."

"That's okay. I'll just have a sandwich."

True to his word, Paul ate a sandwich, played with the dogs for a little while and then kissed me on the cheek and went to bed. It was far too early for me to go to bed so I went into my office and worked for several hours. It actually felt good to deal with someone else's problems for a while.

Chapter Twenty-One

I went into the office the next day and met with Scott. Our meeting was short, though. He had a deposition in Phoenix and didn't have more than fifteen minutes to go over the case basics with me. But in that short time, I understood why Judy was so smitten. He had a way about him that was just plain sexy, and he seemed to be unaware of it which made him all the more attractive. The medical records he gave me took up an entire banker's box. At least I would have something to keep me busy while I waited for the right moment to go back to visit Claudia.

I didn't want another scene at the hospital so I decided I would wait for things to settle down a little before I tried visiting again. I arrived on the floor in the late morning the beginning of the following week and went back to Stephanie's desk.

"Hi, here again, I see," she said when she looked up. "Look, I'm sorry about what happened last week. Her mother came out sometime after you left and I told her what had happened regarding the visitor list. She apologized and said that visitors were allowed as long as they were pre-approved by her. She said she would give the Head Nurse an approved visitors list." She checked the computer screen and frowned. "That's odd. You're still not on there."

I sighed. "I don't believe this."

"I'm sure it's an oversight, Sara. Your sister-in-law and brother-in-law are on the list. I'm sure she meant to put you on, too. We even talked about it. That doesn't make sense to me."

"Well, that makes one of you. Look, my husband is her father. He told me I could see my stepdaughter. Just tell me what room she's in. I'll settle this myself." I was angry and no longer cared what happened. Paul might be taken in by Mona's phony attempt at playing nice but I wasn't having any of it.

Stephanie gave me the room number. As I approached the room, I heard muffled voices. I opened the door a crack, not wanting to intrude if there were other people in there. I didn't want to confront everyone, just Mona. I wasn't prepared for what I saw, though.

Paul and Mona were standing side by side next to Claudia's bed. Claudia was sleeping. Mona was crying softly with her head on my husband's shoulder. He had his arm around her and was talking softly to her. I couldn't hear what he was saying but Mona was nodding and sniffling. He put his hand to her head and touched it in what I felt was a form of endearment. Certainly not the way I expected him to act with the woman who had made our lives – my life – so miserable.

I could feel the blood rush to my face. There was a pounding in my ears and I was afraid I was going to throw up. I ran from the room and back toward the bank of elevators. Stephanie saw me and started to get up to come toward me but luckily, the elevator came at that point and I was able to escape. I waved her off and darted into the elevator as soon as the doors opened. Mercifully, it was empty.

All the way down, my mind played that scene from Claudia's room over and over again. Did I actually see what I thought I saw? Was my husband being affectionate with his ex-wife? And what was he doing there in the middle of the day instead of working?

I had no idea what to do. I got back in my car in the parking lot and just sat there, numb, trying to keep the panic from rising.

My cell phone rang. It was Judy calling from the office.

"H – hello?"

"Sara? Are you okay? You sound awful."

"I'm all right. I'm coming down with a cold. What do you need?" Judy wouldn't be calling on my cell phone if something important hadn't come up.

"The defendant in that case you're working on with Scott is coming in early this afternoon to meet with him and Scott asked me to call you to see if you could sit in. He said to apologize to you for the late notice."

"Sure. I can make it." Why not? I wasn't going to get anything done at home. That was the last place I wanted to be right now.

I drove home, freshened up, and made it to the office in plenty of time for the meeting. I immediately went into Judy's office when I got there. She was going to be in the meeting, too, and wanted to go over some things before we all met. When she saw my face, she came around from behind her desk and hugged me.

"You look awful. Here, sit down. Tell me what's going on. This is not a cold. Is Claudia worse?"

God forgive me, but if that had been the case, I would have been grateful. Instead, my world, as I knew it, was falling apart. I started to tell Judy what had happened just hours before and then completely broke down. When I came to the part where I had seen Paul with his arm around Mona, I could barely talk. Putting it into words made it more real

193

and more upsetting.

Judy kept asking if I was sure about what I had seen. "Maybe there's another explanation."

"What explanation can there be for a man to stand next to a crying woman with his arm around her, consoling her?"

"Well, maybe that's all it was, you know. Just some old fashioned consolation. They do have a child together, after all. And she's very hurt right now."

"Don't take his side. I know Mona. You don't."

Judy threw her hands up in the air. "Okay, don't take it out on me."

"Look, maybe we should just not talk about it anymore. Let's just get into this meeting." I blew my nose and wiped my eyes. "Tell me what I need to know."

Judy went over the details of the meeting with me. Most of it was what Scott and I had already gone over. The client was a doctor accused of botching up a hysterectomy. The details were sketchy right now but from what little she had read, Judy thought we had a good defense. I had gone over the records myself and felt I had a good handle on the case.

The meeting went smoothly. The doctor was a very well-spoken older gentleman who would present well during deposition. Scott went over the process with him, walking him through what was to be expected over the next few months. We made arrangements to get some more records on the patient and Scott told me what he would need from me as the nurse. It was all very routine.

After the meeting, Scott called me into his office.

"Have a seat, Sara. I thought we'd go over things a bit and get your take on the doctor."

I took some charts off a wing chair and sat down. Scott seemed to be a follower of Judy's filing system. There were piles of papers everywhere but at least they were neat piles. The top of his desk, however, unlike Judy's, was uncluttered. He leaned back in his chair behind his desk and loosened his tie. He ran his hand through his black wavy hair. I could see why everyone was so taken with him. His green eyes were piercing and went straight to a woman's soul.

"I think he'll do fine," I said. "He seems to feel pretty confident about how he handled the procedure."

"That was my feeling, too." Scott picked up a picture cube from his desk and played with it. I noticed it contained pictures of two Golden Retrievers. This man was quickly scoring points with me. "I couldn't help but notice that you look ...how can I say this tactfully? A little flat? Are you okay? I don't have to tell you how important it is that you be at the top of your game in this one."

I didn't know if I should have felt flattered that he cared or insulted that he suggested I was less than perfect. I didn't know Scott well enough yet to be able to judge him. Sure, Judy liked him but Judy was thinking with a different part of her anatomy. I looked at Scott and was aware of an unwanted flush, partly from embarrassment, partly from an uncomfortable attraction that was inching its way into a place it had no right to be. For some reason, I wanted this man to like me. I felt myself slipping down a dangerous slope.

"Judy seems to have a high regard for you and I can see why," he continued. "But something tells me that all is not right with you right now. I know we don't know each other that well but if there is something I can do to help...." He put the picture cube down and looked right at me.

I could feel the sweat running down my rib cage and cursed my ovaries. I made a mental note to call my gynecologist. It was definitely time for stronger medicine. "I'm okay, really." God, his eyes reminded me of Paul. "My stepdaughter had an accident a few days ago and it's putting a strain on things. You know, ex-wife in town and all."

Scott smiled. "Ah, yes, the old divorce dance. I know it well." He leaned back in his chair again. "Let me guess. The ex likes to stir things up and get you going. Then you and your husband fight and he doesn't understand why you get your shorts in a knot over her."

My eyes got wide. "How did you know?" I smiled. "Have you been eavesdropping in my kitchen?"

He shook his head. "Not your kitchen. Mine. I've been divorced." He held up two fingers. "Twice."

"Ouch."

"You got that right. And divorce number one caused divorce number two. I used to react pretty much like your husband. My wife would get all worked up over something ex number one did. I would fight with her instead of addressing the problem. Wife number two finally got fed up. Became ex number two."

At last, someone who understood!

I felt myself relax. Before I knew what I was doing, I started pouring my heart out to this man. I told him about trying to visit Claudia and how difficult Mona was making it. I told him what she had done with the visitor's list and how frustrating it was to get Paul to see it. My voice caught at one point. I was afraid I was going to cry and didn't want to appear weak in front of Scott. But the emotions that had all been bottled up in the last few days came rushing out. I was afraid I was making no sense but Scott was kind enough not to say anything about that. He listened as no one had that week. He didn't interrupt. He didn't say I shouldn't be feeling that way.

"On top of it all, I've had my own family stuff to deal with. My father died last year and left my sister and me quite a bit of money. That part hasn't even fully sunk in yet. This probably sounds awful but one of the first things I thought of when I found out how much money I now have was that I didn't want Mona to get any of it. I know she'll try, when she finds out."

"What did your husband say about that?"

I put my head down and said nothing.

"You didn't tell him?"

"I was going to but then his daughter had her accident

196

and I just haven't had a moment when it seemed right."

Scott leaned forward. "If you don't mind, I'd like to offer a little advice. There are ways you can safeguard your money. You and your husband need to look into it. If his ex finds a smart attorney, she could file for more support based on this."

"But I always thought my money couldn't be taken into account when it came to child support."

"Ordinarily, you'd be right but you have an unusual circumstance right now with this accident and her attorney might make the argument that your money makes it easier for your husband to part with his."

My face must have given me away. This had been my biggest fear. As usual, the state of my finances was going to be handed over to Mona. Again.

"Don't look so discouraged, Sara. It's not that bleak. But it is detailed. I used to do a little of this kind of work but not enough that I'd feel comfortable doing this for you, though. I can talk to your attorney or accountant, if you'd like."

"I don't have an attorney or an accountant," I said. I felt like I was admitting that I ate meat to a vegetarian.

Scott shook his head and smiled. I wished he would stop doing that. Did he know the effect it had on women? "Okay, well, how about this? I know a guy back east that I used to give my complicated cases to. Why don't I call him and see if he knows anyone out here. Maybe we can get you set up soon."

"Thanks. I appreciate that."

"Not at all. It's purely selfish on my part. If you're feeling better, I'll get more work out of you." He smiled that captivating smile one more time and I decided to get out of there before my ovaries betrayed me again.

Judy was at the front desk when I passed it on the way out. She and the receptionist were laughing about something but she stopped as soon as she saw me. She put her hand on my arm. "You okay?"

I gave her my best fake smile. "I will be."

"Wanna talk?"

"No, there's nothing more to say. I can't stay. I really should get home. I'll call you." I waved to both of them and fled to my car.

Chapter Twenty-Two

All the way home, I alternated between thoughts of Paul and Mona hugging in Claudia's room and picturing Scott in bed. Both pictures sent my mind twirling.

Paul was home before I was. As soon as I saw his car in the driveway, the anger I had been feeling was replaced by that sick feeling again. The sense of betrayal was overwhelming. There was just no good reason for him to be holding Mona that way. I made up my mind I was going to confront him. If he didn't say the right things, I was prepared to pack and leave. I had had all the Mona drama I was willing to put up with.

My head was a jumble of thoughts as I walked in from the garage. I expected to see Paul in the kitchen but it was empty. The dogs didn't even greet me. He had let them out and I saw them peering at me through the patio door. I opened the door and they jumped all over me in greeting. Something felt off.

"Paul? Where are you?"

"In here." His voice came from the back of the house in the direction of our bedroom. Was he napping? Packing? Panic rose in me but when I rounded the corner, there was no sign of Paul in the bedroom.

"Paul?"

"Over here." He was in the small alcove off our bedroom. He had made that area into his home office and was intently reading something on his computer screen. He looked up as soon as I walked in. Whatever I was about to say died in my throat. He looked awful. He was pale and his eyes were red. I was sure he had been crying. I had only seen Paul cry one other time, when Mona had kidnapped Claudia. Panic was quickly replaced by fear. Was he about to tell me it was all over? That he was going back to Mona?

I wanted to hug him and hear him tell me everything was going to be all right but the sight of him holding Mona flashed across my mind again. I didn't know if I should be angry or afraid. "What's wrong? You look terrible."

Paul extended his hand toward me. I grabbed it and he pulled me toward him. I leaned in and hugged him. He hugged back... hard. He buried his head in my breast. This didn't seem like a man about to leave his wife. I was dumbfounded. "Paul, you're scaring me. What's going on?"

"Claudia may have suffered a stroke."

It took a moment for this to sink in. "A stroke? Wait a minute. When?" I tried to think back to my visit at the hospital. Stephanie hadn't implied that anything was wrong when she checked Claudia's computer file. I pulled back so that I could see his face.

"I don't know. I wasn't there when the doctor spoke to Mona. All she told me is that they're very concerned. We won't know anything more until tomorrow. They're scheduling some more tests for the morning."

"But why a stroke? What happened?"

"I'm not sure. Mona wasn't very clear when she explained it to me. Something about some confusion. I was just looking up symptoms myself to see if I could find out anything."

"Did you talk to her doctor?"

"No."

Typical. Mona says, Paul believes. "So you don't know for sure that she's worse. You just have Mona's word for this?"

Paul's mood changed instantly. "What are you saying? Mona made this up?"

"No, I didn't say that. I'm just saying that Mona has a tendency to exaggerate sometimes. Or, maybe she misunderstood. I'd like to hear this from her doctor, Paul. Maybe it's not as bad as you think. Want me to make some calls?" I walked toward the phone in our bedroom. It was on the end table next to Paul's side of the bed.

Paul walked up behind me and grabbed my hand. "No, let me take care of this. Why must you always take over?"

I backed away from him. I felt as if I had just been slapped. "What? Where did that come from?"

"Look, this is my daughter. Let me handle it."

My concern quickly reverted back to anger. "Does that include consoling Mona?"

"What?"

"I saw you, Paul. I saw you with your arms around Mona this morning."

"What the hell are you talking about?"

"What part of 'I saw you with your arms around Mona' was unclear? I went to the hospital today to see Claudia. I'm still on the banned list, by the way. So I was going to talk to Mona about it. Imagine my surprise when I saw you there with your arms around that bitch instead of being at work!" I was screaming and I didn't care. Both of the dogs had left the room and run for cover.

"You're crazy. I wasn't working because Mona called me to tell me that she was concerned about Claudia. She told me what the doctors had said and I rushed over there. She was upset and I was consoling her, yes. But you seem to forget that my daughter is ill. I don't believe this. After all I just told you, you're still fixated on Mona."

"And why not? You seem to be." The whole scene was becoming surreal. I was a runaway train heading for disaster. "I don't think she'd be above saying something like that even if it weren't true. Look what it got her. Her in your arms."

"You know, Mona has her bad points but you run a pretty close second sometimes. I was consoling the mother of my child. I would think you could understand what I'm feeling right now but as usual it's all about you and what Mona is doing to you. You know I'm getting really sick of this."

He left our bedroom and headed back toward the garage door. I followed him.

"Where are you going?"

"I'm going to the hospital to visit my child." He slammed the door and was gone.

I sat on the sofa and dissolved into tears. I couldn't believe this was happening. In a matter of a few weeks, my life had been totally turned around. I was losing my family. First, my mother, then my father - again. Now, I was losing my husband. Paul was the one person I wanted to be close to right now and he was pulling away from me.

Or was I pushing him? Was he right? Was I confusing my feelings for Mona with the reality of his daughter's illness? He was probably feeling the same way about me that I was about him. I was sure he needed me right now as much as I needed him.

Instead, we were both feeling alone. Mona was the only one gaining from all this. And I was helping her. Paul was right. I needed to stop this insecurity. His daughter was ill. That was all I should be thinking about.

I went to Paul's computer. I wanted to see what he had been looking at. Maybe I could help. After all, it was my job to understand these things. I decided to change my attitude. I would detach from Mona and her drama. I would concentrate only on Claudia and Paul and see how much I could find out. Maybe I could be a liaison between the doctors and Paul and undo the damage that had just happened.

Paul's computer was still on. As he had said, he had been surfing the Internet looking up information on stroke. I read what was on his screen. No wonder he had been so upset. It didn't look good. But that was predicated on Mona's information being accurate. Without talking directly to the neurologist, we didn't know for sure. I refused to believe that Claudia's situation was as bleak as Paul thought. I could not help but feel that Mona the Drama Queen was making more out of this than there was.

I minimized the Internet screen and saw that Paul's email was still up underneath it. I had the uncontrollable urge to peek. It was an invasion, I knew. I rationalized that I needed to have all the information I could if I was going to save my marriage.

I scanned the list. Most of it was work-related. There was also a note from Carol dated from the night before. Innocent enough. Carol emailing Paul was no big deal. Probably telling him how sorry she was about Claudia and offering support. But as soon as I opened the email I knew right away that it was not from Carol. It was from Mona. I read it and felt the walls crashing down.

I couldn't breathe. There it was in black and white, what I had already suspected. I could tell from the icon that Paul had already read it. Whether he had read it before he had seen Mona today was something I would probably never know.

Dearest Paul:

I want to tell you how much it means to me to have you here during this horrible time in my life...our life. Would I be terrible if I told you that this has stirred up all my old feelings for you? Feelings that I had thought were long gone and buried.

Seeing Claudia's life change so quickly has made me realize how fleeting all of our lives really are. How often I have thought about you...and us...and I'm so sorry that I didn't work harder at saving our marriage. I know I could have been a better wife. I regret not having the chance to patch things up with you. If you were to give me half a chance now, I would jump at being your wife again!

Is it really too late for us?

Loving you always,

Mona

The words blurred as I read them, I was crying so hard. How could he have read this and not known what was going on? How could he accuse me of thinking the worst of Mona when it was so plain and in black and white? Why was he doing this to me? To us?

I didn't know what to think or do. I printed out the email before it could be erased. I wasn't going to give Paul the chance to accuse me of making things up again. Then I put the computer screen back to the way I had found it. I didn't want Paul to know I had seen the email until I was ready to confront them both. I hid my copy of it in the bottom of my jewelry box.

After that, I paced.

I wrote imaginary letters to Mona telling her all the things I had longed to over the years.

I cried.

I broke a couple of dishes.

None of it helped. None of it changed the fact that my husband had walked out on me into the arms of a woman who was writing love letters to him.

I tried to watch some television but couldn't concentrate. I drank some wine and eventually fell asleep on the sofa. I woke up at three o'clock in the morning and realized that

Paul had not come home. I didn't think I could feel any worse. I went to bed and slept fitfully for the next few hours.

By morning, Paul still hadn't returned home. Jesse had crawled onto the bed and was sleeping in Paul's place. I reached over and patted him, grateful for the warmth of his body. Toby came over and licked my face. I smiled. Thank God for my boys. I showered and dressed. Over coffee, I tried to decide what to do with my day. There was no point in my staying home. Paul was probably going to stay away until Claudia's tests were done. I didn't expect anyone to keep me informed about Claudia. I knew Paul wasn't going to call. What was there left to say?

I needed something to distract me. Organizing records and doing chronologies was just the thing I needed. However, I didn't want to do it at home. Being alone in that house would force me to dwell on Paul and Mona and that was something I wasn't prepared to handle. I would borrow a page from Paul's book and just not think about it.

I decided to go into the office. I grabbed some files, called Judy, and left her a message that I would be coming in. I called the receptionist and asked for a room to work in. She said the conference room was going to be in use but I could work in the staff library.

When I got there, Judy was out of the office at a deposition with one of the associates. I dropped all my stuff off in the library and went in search of coffee. Cup in hand, I went back to the library, booted up the computer and set to work. Mercifully, the chronology I had decided to work on was more involved that I had anticipated and I was able to lose myself for the next couple of hours.

My growling stomach alerted me to the fact that it was lunchtime. The bowl of cereal I had grabbed before leaving the house that morning had long worn off.

Scott stuck his head in just then. "Hey, I didn't know you were here. How are you doing?"

"Fine. Great." I didn't say *My husband is probably*

205

having an affair with his ex-wife, but other than that I'm
good. "How are you doing?"

"Don't ask. Going nuts, as usual. But a man's gotta eat. I
was just going to go get something. Care to join me?"

"Sure, I'd love to."

Scott drove us to a little Italian place a few blocks away
from the office. It was quiet and cozy. The waiter showed us
to a table in a corner. I got the impression he knew Scott.
After they brought our breadbasket and we ordered a couple
of ice teas, Scott admitted he had an ulterior motive for
asking me out to eat. "Sara, I'm worried about you. I've been
thinking about what we talked about last time and I think
you're in a very difficult position. You also look like hell
today. I know you said you could handle it but I'm not
buying it. I want to know what I can do to help."

"I'm okay, really."

"Sara, I know that look. I used to wear it. All is not well
at home. I can smell it. It's okay if you don't want to tell me.
I respect your privacy but I really am worried about you."

I didn't know what to say. I really yearned to talk about it
with someone. Maybe Scott was the right one. After all, he'd
been there, as he had said.

"You're right. There is more. Yes, my stepdaughter is in
the hospital and I just came into a bunch of money but that's
really not what's bothering me." I laughed then when I
realized the absurdity of what I was saying. "My life sounds
like a bad soap opera right now, doesn't it?"

Scott smiled and I noticed for the first time that he had a
dimple on his left cheek. "Sara, you have no idea." He shook
his head. "Okay, I'll bite. What's the real problem?"

The waiter came and put our food in front of us. I waited
for him to leave. "The real problem is that I think my
husband's ex-wife is still in love with him."

Scott whistled. "Whoa, that's a biggie. How does your
husband feel about that?"

"I don't know. Every time I bring her up, he gets

206

defensive."

"Well, that may be a give-away." He saw the immediate reaction in my eyes and tried to soften what he had just said. "Or it could just mean that he resents the fact that you don't trust him and he's angry that he has to defend himself. Don't jump the gun on this one. This is not the time for you to be making hasty decisions." He reached across the table and patted my hand. I immediately felt the warmth from him and withdrew.

"Has he ever cheated on you before?"

"No."

"Was your marriage good before this?"

"Yes, except for the problems we had because of Mona. We've never fully agreed on ways to handle her and we've fought about her before. This isn't the first time she's tried to win him back. But that was a long time ago."

"Well, she might be using this situation to her advantage. But you don't know that for sure. Just because she feels a certain way doesn't mean your husband does, too. I think you should just give him some distance and some time. This will probably all work out as soon as your stepdaughter is better. You might just be overreacting. If it were me, I would just wait it out."

"You're probably right. I know I'm just being foolish."

We chatted about other things. Scott drove me back to the office and we both went back to work. However, on more than one occasion I just stopped work and thought about how he had looked at lunch. How I felt when he touched my hand. How that dimple showed up when he smiled. I felt like I was in high school all over again. I finally just expelled all thoughts of Scott from my head and concentrated on my chronology. After another hour, I decided to go home and face whatever was there.

Paul was home again. He was in our bedroom taking a nap. I went in and looked at him, sleeping so peacefully in our bed. How could I have doubted him? I loved him. I was going to make this work. I decided to forget Mona's email for now. He couldn't help what she wrote to him. Just because she said something didn't make it true. I had to have more faith in my marriage. Paul had never shown any interest in Mona in all the years I had known him. Why would he start now?

He woke up as if he sensed me there.

Or maybe it was the dog jumping on the bed.

"Hi."

"Hi, yourself. Any word on Claudia?"

"No, I haven't spoken to the doctor yet. The tests were done this morning and he's supposed to come by later this afternoon and talk to me and Mona. I thought I'd come home and shower and get some sleep and then head back. I slept in the chair in Claudia's room and my back feels like it's broken. This bed feels so good. I'm going to sleep for another hour and then go back. I set my alarm clock."

I shooed the dogs out of the room and closed the door, went back to my office and worked. A little over an hour later, Paul appeared in the doorway of my office. He had showered and put on some clean clothes and smelled great. "I'm going back. I'll call you when I find out what's going on." He quickly kissed the top of my head and left. I was alone again and felt miserable.

Paul didn't call until much later. I was in bed trying to concentrate on the TV and not succeeding when the phone rang.

"Hi, it's me."

"How's it going?"

"Ok, I guess. The news regarding Claudia is mixed. Yes, there's a small clot but they think it will dissolve in time and she'll be okay. They have her on anticoagulants. She seems better. They talked to us about rehab. They want us to get it started here before she goes back to New Hampshire. Mona's leaning toward doing that."

How convenient for Mona, I thought but I didn't think I

should share those feelings with Paul. "What do you think should be done?"

"Mona and I need to make some decisions about that, obviously. We're going to go over some of the information they gave us. I can't stand to eat one more bite of hospital food so we're going to go out to get something to eat and go over this stuff. I'll be home later."

I knew it was useless to argue. It seemed obvious to me that they could have come here or even gone to Carol's but if Paul felt that he needed to spend more time alone with Mona, my telling him otherwise was not going to change that. I thought of the email I had in my jewelry box. A cold hand seized me in the chest. My decision to ignore Mona's feelings was not going to be an easy one.

"Whatever you need to do, Paul."

"See? There you go again. Look, I don't have time for this. I'll see you later." And he hung up.

I was confused. I thought I was being understanding but once again, I was wrong. I wondered how Paul would have felt if I had spent this much time with Kevin after Paul and I were married. Paul had never had to deal with an ex. Once Kevin and I divorced, we never had contact again.

I turned off the TV and threw the remote across the room. I was damned if I did and damned if I didn't. I knew then I was not going to win this battle. I had no idea how Paul and I were going to come back from this.

I wanted to just run away and come back when it was over, regardless of the outcome. Running away was only going to throw Paul back into Mona's arms but it looked like that was going to happen anyway. As long as Claudia was in Arizona, Mona would be, too, and there would be no peace. Paul and I were doomed until she left. If it wasn't too late by then.

I was mercifully asleep when Paul came home. I woke up when he came in the room and started to undress. I watched him in the dark and didn't let him know I was awake. He spoke softly to the dogs and scratched them behind their ears. I wished I were them. He crawled into bed and was asleep in minutes. I tossed for a while and then fell asleep myself.

I was awakened by the sound of Paul's alarm clock. I sat up as he started for the shower. "You're up earlier than usual."

"I thought I'd go into the office and try to make up for lost time. I have lots of paperwork to catch up on."

Paul stopped me when he saw me start to get out of bed. "No, don't get up. I'm just going to take a quick shower and leave."

"I thought I'd make us some breakfast. At least some coffee." Paul and I needed some time together.

"No, it's ok. Really. I'll grab something on the way to the office."

I lay back down on the bed. I felt terrible. Paul was not only drifting away. Now he was pushing me away. I had never felt so alone.

I didn't say anything to him while he dressed. I knew no matter what I said, it was going to start an argument, and I didn't want that. So I just watched him and let him go. He kissed me quickly on the cheek before he left as if it was something he felt he was expected to do. I think the dogs were getting more affection from him than I was.

The next few days just drifted one into the other.

Paul worked.

I worked.

Paul visited Claudia (and Mona).

I worked.

The one bright spot was the time I spent with my friends at the office. I confided a lot in Judy. She listened and told me things would get better once Claudia was home. I doubted it but I told myself maybe she was right.

Scott and I spent more and more time together. For the sake of the case, I told myself. I was grateful for his company and found myself looking forward to my time with him. I knew in my heart it was more than just the case. I was afraid I was developing feelings for him. I didn't want to think about it though because if it were true, I knew I would have to deal with that and I wasn't in a mood to deal with anything right now. My emotions were on hold. My only concern was putting one foot in front of the other and getting through each day.

Chapter Twenty-three

Early the following week, over breakfast, Paul told me that Claudia was going to be transferred to the local rehab hospital in Scottsdale. I knew the place. It was one of the better in-patient rehabilitation units around, a little expensive, but if Claudia was going to get better, that was the place for her to be. He said she would be there by the afternoon.

"Claudia's been asking for you. It was probably wrong to ask you to stay away so long."

I almost choked trying to hold back my "I told you so!" Instead, I said, "What did she say exactly?"

Paul hated it when I asked him what people said. "I don't remember. Just something about where were you?" That was about as verbatim as it was going to get.

"So now you're saying it's all right if I go see her?"

"Sara, don't make a big deal out of this, okay? Yes, I was wrong." I gave him a smug look which he accepted. "Yes, you should visit her. But do what you want, okay? I'm not going to play referee between you and Mona. Go, stay, it doesn't matter to me. Do what you want."

"I'll think about it and let you know."

"Fine. I'll talk to you later. I gotta go."

I had already decided I was going to see Claudia the minute Paul had said it was all right. I wasn't going to tell anyone, though. No need to give Mona any warning. I was going to use the element of surprise before she could have me banned again.

I dressed for the event as if I were going out on a date. If I ran into Mona, and I was sure I would, I wanted to be sure I looked like a million bucks. If sweet Mona was feeling so insecure that she didn't want me around, I was going to give her something to feel insecure about.

I arrived at the hospital about an hour after Claudia was transferred there. I checked with the front desk and they easily told me what room she was in. Either there were no restrictions as Paul had told me or Mona hadn't been there yet to work her magic. I found Claudia in her room watching TV. A nurse was just finishing taking her vital signs when I walked in. She smiled at me as she left. Things were actually feeling normal.

I knelt over Claudia, gave her a kiss, and then sat in a chair next to her bed. "You look great," I told her.

Claudia actually didn't look too bad. The nurse in me quickly checked her for any signs of stroke. She moved both legs and hands. When she smiled, her smile looked even to me, a sure sign that things were probably very good. "How are you feeling, Claudia?"

"I'm good." She played with her bed sheet. She looked nervous. "I was wondering when I was going to see you. I thought you were mad at me for some reason."

"Mad? Why would I be mad?"

"Because I wrecked the car that Dad and you had given me."

"Claudia, don't say such a thing. I was worried sick about you."

213

"Then why didn't you visit me the whole time I was in Scottsdale Community? Mom and Dad came every day and even Aunt Carol and Uncle Gregg. But you never came."

I could feel my anger rising. I wanted to explode and scream "Because your stupid jealous mother didn't want me there." But if I said that, she wouldn't believe me and then I would be the bad guy again. I had been set up and I was furious.

Instead, I just swallowed and said, "I think sometimes your mother and I are uncomfortable in each other's presence and I knew your mother needed to be with you. I didn't want to cause her any more stress than what she was already under. So I thought I would wait until we were sure you were okay before I came to see you." Damn! I hated taking the high road and giving Mona so much credit.

"My mother said it was because you were jealous of her and you didn't like me staying in your house."

I felt I was listening to three-year-old Claudia all over again, parroting her mother's lies.

"Claudia, that's just not true. But let's not talk about that, okay? I didn't come here to upset you. I just came to lend you my support and tell you that I love you and I want you to get better as fast as you can."

Claudia looked up and behind me and her face changed instantly. I knew Mona had walked into the room.

"Well, look who's here," I heard her say.

I rose and turned to face her. "Yes, I'm here. It's nice to see Claudia look so good." I felt my legs get rubbery and my hands started to shake. I hated my body for reacting to Mona like this every time I was in her presence.

Mona went over and kissed Claudia. "How's my baby?" I wanted to gag. Then she turned to me. "She was very sick, you know. We almost lost her. If you had been there, you would have known."

I opened my mouth to answer her but the nurse mercifully came in and interrupted.

"I'm going to take Claudia over to Physical Therapy for her assessment," she said. "You're welcome to wait here if you like. She'll be about a half hour." She looked from me to Mona, obviously not sure who either of us was.

Claudia grabbed Mona's hand. "Can my Mom come with me?"

"No, the therapist wants to see you alone at first but she can join us for the last part." The nurse looked at Mona. "I'll come get you when it's time."

Mona nodded at her. "Thank you. I want to be involved in every aspect of my daughter's care."

"Certainly."

Well, I guess Mona had once again pee'd on her territory.

Claudia and the nurse weren't gone two seconds when Mona turned on me. "What the hell are you doing here? What kind of game are you playing?"

I was unprepared for the amount of anger I saw in her face and heard in her voice.

"What are you talking about? I came to see my stepdaughter. What's wrong with that?"

"I know how you feel about her. You never wanted her out here in the first place. If you had taken better care of her, this never would have happened."

I couldn't believe what I was hearing. Mona was blaming me for all this? Is that what all the anger had been about? Or was that just the excuse du jour?

"Look, Mona, Claudia had a car accident in bad weather."

"While you were gallivanting off in New York."

"Where I was had nothing to do with it."

"That just goes to show how much you know about being a mother."

My hands were really shaking but I was determined not to let Mona have the last word. That had happened too many times.

215

"What happened to Claudia could have happened to anyone. I could have been in the car with her and it still would have happened." I didn't think now was the time to mention Claudia's fondness for drinking and driving.

"I wish you *had* been in that car. Maybe we wouldn't be having this conversation now."

"What's that supposed to mean?"

She smiled. "What do you think it means?"

"You're saying you wish it had been me who was hurt? Is that it?"

"You're very perceptive," she said.

That was it. Forget the high road. I wasn't going to take this anymore. Almost twenty years of bottled up anger just erupted. "You know, Mona, you are just about the most hateful, evil woman I have ever come across. Just because you can't hold on to a husband doesn't give you the right to take it out on everyone else."

"What the hell is going on here?" It was Paul. I turned and looked at him. He was looking from me to Mona. "I don't believe this. It sounds like a cat fight out in the hallway."

I went over and stood next to my husband. I had no idea how he was going to react but I hoped he would stand by me.

Mona just sat in the chair and started to cry. "I'm sorry," she said. "I'm just so upset. Seeing Claudia here and then..." she waved her arm to indicate me.

I couldn't believe what I was seeing. And Paul seemed to fall for it. "Why don't you go freshen up, Mona? They told me you can go down to PT and see Claudia soon. I'll meet you there."

She nodded, sniffed into a tissue, and left.

"Well, that performance gets the Academy Award," I said to Paul.

He just glared at me. "What the hell were you thinking, starting a fight with her? Here, of all places."

"Starting a fight? You weren't here. You didn't see the

216

way she attacked me."

Paul put his hand up to stop me. "I don't care who started it. I know Mona's no angel but I expected more of you."

I felt like a child being lectured by her father and I became angrier.

"Don't scold me, Paul. I'm your wife, not your daughter."

"I expected more from my wife. Can't you just put yourself in her shoes, for once? You know how much stress she's been under. How much we've all been under."

Somehow, I didn't think I was included in that group. "You know, Paul, just when I think you can't get any denser, you surprise me yet again. You know what? I'm through with this. You all deserve each other." I turned and left.

This time I didn't cry. I didn't care anymore. It was obvious what was going on. Paul's allegiance had shifted from us to them, plain and simple.

I got in my car but instead of driving home, I drove to the law firm.

Judy was in her office. I plopped myself in the chair and announced, "Stick a fork in me. I'm done."

"I'm assuming this is another chapter in 'As the stomach turns'."

I nodded. "I went to visit Claudia in the hospital today. Mona got me alone in the room and we finally told each other how we felt." I laughed a little. I couldn't believe how detached I felt. It was as if I were telling a story about some other person. "You know, she really doesn't like me."

Judy got up and came over to sit beside me. "I think you're in shock. You're taking this too well. Tell me what happened."

"I don't know. First, I was visiting Claudia. The next thing I know I'm having a fight with her mother. She actually told me that she wished I had been injured in the car accident. Or maybe she wished I had died. She wasn't very specific. But she thinks that I'm the reason this happened, that I didn't take care of Claudia properly. Then Paul walked in, took her side, and told me I'm not being understanding. That *she's* been under stress. Her." I started to cry. "It's over, Judy. I can't take this any longer. I just don't know him anymore."

"I think you're getting hysterical. Let me get you some water."

She came back a few minutes later with a glass of water and Scott.

Scott knelt in front of me and took my hand. "Judy told me what happened. Why don't we go for some coffee? You can't get any work done while you're feeling like this. You need to take care of yourself." He stood and pulled me up with him. I let myself be led out of the office and to my car. "I'll drive," Scott said. "Not that I don't trust you." He smiled and I handed him my keys.

He drove a few blocks away to a small coffee shop. There were only a few customers, most of them at the counter. We took a small table by the window. After the waitress took our order, Scott leaned back in his chair and said, "Okay, tell me everything that happened today."

I repeated the day's events for him, dwelling more on Mona than on Paul.

When I had finished, Scott sighed and said, "Sara, I think you know you have a problem. And I'm certainly not one to offer marital advice. My track record isn't so great, either." He smiled again. Did he know the effect it was having on me? "What I do want to say, though, is that you should protect yourself financially, in case anything untoward happens."

My look must have upset him and he held up his hand. "I'm not saying you and Paul are going to split up over this. But you're in a vulnerable position, even in the best of circumstances. Mona sounds like the kind of woman who will sniff out a free ride if it's there and if she gets wind of your inheritance she may try to go after it."

"How? It's my money, not Paul's."

"I know, but like I said before, sometimes the courts, while they can't tap into your money as the spouse, will say that now Paul has a lot of help with his bills, therefore, he has more disposable income to use for his child."

"But technically, child support is over. Paul and Mona only agreed verbally to work out college between them."

"But now you have a catastrophic circumstance. What if your stepdaughter needs extended care? I'm not saying it will happen, but it could and you should protect yourself. Now. Not after she files. Then, it's too late. It will look like you're trying to hide money."

"Crap." I twisted my paper napkin while I mulled over Scott's words. I was so tired of going into Mona-mode.

Scott patted my hand and took the napkin away. "Look, it's not an impossible task. I told you I know people who do this sort of trust making all the time. I'll call someone for you and we can set something up."

"I appreciate that. I really do."

After that, we just chatted for a while about nothing in particular. While we sipped coffee and munched our danishes, Scott told me some gossip from the office and I pretended to care. I was more interested in just listening to him speak. He had a soothing voice and it was so nice to talk with someone who listened. We got onto the subject of pets and I told him about Jesse and Toby. Scott had an old cat in addition to the two Goldens pictured on his desk. The cat had belonged to him and his last wife and she didn't want it after the divorce.

"That old boy has been with me through thick and thin. It amazes me how attached you can get to an animal. I never considered myself a cat kind of guy but I really love having him around. But he's getting old. I'm going to miss him when he dies."

Suddenly, Scott looked at his watch. "Oops. I have a client coming in to see me in half an hour. I'd better get prepared."

"I'm sorry I took you away from your work."

"Hey, I wanted to do this. I told you I would be here for you. I meant it."

He put his hand on mine and I felt that tingle again. "I think you should go home and just be nice to yourself for the rest of the day. Can you give me a lift back to the office first?"

He left some money on the table and we walked back to my car. This time, he let me drive back to the office. I pulled in to a spot on the side of the building away from traffic. Scott turned to me before getting out of the car. "Are you going to be ok?"

"I'm fine. Honest."

Scott squinted his eyes at me. "You sure?"

"I'm sure. And I want to see someone about this money thing, the sooner the better."

"Good, I'll make some calls after my next appointment. I'll let you know what I find out."

He leaned over to give me a quick hug. Suddenly, we were hugging more intensely. I looked up at him and he kissed me. Then we both quickly withdrew as if we had been burned.

"I'm sorry, Sara. I shouldn't have done that." He let me go and pulled back to his side of the car.

"It's okay." But I knew it wasn't.

"I...I'd better go." Scott hastily got out of the car but he turned around and leaned into the open passenger side window. "Sara, I mean it. I'm sorry. I had no right to do that. It won't happen again."

"It's all right. Forget it. Call me after you talk to the accountant."

"I will."

"Call me," I repeated and then drove off. All the way home I kept feeling his lips on mine and was amazed at how it had made me feel, how I was still feeling. This was wrong.

I was married to Paul. I loved Paul. I wanted my marriage to Paul.

I knew I needed to be careful. I didn't want to throw my marriage away just because things were not so good right now. Doing anything with Scott would certainly ruin everything.

When I got home, the answering machine was blinking. I hit the button. It was Angela. Her voice was trembling.

"Mom is missing. Sara, call me." She had sobbed once and hung up.

Chapter Twenty-Four

My hands shook as I dialed the phone. Please let Mom be okay, I prayed.

Angela answered on the first ring. "Hello."

"Angela, it's me."

"Oh." She sounded disappointed. "I thought you were the police."

"The police? Mom is still missing? What happened?"

"The sitter forgot to lock the front door. She was cleaning up after lunch and she thought Mom was napping. When she went to look in on her, she wasn't in her room. Then she noticed the front door was open. She searched the neighborhood and didn't find her. That's when she called me. I was at a client's home. I rushed back here. When she still wasn't back, I called the police. It's been hours. I'm so scared." Angela sounded numb.

"How long has it been?" I looked at the clock on the microwave. It was four o'clock here. That meant it was seven where Angela...and Mom...were.

"About five hours now. Luckily, we still have a little

time before it gets too dark and it's not cold but still she could be injured somewhere. She could have been hit by a car."

"Don't start worrying about things that haven't even happened yet, Angela. Maybe she's just sitting somewhere. What did the police say?"

"Not much. They said she'll be on the news tonight if we don't find her by then." Angela started crying again. "I can't do this anymore. If...when we find her, we have to place her. Now. I can't go through this again. It was a mistake to wait."

"Don't start thinking like that, Angela. We did what we thought was best at the time. They'll find her. She's going to be okay." I wished I felt as confident as I was trying to sound. There was a click on the phone line.

"Maybe that's the police," Angela said. "Let me take that. I'll call you back." The phone went dead in my hand.

I put the phone back in its cradle and heard Paul's car pull into the garage. The dogs started whimpering when they heard the noise. They were anxious to see Paul. I wished I felt the same.

Paul walked into the kitchen and from the look on his face I could tell he wasn't happy. I decided to take the initiative and smooth things over. "Paul, I'm sorry about this afternoon. If it will make things easier, I won't visit Claudia anymore."

"It doesn't matter now."

"What do you mean? Is Claudia okay?" I suddenly panicked. Could she have taken a turn for the worse? She looked so good when I saw her today.

"She's fine. Mona has decided it's too much to keep Claudia here and deal with everything." He emphasized 'everything'. I knew she meant me. I wondered what had happened after I left. I imagined Mona really laying it on heavy. "She's decided to take Claudia back to New Hampshire for her rehab and recovery."

"When?"

"I don't know. Soon. As soon as she can make arrangements and the doctors will agree she can travel. But that should make you happy."

He threw his keys on the kitchen table and walked into his office. I followed him. "Paul, this isn't what I wanted at all. I can't control Mona's reactions. I'm getting a little tired of being the bad guy all the time." Paul just looked at me. "Why are you letting her come between us?"

"Me? You're the one who's doing this. You're so obsessed over Mona and what she thinks. This is your problem. And now you've made it mine."

"My problem? You don't think the fact that your ex-wife wants you back shouldn't be something I'm concerned about?"

"Why do you keep harping on that?"

Anger flared within me once again. I should have kept my mouth shut but I didn't. "I saw her email, Paul. I saw what she wrote to you."

"You did what?"

He emphasized every word and each one stung like a slap. Paul was livid. His face turned red and I backed up.

"You snooped in my email?" He was shouting now. "Get away from me. I can't believe this." He stormed back into the kitchen, grabbed his car keys off the kitchen counter, and headed for the garage.

I followed him out to his car. "Where are you going? Let me explain."

"Get away from me," he shouted again. He got in his car, slammed the door shut, turned on the ignition, and raced out of the driveway.

I walked slowly back into the house, unable to think. Numb, I sat on the sofa and just stared. I hadn't felt this alone since I had left Kevin. It dawned on me, though, that Paul hadn't denied what I accused Mona of. He didn't deny that she had sent him an email that confirmed her feelings for him. He also hadn't told me that my fears were unfounded.

He didn't even reassure me that his feelings for me were safe. All he had done was get angry that I had read Mona's precious letter to him.

The phone rang. Mom! I grabbed the receiver.

"Angela?"

"No, it's Scott. I have that number for you. Are you okay? You don't sound any better. In fact, you sound worse. Have you been crying?"

"I can't go into it now, Scott. I'm sorry. Things have just gone from bad to worse. But I need that information now more than ever. Give me the number." I wrote down the number and promised Scott I'd call after I made the appointment. I no sooner replaced the phone than it rang again. This time it *was* Angela. Before I could say anything I heard her say, "She's home. She's okay."

"Thank God."

"But we really need to do something, Sara."

"We will. Let me make a reservation and I'll come out and help you get her settled in."

"Thanks, Sara. I really appreciate that. I don't want to do this alone."

"You won't have to. We're going to do this together."

There was no reason for me to hang around and watch my marriage die. I called the airlines and made a reservation to go back to New York in two days. Hopefully, that would give me enough time to get my money situation squared away with the person Scott had recommended. I then called Scott's friend. He had been expecting my call and knew who I was immediately. Scott had apparently filled him in. Marvin said he was able to see me the following morning.

I called Scott back.

"I just wanted to let you know I called that guy you referred me to and I have an appointment to see him tomorrow."

"Great. Why don't we meet up after that? I'll buy you lunch and you can fill me in. That way, if you still have questions, maybe I can help."

"Okay. Where should I meet you?" I wasn't going to let myself sit in a car with him again. Lunch sounded innocent enough but I wasn't so sure.

"How about that coffee shop we went to?"

"All right. I'll call you when I'm finished with the appointment."

Later that night, when Paul was reading in bed, I thought I would take a chance and approach him again. I told him what had happened to my mother.

"So, I made reservations to go back to New York to help Angela settle Mom into the nursing home. I don't think it's fair to make her do it by herself. I know I was just there and we have all this going on with Claudia right now but I really think I need to do this."

Paul had put his book down and listened but it was hard to read his face. "Fine. I'm really sorry about your Mom. It's probably best that you go out there again. It might be good for us to be apart for a while, too."

Hearing Paul say that sent a chill through me. "Is that what you want, Paul?"

"What I want doesn't seem to matter to you."

"Paul, that's not true and you know it." I sat on the bed and put my hand on his leg. "What's happened to us?"

"You let your insecurities get the better of you. Again. You have this vendetta against Mona and you expect me to carry it out for you. That's not going to happen."

"I don't have a vendetta against Mona. I do have a problem with her sending you emails saying that she wants you back. Why don't you see that as a problem?"

"Ignoring the fact that you crossed a line when you read my mail," I started to answer but he held up his hand. "Let me finish. Ignoring that, why would you even believe that just because Mona says something like that, that it would make a difference to me? What does that say about what you think of me?"

I put my head down. I had no answer for that. "Paul, I'm tired of fighting like this. I just want us to go back to the way things were. We love each other. We have a good marriage. Somehow, everything has gotten all twisted around." I couldn't believe that my marriage was falling apart before my eyes and I was helpless to do anything about it. Worse yet, Paul didn't seem to care.

"Look, you have things to take care of and so do I. Claudia is going to be transferred to a rehab hospital in New Hampshire very soon. Let's just get through these next few days and see where we are." He went back to his book. Our conversation was over.

My meeting with Marvin Rockfield went better than I expected. Apparently, I wasn't the only woman in the world who wanted to protect her assets from an ex-wife...or a current husband, for that matter. He went over several options that I could implement. My money was still in New York in the trust fund that my father had set up. Marvin outlined some ways for me to transfer the funds to Arizona and set them up in such a way that they would be untouchable if Mona went after Paul for money to care for Claudia. It would also be my asset only and Paul would have no rights to it should there be a divorce. I felt awful hearing those words out loud. Marvin sensed my discomfort and reassured me that I was only being prudent. Even if nothing happened between Paul and me, this money was still something that I should have complete control over. This was money my father had left to me to do with as I pleased. I was really just following his wishes. Marvin also went over some plans he had drawn up for me so that I could invest some of the money and make the asset grow rather than letting it languish in the bank.

He kept telling me that I was a rich woman and I needed to realize the power and comfort that this could afford me. The way everything else in my life was going, comfort was the last thing I felt. And it had been a long time since I felt powerful. In fact, that was something I was sure I had never felt. It hit me how true it was that money couldn't buy you the things that mattered. If I could, I would have bribed Mona to go away but that wouldn't erase Paul's anger toward me right now. And I wasn't sure how I felt about him, either. I couldn't shake the feeling that he wasn't doing enough to reassure me that Mona meant nothing in all of this. All I had was the vision of him hugging her after she had sent him that email. His response was anger that I had read it. Maybe it was his guilt speaking. Yes, he had said all the right words about how I should trust him and our marriage but words weren't what I needed right now.

Despite feeling that it was something that maybe I shouldn't do, I met Scott for lunch after my meeting. I took the same table we had sat at before and sipped an ice tea while I waited for him to arrive. Scott saw me as soon as he walked in and waved. Why did the man have to be so cute? Or was he too old for cute? Hell, I was too old for cute. I was too old to be doing this, too. Something told me to get up and run for cover but before my mind could get the message to my feet, Scott sat down and was looking right at me.

"Hey, how are you doing? I've been worried about you. You okay?"

"No, not really. I have to admit, I've been better." The waiter came over and offered Scott a menu. He refused the menu and gave him his food and drink order. I gave mine and the waiter left.

"What's wrong?" Scott said.

I told him about Mona's email to Paul. He listened while I spoke and didn't interrupt.

When I had finished, he said, "I can see why you would be upset but you have to look at it in context." Spoken just like a lawyer. Nothing was as it seemed!

"And that would be...."

"That maybe Paul's right. This is all coming from Mona and he's totally innocent. But he's angry that you don't trust him. You know, if you keep punishing him for something he didn't do, he just might do it since he's getting blamed anyway. It happens."

Suddenly, I thought I had an insight into what had happened to Scott's marriage. Maybe he had been through this, too. Maybe that's why he felt like he needed to help. Maybe he wasn't attracted to me at all and I was just building a fantasy in my mind to punish Paul. I really needed to be careful.

"I suppose you could be right but what bothers me is he didn't really deny anything. All he said was that I *should* trust him."

"Why should he deny anything, Sara? You've already tried and convicted him. The only thing left is the sentencing."

I toyed with my napkin. "I don't know. You didn't see them together like I did. Why would he console Mona and place himself in that position knowing how she felt about him?"

"People can control themselves, you know. You said yourself that their daughter was in a bad way. They had just found out that she might be severely injured, more than they had originally thought. They were both very vulnerable and were sharing sadness as two parents, nothing more. Just because Mona feels and wants something, doesn't mean Paul is going to give it to her." He sounded just like Paul and was becoming less attractive by the minute. Did all men belong to the same excuse club? "You might drive him back to her if you're not careful."

I suddenly felt like a real jerk. "I guess I have a lot of thinking to do."

"On the other hand," Scott looked at me very seriously. "I want you to know that I'm here for you. As a friend." I wondered if he was implying there could be more but before I had a chance to think about that, our waiter arrived with our food. As soon as he left, Scott changed the subject. He asked

229

about my mother and told me what questions to go over with the supervisor at the nursing home we were going to place her in. He knew Angela was relying on me to have all the answers and I wasn't even sure what the questions were. He didn't bring up Paul, or failing marriages, or anything else like that again and I was grateful.

I went home to pack and prepare for my trip to New York.

Chapter Twenty-Five

When I arrived at Angela's the next evening, I was horrified at the shape my mother was in. I had no idea she had deteriorated so much in such a short time. Her hair hung around her head like a dry gray halo. Her eyes held no spark. They looked right through me even when I addressed her by name. Her hands shook worse than before. She had no idea how to get from one room to the other. And she had begun to wet and soil herself. She was sitting in a chair wearing diapers.

I looked at Angela in disbelief.

"How could this happen? She wasn't this bad just two weeks ago."

"The doctors think she had a bunch of mini-strokes. They said it's probably going to get worse and quickly. I'm wondering if the place we chose can even handle her now that she's this way."

I couldn't imagine my mother roaming the streets alone like this. No wonder Angela had been so scared.

"They'll be okay with her. They're more used to this than

we are. Some of the other residents looked this bad. Remember? We were thinking Mom was too high functioning to be there. I guess that's no longer true."

Angela made supper for us that night. The mood was somber. Mom brightened up a little but it was so obvious she had no idea who we were. I was amazed at the amount of patience Angela had with her. She treated her like a child and Mom responded the same way. I was having a difficult time reconciling this old woman with the person who had been my mother, the woman who had possibly cheated me out of a father. I wondered if that had been the reason I didn't trust my own husband. I couldn't blame my mother for the mess I was making of my marriage but certainly the seeds had been sown living under her roof.

Angela put my mother to bed and afterwards we sat in her living room and talked. She had poured us both some wine. Feeling sad and mellow, I decided to broach the subject of Eleanor again. I had planned to see her and talk some more about Dad during this trip.

"Angie, I was going to see Eleanor as long as I'm here. Will you go with me this time?"

Angela shook her head. "I can't deal with that now. Let's just get Mom settled tomorrow morning and I'll think about it. Maybe."

We took Mom to Harbor Estates the next morning. I felt as if I were leaving my puppy to be euthanized. I knew she was going to be okay. She was probably far safer there than she was living with Angela. But I couldn't shake the feeling that I might never see her again.

Angela cried the whole time we were there. It was up to me to answer all the questions and sign all the papers. I was grateful to Scott for prepping me as he had. But I felt myself getting more and more angry. I was really getting tired of people leaning on me all the time. Paul, Claudia, Angela, Mom...when did I get to lean? No wonder Scott seemed so attractive.

We stayed and helped Mom get settled in her room. We put some things out that we had packed for her. Some pictures of Angela and me from our school days. Pictures of Michelle. The fact that there were no pictures of Claudia struck me but Mom wouldn't have known who she was anyway. Frankly, I wasn't even sure I cared.

The ride back to Angela's house was deathly quiet. Each of us was inside our own world. I think we both knew this was the beginning of the end for Mom. It was only going to get worse from now on. I finally broke the silence as we were pulling into Angela's driveway.

"Did you give any more thought to seeing Eleanor? Will you come with me?"

"No, Sara. My feelings haven't changed. I'll pass. There's nothing I have to say to her." I opened my mouth to say something but Angela put her hand up. "No, there's nothing you can say to change my mind. Look, this has been a tough day for me. Don't add to it. You want to see Eleanor, you have some sick reason to stay in touch with her, fine. Do it. Just leave me out of it."

We were parked in her driveway by now and I just exited the car without another word. I didn't understand Angela's attitude but I no longer cared. All I wanted to do was spend a little time with Eleanor and hopefully get some answers. Then I wanted to go home and see if there was anything left of my marriage.

Eleanor seemed a little cool when I called but it might have been my imagination. She agreed to meet with me and we set a time for later than afternoon. This time, I agreed to meet her in her home. Frankly, I was curious to see where she and Dad had lived.

I found her house easily. As it turned out, she was only twenty minutes from Angela, closer than the tearoom where I had met Eleanor previously. The house was a large brick house with a winding stone walkway to the front porch. Flowers were in bloom in window boxes hung from the railing. As I walked up to the front door, a calico cat watched me from the front window.

I rang the bell and waited. The cat jumped down from its perch and the door opened. I tried to breathe normally. I was experiencing the same sensations I did whenever I had to be in Mona's presence.

Eleanor smiled when she saw me. She was dressed as well as she had been when we met the two other times but more casually this time. She was wearing jeans and a sweater. I don't think I ever saw my mother in jeans and the contrast startled me.

"Hi, Sara." She opened the door wider. "Come in." I noticed she did not attempt to hug me.

"Thank you for seeing me on such short notice."

"That's all right. I have to say I was curious when you called. I really never expected to hear from you again." The front door opened into a small foyer. To the left was a large living room and Eleanor gestured toward it. "Why don't we sit down?"

I sat on the sofa Eleanor had indicated. She had a tea set on the coffee table all ready for us with a plate of cookies. She took a seat next to me on the sofa and poured tea for both of us. "I hope this is okay. I usually have a cup of tea this time of day."

"This is fine. Thank you," I said taking the cup from her. My eyes scanned the room. There were pictures everywhere. On the walls. On the end tables. I was dying to get up and grab one. I knew my Dad had to be in some of them. Eleanor saw me eyeing the photos and picked up the nearest one to her. She handed it to me with reverence.

"This is your father. It was taken just before he died." I looked at the couple in the photo. An older man I never would have recognized was sitting next to Eleanor on a bench in someone's back yard. He had his arm around her and they were smiling.

"My daughter took that," she said.

My head shot up when she said that. "Your daughter?" Eleanor did not have any children when I knew her. That had to mean...

"Yes, Sara, you have a sister. You met her. Maria from the tea shop."

Maria! No wonder she looked familiar. And the way she had hovered over us the entire time we were there, acting so protective of Eleanor. A sister. Daddy's daughter.

Tears formed and ran down my cheeks. All the emotions I had bottled up finally surfaced and spilled over. It was too much. Putting my mother in the home, fearing my marriage was over, and now this.

"I'm sorry," I said. I handed the picture frame back to Eleanor. "I'm feeling a little overwhelmed right now."

Eleanor moved closer to me and put her arm around me. "It's all right," she said. "I understand."

I pulled away and looked at her. "No, I don't think you do at all."

"What do you mean?"

"I want to know why my father stopped seeing me and my sister."

Eleanor sighed. "I've both dreaded and wished for this day." She poured herself some more tea while she gathered her thoughts. "Your father and I used to talk a lot about the day when you and Angela would come around. What we would say. How we would handle it. Your father knew how angry I was with you and your sister. I didn't think I would ever forgive you for turning on him the way you two did."

"Wait a minute. What do you mean 'we turned on him'? He left us. He just disappeared from our lives." I was hesitant to go on but knew it finally had to be said. "My mother told us he had died. Are you saying now that he had nothing to do with that?" Something was very wrong. I was feeling light-headed.

Eleanor erupted. "Your mother is the one who told you that?" She got up and paced the room. "I knew it. I just knew

235

it. I always said something like that had to have happened. Your father wouldn't believe me."

I suddenly had a flash of Paul and me arguing about Mona. Eleanor and I had more in common than I had thought. I was starting to feel compassion for her. Maybe she and I were kindred spirits.

Eleanor stopped pacing and faced me. "Sara, you and I are going to have to trust each other a little if we're going to make any sense out of this. I would like to resolve this once and for all. We don't have to ever have anything to do with each other again after today but I really would like to put this behind me. Finally. Do you think we can do that?"

I nodded. I watched her as she went to the drawer in her desk and pulled out a photo album.

"Your father and I made this in case you and your sister ever came back. These are pictures of your father...and us... over the years."

She sat next to me and opened the book on her lap. Slowly, she went through it page by page. She stopped at every picture and explained to me what each one meant, where it was taken, who was in it. By the time she had finished I felt as if I had gotten part of my past back.

But it made no sense that someone who didn't want anything to do with me would go to all this trouble. Even though I thought I already knew the answer, I had to say the words out loud. "Eleanor, why didn't my father keep in touch with me?"

"Sara, this is going to be difficult without me saying anything bad about your mother. You may not want to hear what I have to say."

"Just say it. It's been long enough. I want the truth no matter what it is."

Eleanor sighed again and looked down at her hands. She seemed to make a decision. "Your mother never accepted your father leaving her. She was determined to make his life hell as long as he and I were together. She blamed me for their problems even though I didn't even meet your father until after their divorce. I even thought of leaving your father so that he wouldn't have to choose. But he wouldn't hear of it. You have to remember what kind of times we lived in then. It was a long time ago. Fathers didn't have the rights that they do now." I laughed inwardly. If she only knew.

She continued. "Your mother didn't want me in your life. When she found out I was pregnant, she threatened to take you kids away where your father would never see you girls again. He promised to bow out if she promised to stay. She said she would. Your father's plan was to keep his distance but keep an eye on things. He paid child support directly to your mother. He wrote to you girls but your mother insisted that he not call until you were older and could make the decision for yourselves whether or not to keep in touch with him. I guess she was hoping that would give her time to sway you to her way of thinking. He did send you presents and cards, though."

"We never got those." Eleanor smiled but it wasn't a smile of happiness. "You're saying she just didn't give them to us?" She nodded. I shook my head. "I'm having so much trouble with this."

"What else do you remember?"

"I remember we didn't see Daddy for a while. Mom kept saying a visit was coming up but it never did. Then one day she just told us Daddy got sick and that he was gone." Another tear eased its way down my cheek.

Eleanor squeezed my hand. "It's okay, Sara. You didn't want to believe that your mother could have lied to you."

I nodded. Words were stuck in my throat. I didn't trust myself to speak.

"But now we both know that she did. I wish now your father had been more aggressive. Many times, I asked him to get in touch, to call even when he said he had promised not to. He never thought your mother would go to the lengths she did. But it makes sense now. We wondered why you girls didn't get in touch with us when you got older. Your father always assumed you would. You didn't live that far away. It just broke his heart to have you so close and not be able to see you or talk with you. He was devastated. I finally convinced him to move farther away. We needed to start over. We needed to get on with our lives." She shook her head. "And all that time, when he was hoping you'd come back to him, you had no reason to even try."

If my mother had been in that room at that moment, I know I would have said some very nasty things to her. My mind was a jumble of emotions. I was so angry for losing my father because of her lying. Part of me could understand her desperation. My mother felt she had lost her husband to another woman. She was afraid of losing her children - all she had, in her mind - to that woman as well. At that moment, I even felt a twinge of sympathy and understanding for Mona. But I would never understand…or accept…what my mother had done. What either of them had done.

Eleanor spoke again. "When your father learned that he was dying, he made me promise that I would find you girls. He wanted you to know how much he loved you even if you didn't want to hear it. We knew he didn't have long. His cancer was very aggressive." She put her head down. "You feel you have forever and then time just runs out." She stopped for a moment. "Anyway, we set up a trust for you and Angela and the attorney was commissioned to hire a detective to find both of you. I think your father was hoping the news would come back in time before he died. But it didn't. He died last year, right before Christmas. A few months later, the detective tracked down Angela and then, later, you called. You know the rest."

I kept shaking my head. "I don't know what to say, Eleanor. I knew Mom hated you. I knew how she felt about Dad and you but I didn't think anyone would go to such lengths." Then I thought of Mona. Maybe my mother wasn't so unusual after all.

Now it was Eleanor's turn to be confused. "I still don't understand something. If you knew your mother had told you what she did and you also knew your father had been alive, why didn't you confront your mother before today? What did she say about all this?"

"Because life plays mean tricks on us sometimes." I told her about my mother, what she had become, how Angela and I had just placed her in a nursing home.

"I'm sorry, Sara. I'm sorry for you to have to go through that. But I'd be lying if I said that I felt sorry for Helen. She hurt Peter very much. She stole his daughters from him. Maybe this is her karma."

A thought crossed my mind then. "Eleanor, how about another pot of tea? I need your opinion on something."

Over the next hour, I discussed Paul and his ex-wife with Eleanor. She was so easy to talk to. I found myself pouring out my soul to her about all the problems I was having dealing with Mona and Claudia and how it had come between Paul and me.

Eleanor listened without saying much. She nodded here and there when I talked about the things Mona had done over the years. Finally, she spoke. "Sara, I hope you don't take any of this the wrong way. I know exactly where you're coming from because I've been there. I was the outsider just like you are. Your mother would have loved nothing better if I just left your father and everything could go back to the way it had been. Your mother, like Mona, was convinced that I was standing between her and your father getting back together. Nothing could have been further from the truth. If I had left your father, he still would not have gone back to Helen. That part of his life was over. Once he took that step to leave her, it was as if a big weight had lifted. He knew what life without her was like and he liked it, with me or without me.

"I imagine it's the same with Paul. You really need to stop tormenting yourself over this. He left Mona. He married you. Those are two separate issues. What she does or doesn't do, especially after all these years, isn't going to suddenly make him wake up and realize he wants to be with her. What may happen though is that you both wind up alone."

I knew Eleanor was right. She had come into my life at just the right time. "I think I have trouble dealing with Mona because she reminds me so much of my mother."

"You need to forgive them both and move on. I had to. It will eat you up if you don't. Don't give her...or Mona...that kind of hold over you."

"But how? I can sympathize with my mother somewhat. But Mona's different."

"Is she? Your mother was an unhappy person who lashed out at what she thought was the source of her unhappiness. Mona is doing the same thing."

"It doesn't justify her actions."

"No, but who will it hurt now to continue to be angry with her? Her? You? Is that what you want? To turn into a bitter old woman?"

She didn't say it but I knew the question was did I want to turn into my mother? I knew I didn't. It was the last thing I wanted.

"You're giving Mona more power than she deserves. We are all on the same road, just in different places. Your mother felt she was doing the best she could under the circumstances and I'm sure Mona feels that way, too. You're the one who is in the position to determine how that affects you. You choose what you want and then decide nothing and no one is going to come between you and what you want...as long as you don't hurt anyone else in the process."

I knew what I wanted was Paul and our marriage. That was where my heart lay and that was what I was going to keep. I could see why my father fell in love with this woman. She was gentle and loving, but strong, something my father had missed in his marriage to my mother. I felt so much better just being in her presence. I knew he must have felt it, too. Eleanor hugged me. "I know this has been hard for you. But I hope you'll find some peace now."

I stayed with Eleanor a little longer. Then, with promises to keep in touch, and meaning it this time, I headed back to Angela's house.

Chapter Twenty-Six

Angela was in the living room reading a book. "I thought we'd go out to eat, if that's ok," she said. "That's fine. Can we talk first?" I put the picture album that Eleanor had given me on the coffee table and sat across from Angela. I could tell by the look on her face that she wasn't going to be too receptive so I gave her the condensed version of my visit with Eleanor. When I finished, Angela didn't say a word. She blinked and seemed to be processing the whole thing.

"Well, say something."

"Let me get this straight. Our father was alive all that time and didn't come forward? He left it up to us to get in touch with him? What a crock. Don't tell me you actually believe that old woman?"

I was speechless. I couldn't believe what I was hearing. "Daddy didn't know that we thought he was dead. Mom did that, or did you forget?"

"That doesn't matter. He didn't have to agree to her demands. He just didn't care."

"But he wrote to us."

"I didn't get any letters. Did you?"

"Mom must have kept them from us."

"Sara, wake up. Eleanor's lying to you. And how are we going to disprove anything she says now? Of course, she wants us to believe they did all the right things. They didn't have to pick up the pieces. Mom did. We did. I did."

"But Angela, Dad was afraid."

"Afraid? Afraid of what? Rejection? He rejected us. He should have been afraid." All of a sudden, Angela's remarks were starting to make sense. Had I wanted to believe Eleanor so much that I was blind to the fact that she could possibly have been lying to me? I was so caught up in my own thoughts, I didn't even bother to answer Angela. She took this as license to go on.

"I don't believe any of it," she said. "And I certainly want nothing to do with her. I'm not going to play family with Eleanor or her little brat."

Angela sounded too much like my mother. "Angela! Where is this anger coming from? Dad couldn't have known what Mom had done and she was the one pulling all the strings, remember? Just because she's a helpless old lady now doesn't mean she's any less to blame for the part she played in all of this."

"I don't care and I don't want to talk about it."

"Why?"

"Why? Because we had a father who abandoned us. Now you tell me he had another child. They all grew up together as a family and we didn't. So he left us money. Is that supposed to make all the rest go away? Frankly, that's the least he could have done. But that doesn't buy him forgiveness."

"I give up. It's obvious that it's more important for you to hang onto your anger than to grow up for once and see life for what it is. I'm sorry you feel this way. I'm sorry you feel you have a grudge to bear. But you know what? You're not

243

the only one with a problem. Maybe if you looked beyond your own nose once in a while you would see things differently."

"What's the matter? Do you think you're special because you have to deal with your husband's ex-wife? At least you still have a husband. You're not raising a child all by yourself."

"Okay, here we go. Sad song number thirty-nine. You're not raising a child all by yourself, Angela. In case you haven't noticed, Michelle is in college and doesn't even live here anymore. You chose to keep Mom here all this time on your own. I offered to help you place her a long time ago. This is what you chose. And what's wrong in my life right now is none of your business."

I didn't want Angela to see me cry. I went to my room and slammed the door. I heard her rummaging around in the kitchen. For a moment, I thought she was going to come in and apologize. I had myself all set for a hug when I heard the front door close. The next sound was her car driving off. So much for sisterly love. Angela just wasn't going to change. I resigned myself to this and was glad Mom was placed. Now I wouldn't have to deal with Angela so much. But I mourned the loss of my sister. Even as she was, she was all I had now. I might have a sister through Eleanor but I didn't know Maria. I had no memories to share with her. She was a stranger and always would be.

I packed my things while she was gone. I put the picture album in my suitcase. I did not intend to show it to Angela now. I was afraid she would rip it up.

Angela was gone for hours. I had no idea where she was. I made a sandwich and watched some television. Four hours after she had left, Angela returned.

"Where did you go?"

"I went to see Mom."

"How was she?"

"Fine. She seems to be settling in okay."

"Good. Can we talk?"

"There's nothing to talk about. I don't want to deal with this anymore. It's over and done. Nothing is going to change now. Mom doesn't even know who we are half the time. There's no point in any of this."

"But we can be friends with Eleanor. With Maria."

"I don't want that. You do what you want. I'm going to bed."

"I'm going back to Arizona tomorrow."

"Fine. Suit yourself. I guess there is nothing else for you to do here. Good night."

"Angela...are you going to be all right? You know there's more to life than taking care of Mom. You have your whole life ahead of you. Why don't you think about coming out to Arizona to visit? You'd love it there."

"No, I need to concentrate on my business and I want to be around here for a while. Mom might need me."

"Angela..." but I let it go. Angela needed Mom to need her. It was going to be hard on her to be alone now but Angela seemed to want to stew in her misery. There was nothing I could do about it. She was her mother's child, after all.

Chapter Twenty-Seven

I begged off visiting Mom with Angela the next morning. Instead, I took a cab to the airport. I didn't want to see my mother the way she was. I wanted to remember her as she had been. Yes, she had been a little more than mean but she had been alive. Now she was just the walking dead.

I figured I would be getting home at the same time as Paul, assuming he had gone to work. I had no way of knowing if Paul would be home when I got there and I had no idea what I would be walking into. He hadn't called me at all while I was away and I hadn't tried to reach him, either. I wondered what I was coming back to.

The cab I grabbed at Sky Harbor Airport left me off at the curb outside my home. I stood in the driveway a moment, almost afraid to go inside. There were no cars visible and the garage door was down. I let myself in the front door with my key and was welcomed by the dogs. I called for Paul but got no answer. Dropping my suitcase in the hallway, I headed into the kitchen. The mail was on the countertop in a pile so that meant Paul had at least come home at some point that day. Where was he now?

I sorted through the mail but didn't see anything interesting. I wandered through the rooms and thought how much I would miss this house. This was silly. Paul and I needed to talk and I had to find him. I called his office.

"Weber Construction," said his receptionist.

"Hi, Meg, is Paul there?"

"Why, no, he's been at the new building site all day. He wasn't planning on coming back here today." She said it in a way that implied I should have known that.

"Right, of course. I forgot. I've been out of town."

"Paul mentioned you were back east. Welcome home."

"Thanks."

Well, that had gotten me nowhere. I had no idea where to start looking. I certainly didn't want to run into him if he was with Mona. But Eleanor's words kept coming back to me.

"You choose what you want and then decide nothing and no one is going to come between you and what you want."

I chose Paul and my marriage and I was going to get him back. I decided to swallow my pride, drive over to Carol's, and see if she knew where everyone was. If Mona was there, so be it.

I could feel the tension mount in my stomach as soon as I saw Carol's house. My resolve about possibly facing Mona was starting to waver. I wasn't looking forward to seeing her again after our confrontation in Claudia's room. I also didn't want to give her the satisfaction that I didn't know where my own husband was. But things were going to have to be resolved. Might as well be now. If Mona was here, I was going to take it as a sign that we should settle things once and for all. It seemed to be my week for getting things done.

Paul's car wasn't in the driveway. I rang the bell and heard footsteps come to the door. My heart sank when I saw Mona open the door. She seemed as unhappy to see me as I was to see her.

She just stood there without saying a word. It was obvious she was still intent on making me as uncomfortable as possible. Fine, I was up to it.

"Hi, Mona. Is Carol home?"

"No, she's not."

"Do you know when she's going to be back?"

"Yes."

"Mind sharing that with me?"

"Yes, I do, as a matter of fact. I'm not sure she wants me to give that information out."

"You're never going to change are you?"

"I don't know what you mean."

"Sure you do. You're not stupid." I pushed myself past Mona into the living room and sat on the sofa.

Mona didn't close the door but she turned to look at me. "What do you think you're doing?"

"I'm waiting for my sister-in-law. What does it look like I'm doing?"

"I think you're trying to make a pathetic attempt to show me that you belong here."

"I'm not the one who's pathetic." I felt like I was back in high school and dealing with the class bully.

She closed the door and stood in front of me. "You think the whole world revolves around you, don't you? You think you're just the perfect little wife."

"I'm far from perfect but I am Paul's wife and it's about time you got that through your thick head."

"Oh, I know you're Paul's wife...for now."

"Is that a threat?"

"No, it's a fact." Mona had a smug look on her face that I yearned to slap off. "I'm the mother of his child and I always will be. That's a bond we'll always have. Paul and I made a child together."

"And you and Paul made a mess of things together, too." A flicker of confusion crossed Mona's face and I forged on. "Claudia was drinking the night she had her accident. As you yourself admitted, that wasn't the first time. She was already messed up when you sent her to us. If I were her mother, I'd be thinking I bore some responsibility for that."

"You have no right to speak about Claudia like that. How dare you lecture me!"

I was having that surreal feeling again but this time I was watching myself do what I had always wanted to do and never had the nerve to do before. I was nervous and glad I was still sitting. I kept going. "And in case you didn't notice, Paul divorced you years ago. So the only bond the two of you have is a daughter with problems." If Mona wanted a battle, she was going to get one.

Mona's cheeks were flushed. She clenched her fists at her sides. "When Paul and I separated, we would have worked things out if you hadn't interfered. There wouldn't have been a divorce. You're the one who destroyed things." She smiled. "But it seems to me you're about to get what you deserve. Paul and I are going to work this out this time and things are going to go back to the way they were supposed to be."

"I don't think so, Mona," said a familiar male voice.

We both looked toward the door and saw Paul standing there.

Paul looked at me. "I saw your suitcase at home."

"How did you know I was here?"

"I didn't. I came over here to talk to Mona about the travel arrangements for Claudia. Then I saw your car here and ..." he didn't finish but I knew what he meant. He knew Mona and I being in the same room was not a good idea.

He looked back at Mona. "So tell me more about how things are going to work out between us, Mona."

Mona's face got red. "What I meant was...."

"I know what you meant." Paul's voice gave away how hard it was for him to maintain control. Paul hated to be played for a fool and it was obvious to me, and I'm sure to Mona as well, that he was trying very hard not to give full vent to his anger. "It's obvious what you meant. My wife knew what you meant all along. But I was too dumb to see it. Instead, I blamed her when I should have been blaming you. You've been exploiting this situation for all it was worth. And I was too naïve to see it. You've been doing a lot of things I've been too naïve to see. Or maybe I didn't want to see them. But that's over, Mona."

I looked at Mona. Her initial fear of Paul's reaction was now turning to anger. Anger at being found out.

Anger at having Paul turn on her.

Anger at losing.

"What about our daughter? You owe us...."

"I owe my daughter a good life. I owe her my love. I owe her my support, financial now and emotional for the rest of her life." He pointed his finger at her. "I owe you nothing."

Paul looked at me again and I could see in his eyes what I had been missing. He walked over to the sofa where I was still sitting and put his hand out to me to lift me up. He kissed me on the mouth. Then he looked at Mona.

"I'm taking my wife home. Call me when the arrangements have been made for Claudia's transfer. You know where to reach me."

He put his arm around my waist and we walked out together. I wanted to turn around and see the look on Mona's face but I didn't dare. On the way to the car, Paul kissed the top of my head as he hugged me close to his side. I leaned in and smelled his cologne. It smelled like heaven.

"Did I do good?" he asked.

I looked up into the fuzzy face that I loved. "You did great. I love you, baby."

"I love you, too. Look, I know I behaved miserably and I can't tell you how sorry I am."

"You're back now. We're back now. That's all I care about. I'm sorry I read your email. It's just...."

"Forget it. We can talk about all that some other time. Let's just be friends again, okay?"

I couldn't help but smile. "Of course, my friendship will have to be bought."

"You got it. Whatever you want."

"Let's start with jewelry and sexual favors, what do you think?"

He kissed me again. "You got it."

We had to drive home in our separate cars but I smiled all the way. I couldn't wait to be back in our house and hug Paul again. It was so good to be in love and to finally feel that the devil that was Mona had been exorcised. It couldn't have gone any better if I had scripted it myself. I wondered what had caused the change in Paul but decided I didn't really care.

Paul was home a few minutes before me and I found him going through the mail in the kitchen.

I grabbed the mail out of his hands and hugged him again. "That can wait," I said. "Tell me again how wrong you were and how much you love me."

Paul smiled. "I'm not going to live this down for a while, am I?"

"Probably never." I pulled away a little then. "Paul, let's be serious for a minute. I know I bear some responsibility for all this, too. I'm sorry for the way I acted. I want this to work. I love you."

He kissed me again. "I love you, too."

"What's going to happen now? It feels like we're back to the old days with Mona. What's going to happen with Claudia?"

"Claudia's going to go back to New Hampshire to recover and Mona can take care of herself." Paul looked into my eyes. "You didn't really think I was going to go back to her, did you? Don't you have more faith in me, in us, than that?"

"I let my fears get the better of me, I admit that. That was wrong. But I've had a chance to do some serious thinking in the last couple of days and I think I'm in a better place now."

Paul kissed my nose. "Good. Let's hope you stay there." He picked up the stack of letters on the counter and started sorting through them again. "Oh, by the way, there was a call for you while you were gone."

"Oh? Who?"

"Some lawyer from your office named Scott. We had a pretty interesting conversation."

I felt the blood rush to my feet. "What did he want?"

"Not much. Just said to call him when you got home. Something about a case you were working on. But we got to talking. He seems like a really nice guy."

"What did you talk about?"

"This and that. Work. Dogs." He looked at me and smiled. "Wives."

He pulled me toward him again. "You know, for a divorced guy, he's got some pretty good ideas on marriages and keeping them."

Paul kissed me and that told me all I needed to know. I sent a silent prayer asking God to bless Scott and Eleanor.

Joy Collins has wanted to be a writer since she was a child. Educated as a nurse, she has written a health newsletter for Baby Boomers, as well as many medical articles for journals and web sites. But making up stories has always been her passion. Her debut novel *Second Chance* centers on the many pitfalls of living in a stepfamily. *Coming Together* is her second novel and she is now at work on her third.

Joy shares her Arizona home with her husband and several fur-kids. For more information, visit her at www.joycollins.com.